Murder
Comes to Call

Books by Jessica Ellicott

MURDER IN AN ENGLISH VILLAGE

MURDER FLIES THE COOP

MURDER CUTS THE MUSTARD

MURDER COMES TO CALL

Published by Kensington Publishing Corporation

Murder
Comes to Call

Jessica Ellicott

KENSINGTON BOOKS
www.kensingtonbooks.com

KENSINGTON BOOKS are published by

Kensington Publishing Corp.
119 West 40th Street
New York, NY 10018

Copyright © 2020 by Jessie Crockett

All Kensington titles, imprints, and distributed lines are available at special quantity discounts for bulk purchases for sales promotion, premiums, fund-raising, educational, or institutional use. Special book excerpts or customized printings can also be created to fit specific needs. For details, write or phone the office of the Kensington Special Sales Manager: Attn. Special Sales Department. Kensington Publishing Corp., 119 West 40th Street, New York, NY 10018. Phone: 1-800-221-2647.

Library of Congress Card Catalogue Number: 2020939481

Kensington and the K logo Reg. U.S. Pat. & TM Off.

ISBN-13: 978-1-4967-2484-7
ISBN-10: 1-4967-2484-4
First Kensington Hardcover Edition: November 2020

eISBN-13: 978-1-4967-2490-8 (ebook)
eISBN-10: 1-4967-2490-9 (ebook)

10 9 8 7 6 5 4 3 2 1

Printed in the United States of America

Murder
Comes to Call

Chapter 1

Beryl Helliwell was not in the habit of being put out. In fact, she usually took new circumstances in stride. For the most part, she felt that experiences most others found irritating were simply opportunities to learn something new. Either about herself, about a foreign culture, or about the way one's fellow man comported him or herself under duress. But as she gazed about the magistrates' court, she felt a sense of unexpected effrontery. Never could she have imagined being called upon to answer a charge of reckless motoring.

In most of the places in the world Beryl visited, her daring feats of speed were encouraged and, more often than not, covered by the press, which described her heroics with glowing accolades. Her mind boggled, yes, simply boggled, at the notion of being required to justify her prowess behind the wheel. She could put it down only to professional rivalry on the part of Constable Doris Gibbs.

Nothing else could possibly explain it. When Constable Gibbs had flagged her down at the side of the road, Beryl had naturally assumed the police officer was desirous of procuring a lift.

Beryl had never been so astonished in her life than when the constable had produced a citation pad and commenced to fill it in.

Which was why she found herself on a fine June day within-doors, simply sitting in the local magistrates' court, awaiting her turn before the bench. The room felt stuffy and overheated. Warm rays from the sun slanted through the window and filled the chamber with light. Workingmen with battered hats and scuffed boots piled into the chairs set out about the room. Next to her, a man smelling decidedly of barnyard shifted nervously from one buttock to the other. Most proceedings held little interest. Poachers, mischief-makers, and those involved in youthful high jinks paraded before the bench without much drama.

"Declan O'Shea, please approach the bench," a voice boomed from the front of the room. What Beryl considered a fine specimen of a young man rose from his seat at the far side of the court. With his head of glossy black hair held high, he stepped before the bench and came to a stop in a wide stance, as if bracing himself.

Throughout the proceedings Beryl had taken some interest in the role her friend Charles Jarvis played. Charles held the distinction of being the only solicitor in the village of Walmsley Parva. Charles seemed to be acting in an advisory capacity to the magistrate. She hoped that with Charles involved in the proceedings, she might have a real chance of getting off lightly. From the scowl on the magistrate's face, it did not look as though the young man standing in front of him had any chance of doing so.

"I see here you are charged with disorderly conduct and simple assault as well as public drunkenness," the magistrate, Gordon Faraday, announced upon glancing at the papers in front of him. "What have you to say for yourself?"

"I say it was all made up," Declan O'Shea said. Beryl leaned forward as she caught the lilt in his voice. Not only was the young man handsome, but he also had just the sort of accent that never failed to catch her attention. If she had to guess, she would say that Declan O'Shea had not long quit Ireland.

"According to Constable Gibbs, you were seen shouting at a fellow member of the public just outside the pub on Tuesday last." The magistrate shuffled his papers and adjusted the pair of wire-rimmed spectacles perched across the bridge of his nose. "She reports you stank of liquor and were exceedingly abusive when approached."

"I had just left the pub, so it would have been surprising if the smell of liquor had not been on my breath," Declan O'Shea said.

Beryl watched with interest as the magistrate's face became suffused with color. He was by no means a young man and tended strongly towards corpulence. Beryl wondered if her case would be dismissed should the magistrate succumb to some sort of apoplectic fit. She decided such hopes were unworthy of her and returned her attention to the scene unfolding before the bench.

"I caution you to consider how you speak to your betters. Although I must say, I would expect nothing less than this sort of arrogant and unprincipled behavior from one such as yourself. After all, has anyone ever heard of an Irishman who doesn't stink of liquor and cause trouble wherever he goes?" Magistrate Faraday seemed to be addressing the courtroom as a whole.

Beryl was not surprised at the reaction of the assembled crowd. Laughter and cheers rippled through the room. Beryl heard a number of ethnic slurs bandied about.

The political climate in Ireland was tumultuous, to say the least. People in England, by and large, did not hold the Irish population in high esteem under the best of circumstances, and talks of Irish independence had done little to raise their opinion of them. Still, such obvious prejudice from the court left Beryl feeling rebellious herself. As an American, she had very little patience with the idea of the British telling any other country it belonged to them. She was relieved to see a flicker of discomfort cross Charles Jarvis's face. He leaned towards the magistrate and whispered something in his ear.

Magistrate Faraday shook his head at Charles and returned his attention to the accused. "I'm sentencing you to a two-pound fine, to be paid in full a fortnight from today. What's the next case?" he said, turning to Charles once more.

"Where am I supposed to get two pounds in a fortnight?" Declan O'Shea shouted. "I barely earn enough to keep body and soul together. There's nothing left over for things like fines."

"There certainly seems to be enough left over to pay for spirits at the pub," the magistrate said. "I suggest you curtail your drinking and whatever other debauchery you get up to. If you don't pay the fine in a fortnight, you will serve time in jail."

"It won't matter how I cut expenses. I don't earn enough to pay off such a large fine so quickly. You just have it in for me, don't you?" Declan O'Shea said. The young man began waving his arms about wildly in the air. He took two steps towards the bench. The magistrate slid his spectacles down his nose and peered over the top of them from behind the relative safety of his ornate wooden barrier.

"I can double it if I have any sense that you are threatening an officer of the court." The magistrate cocked one shaggy eyebrow, as if daring the young Irishman to deliver an impertinent retort or to launch into a physical altercation.

Beryl released a deep breath, hardly aware she had been holding it. There was something very compelling about the plight of the young man. Beryl thought it had more to do with the unfair treatment she felt he was receiving than any swayed emotion she may have felt on account of his good looks. At least she hoped that was the case.

Declan O'Shea shook his head silently, as if he did not trust himself to reply. The magistrate barked out that he was dismissed and called for the next case, which happened to be Beryl's own. As she rose, she managed to catch the young man's eye. He slowed his step as she approached the bench to take his place in front of it. As they passed, she paused and leaned towards him and whispered for him to wait for her in front of the court building. For her trouble, she perceived the briefest of nods before he passed on.

Beryl had dressed carefully for the occasion. She generally preferred clothing of a dramatic variety, and today was no exception. Clothed from head to toe in a daring scarlet silk trouser ensemble with a floating duster jacket, a smart driving cap, and matching leather gloves, she felt she looked the part of a supremely competent motorist. She donned her brightest smile and trained it at the magistrate. Even from across the bench, she could feel him softening under the warmth of her smile.

Although Beryl was not a vain woman, she was well aware that her appearance played a part in her success. The newspapers seemed to be far more interested in featuring photographs of attractive and stylish women in their pages than they did more conservative and modest specimens. So, Beryl had cultivated a persona that had served her extraordinarily well for years. Brighter colors, daring hairdos, and exaggerated American warmth were part of her reputation. She saw no reason to hold back now.

"Miss Helliwell, I see you have been charged with excessive speed and dangerous motoring. I assume you have a good reason to have been clipping along at such a shocking rate of speed," the magistrate said.

"But of course I have, Your Honor," Beryl said, not quite sure that it was the way to address a magistrate.

"Well, what is it, then?" the magistrate stated, leaning forward.

Beryl could feel the other assembled persons in the courtroom leaning forward, as well. Not for the first time, she found herself the only woman in a room. She had shocked her dear friend Edwina by frequenting the Dove and Duck, Walmsley Parva's local pub, where she frequently found herself in the very same state of affairs. But it wasn't just withindoors that she found herself the sole female amongst a gaggle of men. When one spent one's life building a reputation as a daredevil adventuress, one tended to suffer from a lack of feminine companionship. She had undertaken safaris, Arctic treks, and hot-air ballooning escapades without other members of the fair sex. If there was one thing Beryl knew, it was how to play to this sort of an audience.

"I had just gotten my automobile back from Blackburn's garage. The engine had been playing up a bit, and there was no way to be sure things were corrected without putting the old bus through its paces," Beryl said, turning towards the rest of the courtroom, as if to include them in her assessment of the situation. "I couldn't very well do that by poking along at a snail's pace, now could I?" she asked, batting her long eyelashes at the magistrate.

"Although that very well may be true, Constable Gibbs cited you with exceeding the speed by at least ten miles per hour. By my calculations, that would put you at an astonishing clip of forty-five miles per hour," the magistrate said, his face once more suffusing with color.

"I can't see how Constable Gibbs could have any real sense of how fast I was going, as she was simply standing on the side of the road. In my experience, those who stand about stationary always feel that those who are moving are doing so far more quickly than they really are," Beryl said.

"Are you saying that the constable has falsified this report?" the magistrate asked.

"I am suggesting no such thing. I am simply stating that the constable has no possible way of knowing exactly how fast I was going. I doubt very much I had exceeded the speed limit by ten miles per hour," Beryl said.

"So, you deny the charge that you were driving recklessly?" the magistrate asked.

"I never drive recklessly, not in the least," Beryl said. "In fact, I would go on record as saying I am the most capable and qualified driver in the entire district. Although I have set many a record for land speed, I have never been involved in a motoring accident. At least not one that was my fault."

Beryl could hear whispers and guffaws swelling up behind her. It was one thing to be accused of exceeding the posted speed. It was quite another to be called incompetent. Upon that subject she could not rest easy. Beryl was always happy to be called foolhardy, but she certainly did not care to be called incapable.

"I like a woman with a bit of spirit," the magistrate said. "Are you prepared to prove your motoring prowess?" Beryl noticed a twinkle in the magistrate's eyes and felt good about her chances of avoiding a fine. Even though she and her dear friend Edwina Davenport were on far sounder financial footing than they had been in the recent past, she still did not enjoy the idea of forking over some of their hard-earned cash for something so insulting as a speeding fine.

"What did you have in mind?" Beryl asked, giving her long eyelashes an extra bat. Although she had no intention of pursuing a romantic entanglement with the magistrate and all his many chins, she saw no reason not to stroke his ego as he came to a decision.

"I should think the matter could be easily settled by you offering me a lift when the proceedings are complete for the day. It is only about half a mile out of the village to reach Groveton Hall, but I should think it would prove sufficient to test your abilities behind the wheel," the magistrate said.

From the lecherous look in the magistrate's eyes, Beryl was quite certain that should she accept his offer, she would be wise to insist that he occupy a spot on the backseat of her automobile while she remained in the driver's seat. It would be wiser still to insist on a chaperone of some sort. Preferably his wife. Unfortunately, she did not appear to be at hand.

"A sort of road test is what you're suggesting?" Beryl asked.

"I suppose that it is."

"Or even a trial by combat. Of course, I shall have to request a witness to the proceedings," Beryl said.

The magistrate looked visibly deflated. "And who do you suggest?" he asked.

"I should think that the most impartial observer and certainly the most trustworthy would be your legal advisor, Mr. Charles Jarvis," Beryl said. Charles sat up a little straighter in his chair. His normally erect posture took on an even stiffer look. Charles, Beryl happened to know, was a great fan of motorcars and was always eager to accept her suggestion of a ride out into the country. "After all, you would want someone to support your rather unorthodox manner of meting out justice, would you not?"

"Quite right." Magistrate Faraday turned towards Charles and cleared his throat. "I assume you have no engagements that will keep you from accompanying us at the close of court this afternoon. A bachelor like yourself is the captain of his own time, isn't he?"

"I would be happy to oblige," Charles said, the slightest trace of a smile enlivening his slim face.

The magistrate dismissed her with instructions to meet him

in front of the courthouse in an hour's time. She gave him a final dazzling smile before turning to face the rest of the audience in the court. She nodded and winked at those assembled, hoping the magistrate would be in a good enough mood to go easy on all the rest of them. Adjusting her hat, she strode out of the courtroom with her head held high.

As she stepped out into the bright sunshine, she looked up and down the street for Declan O'Shea. She caught sight of him at the corner, grinding a cigarette stub out beneath his foot. Beryl stepped quickly down the courthouse steps, then sauntered towards the young man, giving him enough time to enjoy her approach. Even though Beryl was at an age when many women began to give up on the pursuit of romance, she did not think it was in her best interest to do so. Not only was it good for her celebrity to be considered attractive and glamorous, but she also had no interest in being put out to pasture on any front just yet. In fact, she oftentimes felt as though her real purpose in life had just gotten under way.

Only months before, she and her finishing-school friend Edwina had become reacquainted and, through a bizarre set of circumstances, had decided to open a private enquiry agency. Beryl found that she and Edwina had a knack for solving cases together, and slowly but surely, their business was growing. Financially, the pickings were still quite slim, but thanks to an influx of funding from a silent partner, their fortunes appeared to be on the rise.

Beryl had made her name for herself by cavorting about the globe as a solo transcontinental pilot, a race-car driver, and even a hot-air balloonist. But nothing she had turned her hand to before had given her the same sense of excitement and accomplishment that tracking down criminals seemed to do.

Beryl suspected her contentment with her new undertaking had as much to do with renewing her friendship with Edwina as it did with the aspects of the business itself. There was something about sharing adventures with a true companion that made them all the more worthwhile.

Declan O'Shea looked like he could use a bit of company himself. He did not look like a happy man. When he noticed her approaching, he swept his tweed cap from his head and sketched a slight bow.

"Now, what could I have possibly done to warrant the attention of the famous Beryl Helliwell?" he said as she came to a stop in front of him.

"I am always eager to assist my fellow man, especially if I feel he has been maligned. Don't you know Americans always root for the underdog?" she said. "But if I had to say exactly what caught my attention, I would have to confess it was your accent."

"I rather like yours, as well," he said with a wink. Deep dimples appeared on either side of his mouth as he smiled. "So, tell me what you had in mind to help me with my problem. You don't need me to join a crew planning to rob a bank, do you?"

"Although that does sound intriguing, I find that my efforts are firmly on the side of upholding the law at present rather than breaking it," Beryl lied. Even though she and Edwina were firmly committed to bringing criminals to justice, she was not above using somewhat illegal means to do so.

"Well, I can't think of any legal means of earning that much money that quickly," he said. He drew out a pack of cigarettes and offered one to Beryl. She shook her platinum head. Smoking had never been something that appealed to her.

"You look like a man with a strong back," she said, flicking her gaze brazenly over his taut form. "Have you ever done any gardening?"

Declan struck a match and lit his cigarette, drawing in a deep breath, before responding. "I don't know a turnip from a tulip, but I have a strong back, that's true. And I know how to dig, how to trundle a barrow, and how to show up on time."

Beryl reached into her small handbag and withdrew a calling card. She offered it to Declan before wondering if he could read it.

"The Beeches, Windhurst Lane, Walmsley Parva," he read aloud. "Is this a place that needs someone to oblige in the garden? It sounds a bit too posh for someone who knows next to nothing about plants."

"We already have a gardener, but he could use the help of a younger man. He and my business partner, Edwina, have some ambitious plans to renovate the gardens around the property, and we've been looking for someone such as yourself to do some of the grunt work. If Simpkins likes the look of you, you could earn the money you need for your fine in short order," Beryl said.

"Much obliged, miss," Declan said. "When would you like for me to stop by for Simpkins to decide if he approves of me?"

"I would have said straightaway, but I find that I am unfortunately engaged in the transportation of the magistrate to his home after the close of court today. Shall we say tomorrow morning?" Beryl asked.

"I'll call on him tomorrow, then." Declan tipped his hat and strode away without a backwards glance.

When her jobbing gardener, Simpkins, had come into an unexpected and decidedly vulgar quantity of money by way of an unexpected inheritance three weeks earlier, Edwina had feared his newfound wealth would change the status quo at the Beeches for the worse. However, since becoming a man of significant means, Simpkins had found only two ways to display his wealth. Rather than being known as someone who couldn't quite reach his pockets, he had become famous for standing rounds for the other tipplers down at the Dove and Duck.

Edwina knew of this only because Beryl had remarked upon

it one evening, before heading out to the local watering hole herself. Edwina never stepped foot in the place. Whilst she had become someone far less concerned with what society thought of her than she had ever been before, there were some standards she was not inclined to abandon.

That being said, it gave her no small degree of satisfaction to consider the astonished look that would surely be on the face of her mother's ghost should that paragon of society look down on the antics her daughter had been up to recently. It gave her a thrill every time she remembered that she had become a private enquiry agent and had proved to be quite a successful one.

Which brought to mind the second indulgence in which Simpkins seemed determined to partake. From her seat behind her desk in the morning room, a space she had commandeered recently as the center of business operations, she could hear the sound of a newfangled carpet cleaner being piloted about the hallway carpet runner by a woman Simpkins had hired to do the heavier aspects of the housekeeping. Since moving into one of the spare bedrooms at the Beeches, he had insisted on contributing to the household finances.

Simpkins, being a lifelong gardener, had not stopped at applying his generosity withindoors. As soon as he had been assured that his inheritance was forthcoming, Simpkins had set about making plans for renovating the gardens at the Beeches. His father had been the head gardener on the property when Simpkins was a boy, and Simpkins had grown up with Edwina's mother. Edwina had only recently come to realize how profoundly affected Simpkins had been by the reduction in fortunes the Great War had laid at her feet.

Between the death duties the government required after she lost each of her parents as well as her brother and the fact that her shares were no longer performing in a way one could even optimistically call paltry, Edwina had simply not had the financial wherewithal to maintain the staff required to keep the gardens in trim.

She had herself felt agonies of remorse every time she saw the overgrown shrubberies and the herbaceous borders in need of weeding, but she had not realized how distressed such things had made Simpkins. She had always attributed his lackadaisical attitude to sheer indolence, but she had come to wonder if rather it was that he had felt helpless and overwhelmed. Since he had come into money, he had completely thrown himself into the renovation project. Unfortunately, despite the amount of money he had to spend on the place, it was proving difficult to find willing workers to assist with his schemes.

Although everyone seemed to be facing difficult finances, the working class, from which strong backs and eager hands were to be found, had also been seriously affected by the aftermath of war. Not only had so many young men been lost on the battlefield, those who had returned were often in no shape physically to perform such duties. Even those young men who were capable of hard labor had discovered they vastly preferred working in factories to working the land or remaining in service to those who considered themselves their betters.

Edwina could not blame them. So many of society's conventions had been shaken off in the past few years that Edwina could hardly remember how life had been before. That is, until she heard the aspirating machine switch off, followed by a discreet knocking on her door.

"What is it, Beddoes?" Edwina asked after inviting the maid to enter the morning room.

"There's a man at the door to see you, miss," she said. "He insisted on speaking to the head of the household."

"Do you think he is here on business?" Edwina said. She peered down at her diary but did not notice any appointments scheduled for the day. In fact, whilst she was very proud of their accomplishments, the sad truth of the matter was they were not teeming with clients at present. She was rather afraid it might be some time before another problem in the village required solving. After all, it was not as though Walmsley Parva was a steaming hotbed of criminal activity.

"He didn't say, miss. He's just asked to speak with the head of the household." Beddoes lowered her voice. "He seemed rather official."

"Then I suppose you'd best show him in," Edwina said, closing her diary and arranging a few items on her desk to appear busier than she actually was. There was no need to let an outsider know she spent much of her time at the desk working on her novel rather than on business affairs.

A slim man of average height entered the room, looking as though he were on a mission. In his hand he held a clipboard. She gestured to the seat across the desk from her and waited for him to deposit himself with surprising grace down onto it.

"I understand you wish to speak with the head of the household," Edwina said. "May I ask your business?"

"Allow me to introduce myself. My name is Terrence Crossley, and I've been appointed by the registrar-general to act as a census taker for the Walmsley Parva district. I am here to deliver your census schedule and answer any questions about how best to fill it out," the man said. He gestured to a stack of papers affixed to his clipboard.

The census, of course, Edwina thought. It was overdue by two months. Unrest and agitation on the part of the working classes had caused the registrar-general's office to delay the census for fear that those inclined to strike for more pay and better benefits would refuse to participate as a bargaining tactic. Edwina had completely forgotten that the census was due to be taken in June. But now that the census taker had come to call, Edwina felt an uneasy sensation fill her stomach and her chest.

She was overwhelmed by the memory of the census taken in 1911 and by how much had changed since then. She felt a twinge of melancholy as she recalled it had been the first and only census taken in which her mother listed herself as the head of household. Edwina had tried at the time to convince her mother not to fill in the form. She had agreed with the many women who had argued that if they were not allowed to vote, they were not required to answer the government's impertinent questions, either.

Her mother had not agreed, and in an entirely unprecedented occurrence, the two of them had quarreled spectacularly. Her mother had sulked extravagantly by taking to her bed with an impressive variety of imaginary ailments. Her main objective had been to create as much fuss as possible for those around her, which, given their financial difficulties, amounted solely to Edwina. It had taken some weeks before her mother had condescended to take her meals in the dining room or to perform any duties more arduous than replying to her post.

And here Edwina was, ten years later, serving as the head of household at the Beeches. She could, without consulting anyone, fill in the census in any way she chose. But what exactly did she wish to have noted down on an official form?

Since Beryl had taken up residence in her guest room several months earlier, Edwina had found her notions of how the world worked repeatedly called into question. She did not like to think of herself as narrow minded, but the time spent with her iconoclastic friend had shown her that some of the things she had always felt were simply the way the world worked were perhaps unjustifiable.

She liked the way she had started to think of the world around her. She was proud of the business they had built together and appreciated the way that Beryl had encouraged her to consider her worth as extending far beyond the confines of traditional English village spinster.

What she had not grown accustomed to was the notion that Simpkins had come to be a member of the household in a real sense. Of course, she was used to him being on the property. How could she not be? After all, his father before him had been the head gardener at the Beeches, and Simpkins had grown up following in Edwina's mother's wake.

But she was still becoming accustomed to his face at the breakfast table each morning. Without consulting Edwina, Beryl had spontaneously moved him into one of the spare rooms only a few weeks earlier. Edwina had agreed at the time that the man needed looking after. He had received two shocking pieces of news in short order and was not as young as he used to be. The two women had agreed he required supervision until he got back on his feet once more.

What Edwina had not agreed to was an extended, one might even say permanent, accommodation for the irascible elderly man. But somehow, he had inveigled himself into their lives in such a way that it seemed impossible to extract him. One moment he was sleeping rough in her garden shed, and the next he was installed in the blue bedroom at the back of the house, as if he had always been there.

The situation was exceedingly awkward. One could not accept one's jobbing gardener's generous, yet secret, donation of cash for their fledgling business with one breath and turn him out on the street with another. If he was good enough to invest as a silent partner in Helliwell and Davenport, Private Enquiry Agents, was he not good enough to park his hobnailed boots beneath her kitchen table? Still, the notion of officialdom, in the trappings of the census, brought Edwina's feelings of misgivings to the surface.

It was one thing to keep her head held high as she walked the high street, knowing village gossips like Prudence Rathbone and Minnie Mumford were whispering behind their hands about her unorthodox living arrangements. It was quite another to consider she would have set down such information for posterity. Any qualms she was considering were magnified as the census taker cleared his throat and tapped his broad, blunt finger on the census schedule.

"Do you have any questions concerning the manner in which you are to fill this out?" he asked. "I'm certainly happy to oblige you if you require any assistance with the instructions or even with the reading of the document."

Edwina sprang to her feet and drew herself up to her full height. Admitting to sheltering her gardener only a few yards down the corridor from her own bedchamber was one thing. Being perceived as someone who was illiterate was an entirely other matter indeed.

"I assure you I am neither so aged that my eyes do not permit me to distinguish the letters nor so feebleminded as to not possess the ability to comprehend the contents of a government form," Edwina said. "I assume you intend to return to collect it at some point?"

Mr. Crossley stood. "Indeed, I do. The official census is to be taken in such a way as to reflect the persons domiciled in this residence on Sunday night. I shall make my rounds in Walmsley Parva beginning Tuesday morning in order to give residents sufficient time to complete the schedule."

"I will be sure it's ready whenever you arrive. Now, if there's nothing else, my maid will see you out," Edwina said, gesturing towards the door.

Her proclamation lost some of its punch when Beddoes did not answer the ringing of the bellpull and Edwina was forced to escort Mr. Crossley to the door herself. Beddoes was not to be faulted for her inattention to her mistress's call. Edwina could hear the sound of the carpet cleaner as the maid had turned her attentions to one of the rooms on the second floor.

With a feeling of impatience, she closed the door behind her caller, returned to the morning room, and seated herself at the desk once more. The world of her novel was ever so much more pleasant to contemplate than the census and all the fraught decisions it presented. Edwina resolved to put off any ruminating upon it for the time being and, with a far lighter heart, began tapping away once more on the typewriter.

Chapter 2

Edwina tucked the census schedule into her letter rack and took herself firmly in hand. There was only one way to stop thinking about things over which one had no control, and that, Edwina knew, was to take action on those things that one could affect. Upsets of most sorts required soothing, and the most soothing thing Edwina could think of was a trip to her local knitting shop, the Woolery. She stepped briskly into the hallway and retrieved her third-best hat from the hall tree. Adjusting it in the wavy glass, she gave her appearance a cursory glance.

It still felt odd to place a hat upon a head of bobbed hair. Although she had not regretted lopping off her far longer locks, she was still not entirely accustomed to the sensation of a line of hair tickling the nape of her neck. In fact, by ridding herself of so much hair, she had found the range of hats she could wear had increased enormously. She leaned forward and was not entirely displeased with what she saw reflected in the glass.

Perhaps Beryl's far more daring sense of style was rubbing off on her a wee bit. She couldn't help but notice she looked rather jaunty with her wide-brimmed hat and gently waved hair. Whilst there were roses in her cheeks, she thought they were perhaps due more to the distress caused by the census taker's visit than to any youthful blushes. One could hardly expect that, considering she was well into her forties.

Edwina gathered up her shopping basket and slipped it over her arm. She whistled for Crumpet, her dear little Norwich terrier, and retrieved his lead from its hook near the door. The warm sun beat down on her shoulders as she and Crumpet made their way to the high street. The Beeches was not far outside the village proper, but the walk was long enough that she was grateful to escape from the heat of the day when she crossed the threshold of the Woolery.

She felt her shoulders creep down away from her ears as she glanced around the small shop, filled to the scuppers with skeins of wool, silk, and cotton. Running her hand over a plump ball of red worsted, Edwina imagined herself sporting a cheery beret when autumn came to call. She pictured herself coasting on her bicycle along one of the many lanes in the village, with such a stylish hat perched upon her smooth cap of shorn hair.

She placed two balls of the irresistible red wool into her basket, then made her way to the table where booklets of knitting patterns were displayed. Crumpet stretched out on a small rug in a corner of the shop, as if he knew his mistress would be some time. As Edwina began to look over the booklets, she heard footfalls coming from the back room.

Mrs. Dunbarton, the proprietress of the Woolery, pushed aside the curtain that shielded the private space at the back of the shop from the storefront, and stepped into the room. Mrs. Dunbarton was a plump little woman with a welcoming and cheerful demeanor. Edwina had spent many happy hours in her company, perusing the shop and discussing the Woolery's latest offerings as well as her own various projects. Mrs. Dunbarton could always be counted on to locate just one more ball of the yarn needed to complete a project as well as to help sort out any problems when a pattern had somehow, inexplicably, gone wrong.

"Miss Davenport, how lovely to see you this afternoon. I don't mind telling you, you gave me a bit of a turn when I heard you out here in the shop," she said, taking a tentative step in Edwina's direction.

Edwina gave Mrs. Dunbarton her full attention. The proprietress of the Woolery was not a woman easily rattled. With her shrewd blue eyes and competent air, she seemed to take life very much in stride. Many was the time Edwina had watched as she soothed a nervous new knitter determined to do her bit for the war effort by taking on the task of knitting socks for the soldiers, regardless of her level of skill or her aptitude for such a project. No one without nerves of steel could have wrangled the volunteer needlewomen of Walmsley Parva as Mrs. Dunbarton had done. The fact that she was feeling spooked gave Edwina pause.

"Is the shop not open?" Edwina asked. She glanced down at her basket and hoped fervently she would be able to purchase the two balls of yarn. She was already itching to cast it on and to feel it rhythmically running through her fingers.

"Yes, the shop is open. I just didn't hear you come in until I heard your footsteps creaking the floorboards. I confess I've been more nervous than usual lately with the burglary and all," she said.

"I didn't know that you had been burgled," Edwina said, glancing about the shop.

Everything looked as it always did. Baskets and shelves filled in a higgledy-piggledy manner with quantities of sumptuous fiber dotted the small shop. The counter where orders were written up and payments were made looked much as usual, as well. The familiar scarred wooden table ringed with six chairs filled the far corner of the room. Nothing seemed the least bit out of place.

"It wasn't here at the shop," Mrs. Dunbarton said. "It was my house. Someone broke in whilst I was here minding the shop."

She reminded Edwina of a hickory walking stick. Stout, sturdy, and unlikely to break. It crossed her mind that it might have been in the burglar's best interest not to enter Mrs. Dunbarton's home whilst she was within. He or she might have come off the worse for the attempt.

Doris Gibbs, the local constable, had been kept busy over the past few days by a spate of uncharacteristic burglaries in the village. Walmsley Parva was not normally the sort of village in which one needed to lock one's doors. Edwina hated to think that a need for greater security was one more of the many changes to daily life that could be attributed to the war.

So many people had moved on, whilst strangers had filled their places in rural communities like Walmsley Parva. One did not know one's neighbors quite so well as one had in the past. Many of the larger homes and estates in the surrounding area had been sold to the sorts of people who had the money for weekend homes in the country. It was not a fashion of which Edwina approved. The village was better off, in her opinion, when the residents were full-time inhabitants rather than those who motored down at the weekend in order to show off their quaint country cottage to a bevy of city-dwelling friends.

Beryl, of course, Edwina thought, would be inclined to see the positive side to an outbreak of criminality. Edwina was quite sure her friend would view it as an opportunity to grow their business. As much as Edwina was delighted by the notion that she had become a capable businesswoman, she was not entirely comfortable with her success being at the expense of the quality of life in her beloved village. It was one thing for Beryl to calmly, and one might even say coldly, see the bright side of the situation. But Edwina, a lifelong resident of Walmsley Parva, could do nothing but regret her ever-expanding knowledge of the seamy underside of country life.

"Did the burglar take anything?" Edwina asked. Even though she was distressed to think that a determined burglar had infiltrated her community, she was, of course, curious about the details.

"As a matter of fact, I did lose several items of some value," Mrs. Dunbarton said. "A few pieces of silver and bits of jewelry, as well as three or four jars of my best preserves." Mrs. Dunbarton shook her head in disbelief.

"What a strange combination of items," Edwina said. "Did you report it to Constable Gibbs?"

"Yes, I did. As soon as it happened," Mrs. Dunbarton said.

"Does the constable have any leads?" Edwina could not help but feel a small thrill of competitiveness surge through her. It was a quality she did not realize she possessed until she and Beryl had begun solving cases together. Although she had no bone to pick with the village constable, neither was she on particularly friendly terms with the other woman. Whilst she admired Doris Gibbs for being that rare thing, a female constable, that did not mean she was required to like her.

Doris had managed to hold on to her job as the local law enforcement officer even after the war had ended. She had assumed her post because of the lack of men available to do the job, but it was her own grit and determination that allowed her to keep it despite qualified men becoming available once more. Yes, Edwina had to admit she admired Doris for her resolve, even if she did not always approve of her enforcement of her duties or her aptitude for the tasks at hand. It came as no surprise to Edwina when she heard Mrs. Dunbarton's response.

"Constable Gibbs simply wrote a few things down on a pad of paper and admonished me to be more careful and consistent about locking my doors. When I asked her if there was any chance I'd get my things back, she told me I should not count on it," Mrs. Dunbarton said.

"How many robberies does that make in the village?" Edwina asked.

"I'm not sure how many people have been burgled besides myself and one of my customers. Do you know Mrs. Corby?" Mrs. Dunbarton asked.

"Certainly, I do. The elderly lady who lives out on Preble Lane?" Edwina asked.

"Yes, that's her. She telephoned in to order some yarn just this morning and told me she thought she had heard someone trying to break into her place yesterday," Mrs. Dunbarton said, shaking her head. "I don't know what the world is coming to when an elderly shut-in is afraid to be in her own home."

Edwina knew that Mrs. Corby was hardly a meek and mild shut-in. Even though she was rather elderly, she was a querulous and unpleasant hypochondriac, one whom Edwina had done her best to avoid. Edwina had little doubt Mrs. Corby would outlive all her contemporaries and most of the younger generation besides.

"You say someone tried to enter the home. So, she was not actually burgled?" Edwina asked.

"Apparently not. I don't know all the details. The primary purpose of our telephone call was to sort out her yarn order. I promised I would deliver it today, but after the burglary I got a little bit behind here at the shop, and I'm not sure when I'm going to be able to take it over to her," Mrs. Dunbarton said, gazing around.

Edwina knew a hint when she heard one. Still, the thought of a trip out to see Mrs. Corby left her feeling decidedly cool. Mrs. Dunbarton seemed to sense her lack of enthusiasm and knew just how to entice her to change her mind.

"I received rather a large order of new wool from a supplier in Scotland, which I wanted to be able to get out on the shelves by the end of business today."

"You know, I would be happy to deliver her order for you if you'd like," Edwina said. "Especially if it meant I might go into the back room, where I could take a peek at your latest offerings before they end up on the shelves."

"Follow me. It would be an enormous help, and there's some robin's egg–blue double knitting weight wool that I think would interest you very much."

Edwina busied herself looking through the sacks of new yarns, whilst Mrs. Dunbarton wrapped up the parcel to be delivered in brown paper and sturdy twine. Edwina selected several skeins of the good Scottish wool. She often liked to work on Fair Isle patterns, and the colors she spied amongst the new stock inspired her to plan a project she had not previously considered.

Although Edwina did not consider herself a slave to fashion, she had been just as intrigued as all the knitters of her acquaintance by the beautiful multicolored sweater His Royal Highness Edward, Prince of Wales, had been wearing after a recent trip to Scotland. She thought it would be a great deal of fun to try creating one herself. With her market basket overflowing with a great many skeins, she whistled for Crumpet, bade her good-byes, and headed off not only to deliver Mrs. Corby's yarn but also to snoop around just a bit about the burglary.

Edwina tied Crumpet's lead to the fence railing and opened the latch on Mrs. Corby's front gate. She felt her feet slow as she approached the front steps. The past snuck up on one in surprising ways. Edwina had loved her mother but, if she were to be entirely honest, had found her continual carping about her ill health to be rather a trial. In fact, Edwina had become so used to dismissing the older woman's complaints, at least within the privacy of her own mind, that she had been taken completely by surprise when her mother contracted a very real case of influenza and unceremoniously succumbed to it. It seemed ironic to Edwina that the one illness that had proved fatal to her mother was the one that had caused the least amount of fuss.

Out of the corner of her eye, Edwina detected a faint motion. A gnarled hand twitching back the curtain hanging in the window. She gave herself a shake and took herself in hand. Edwina believed in living up to her commitments, even the unpleasant ones. The day was a fair one, and warm, and the front window was open.

Mrs. Corby was hardly a shut-in. She claimed to have lost her footing in her garden the previous week and to have badly wrenched her ankle. According to Prudence Rathbone, who made it her business to know everyone else's, the poor woman would be laid up for some weeks. Prudence had it on good authority, by which, Edwina assumed, she meant a relentless grilling of the local nurse when she had come into Prudence's post office–cum-sweetshop-cum-stationer. According to Prudence, Mrs. Corby had been advised to elevate her leg and to remain off her feet as much as possible. Edwina could well imagine that faced with the same admonishment from the doctor, she, too, would start on a new knitting project.

"Hello, Mrs. Corby. It's Edwina Davenport here, delivering your yarn order from the Woolery."

"You've likely heard about my episode in the garden. Let yourself in, won't you?" Mrs. Corby called through the open window.

Edwina mounted the steps and pushed open the heavy, creaking front door. As she stepped into the dimly lit front hallway, she felt a wave of gratitude for Beryl's arrival. A solitary cardigan hung on a single peg on the wall near the door. One pair of shoes sat pressed against the wall. Edwina felt a startling rush of pity for the elderly woman, who lived alone. Edwina knew how lonely that could be and was cheered to think the hall tree at the Beeches now groaned under the myriad of garments that Beryl and Simpkins had added to it over the past weeks. Edwina had been expecting to end up rather like Mrs. Corby, a solitary woman alone in the world.

"I'm right in here," Mrs. Corby called out. "What brings you by to see a sick old woman like me?"

"I have the yarn you ordered from the Woolery, along with rather a large quantity I purchased for myself," Edwina said.

She took a seat in a chair opposite the elderly woman and handed her the paper-wrapped parcel.

Mrs. Corby carefully picked at the string with her gnarled fingers. The older lady pulled the yarn from the parcel a skein at a time and held it up to the light filtering in through the window. Even from a few paces away, Edwina could see the flecks of indigo and scarlet heathering the balls of soft grey wool.

Mrs. Corby sat with her feet propped up on an ottoman, a woolen blanket draped over her legs despite the warmth of the day. She had a lacy shawl draped across her shoulders, and Edwina assumed it was one of her own making. Quite likely, it was of her own design, as well. Even though Mrs. Corby was not easy to admire in many ways, Edwina thought very highly of her skill as a knitter and pattern designer. In fact, the older woman had designed a helmet liner for the soldiers during the war that had proved easy for knitters to produce and comfortable for the soldiers to wear.

Mrs. Corby cleared her throat and trained her gimlet eye on Edwina. "I expect it would be too much to expect you to make me a cup of tea whilst you're here," she said with a tone of reproof in her voice.

Edwina nodded and, with a sense of relief, hurried off to the kitchen. As she gazed about the room, she noticed things seemed neat and tidy. She wondered how someone as incapacitated as Mrs. Corby claimed to be was able to take care of the washing-up so efficiently. After all, it wasn't as though it was easy to acquire domestic servants. Even if the war years had not dissuaded so much of the population from pursuing jobs in service, she very much doubted Mrs. Corby would be in any position to afford to hire one should any servants be available to be had. Her home was an exceedingly modest one by the standards of her class, and Edwina knew from her own difficult experiences how the severe downturn in the economy had caused difficulties even for those who had previously felt carefree concerning economic matters.

As she filled the copper teakettle and then placed it on the hob, Edwina glanced out through the back window. She wondered what sort of foolish burglar would be interested in entering such a modest establishment. Lost in thought, she was surprised to hear Mrs. Corby call out that she should rummage through the cupboards for a packet of biscuits to add to the tea tray. By the time she had sorted out the refreshments, Mrs. Corby had asked her what the delay was three separate times. With a sigh, Edwina hoisted the tea tray and carried it back to the parlor.

She placed it on a side table within easy reach of the elderly woman and proceeded to pour out a cup for her hostess. Noticing the other woman neither smiled nor thanked her for her efforts, she poured a second cup for herself and settled back in her chair, determined to leave at the earliest available opportunity.

"I suppose you heard about my burglary?" Mrs. Corby said.

If there was one thing Edwina knew about elderly ladies, it was that they liked to be the first with the news. There was no reason to spoil Mrs. Corby's pleasure even if she was a difficult person. In fact, Edwina thought, perhaps she might prove less difficult if she derived more pleasure from life. She slowly raised her eyebrows in mock surprise and peered at Mrs. Corby over the rim of her teacup. Mrs. Corby could interpret her expression as she saw fit, and Edwina's conscience would be clear. It could hardly be considered a lie, could it?

Mrs. Corby took the bait. "I've never been so scared in all my life," she said, placing her teacup on its saucer with a clatter. "Bold as brass, he was. I should have thought any self-respecting burglar would know enough to sneak into a house when no one was home. Or at least under the cover of darkness."

"You mean someone broke into your house when you were awake and at home?" Edwina said, scarcely believing such a thing could be true. Even though the rash of burglaries was disturbing, no one had previously reported being home when one had occurred.

"In fact, he did not actually break in. I heard him rattling the doorknob and pressing against it. It was a good thing I had left the key turned in the lock that day. If it hadn't been for my accident, I would have been more inclined to go about my normal routine. Every day I unlock all the doors as soon as I awaken. Fires, you see," Mrs. Corby said with a knowing nod.

"Fires?" Edwina asked.

"Yes, of course, girl," Mrs. Corby said with a scowl. "Didn't your mother teach you anything? Unlock the doors as soon as you start your day, in case a fire breaks out in the house. You wouldn't want to be burnt alive because you couldn't open your door and escape quickly enough."

Edwina had not considered the possibility of perishing in her own home from fire. She knew it was a possibility, but it was not amongst her chief concerns.

"I shall be sure to keep your advice in mind," Edwina said. "But it occurs to you that you benefited from deviating from your usual course on that particular day?"

"I was most fortunate indeed. For all I know, the man could

have murdered me in my bed," Mrs. Corby said. Edwina did not remind the elderly woman that she had admitted to having arisen before the attempted burglary occurred.

"Did you get a good look at him?" Edwina asked.

"Unfortunately, I didn't manage to catch even a glimpse of him. I'm not as fast on my feet as I used to be, and with this dreadful wrench to my ankle, I'm even more slowed down than usual. I don't mind telling you I felt frozen in place when I first heard the rattling of the doorknob. It took me a moment to collect myself and decide to creep towards the window."

Edwina thought of the elderly woman's lookout spot near the window and that gnarled hand twitching the net curtain. She wondered if Mrs. Corby had seen more than she was letting on, for some reason of her own. Could her eyesight be failing? Or perhaps it was as she said, that she had simply not yet installed herself in her favorite perch when the incident had occurred.

"What led you to believe it was a man if you did not see the intruder?" Edwina felt surprised to realize she was offended by the assumption that a woman could not be a burglar. Edwina had known of many pilfering domestic servants. Not her own, mind you, but those who worked in the households of others. Suddenly she wondered about the reliability of Beddoes. So far nothing seemed to have gone missing from the household, but really, what did one know about her?

"Of course it was a man. No self-respecting woman would go about letting herself into another woman's house without an invitation. At least not in my day she wouldn't." Mrs. Corby let out a deep, shuddering sigh, as if the madness of the modern world exhausted her.

"Did you report the prowler to Constable Gibbs?" Edwina asked.

"I telephoned her right away. Not that it did me any good whatsoever. To think I opened my front door and entertained a member of the constabulary in my dressing gown, only to have it come to naught," Mrs. Corby said.

After a tedious further half hour of listening to the way the world had fallen into a lamentable state, Edwina managed to make her excuses, collect Crumpet, and walk back to the Beeches.

Chapter 3

Although Beryl was always up for an adventure, she was not inclined to be an early riser unless the circumstances absolutely called for it. So, it was not her habit to find herself standing in the garden of the Beeches as the morning light still filtered softly through the leafy canopy of the trees. Beryl vastly preferred the hours of the owl to those of the lark and did not find that the early morning twitter of birds pleased her in the least. However, she knew that the fault was entirely her own as she felt the damp dew that clung to the grass seeping through her satin slippers.

Simpkins looked no worse the wear, despite the earliness of the hour. For a man his age, he held his liquor impressively and rarely seemed to show the aftereffects of a night of excess to any great degree the next morning. Although, to be fair, he always looked so disreputable, it might be difficult to tell whether he had spent the evening before well into his cups.

Declan O'Shea, on the other hand, looked the picture of health as he stood awaiting Simpkins's inspection. Simpkins looked him up and down with an appraising glance. Although

Beryl had known Simpkins for only a few months, she had formed a positive opinion of him. He made for a jovial and entertaining companion on jaunts to the pub and also provided another perspective on how best to support Edwina.

Beryl had noticed that Simpkins deliberately cultivated an adversarial relationship with his employer. What she had also come to realize was that it benefited Edwina enormously to have someone needling her from time to time. As much as she hated to admit it, Edwina was as often encouraged to make changes based on a contrary attitude towards Simpkins's suggestions as she was to simply adopt those made by Beryl herself.

In the time Edwina had known him, Simpkins had been the sole gardener at the Beeches. Over the years, the entire property had taken on an air of dishevelment, much like Simpkins himself. With dwindling funds for their upkeep, the once meticulously maintained sprawling gardens were now far more modest in scope and did not easily bear close scrutiny. Although Edwina was an avid gardener and an able plants woman, the grounds were simply too much for her to maintain aided solely by an aging man with an inclination towards indolence.

Watching Simpkins appraise the fitness of a potential employee gave Beryl an entirely new perspective on him. In her mind's eye, the years fell away from him, and she could imagine a far younger Simpkins with a much larger budget for upkeep marshaling a small troop of eager young workers to do his bidding. She wondered if the sudden influx of cash Simpkins was able to provide to the property might cause the years to fall away from the gardens, as well. For all their sakes, she fervently hoped so.

Beryl was of the firm opinion that success was drawn to success. If she and Edwina wanted their private enquiry agency to reach the heights she had planned for it, appearing to be housed on a property tottering on its last legs was not in their best interest. No, it would be far better for the gardens to elicit envy and admiration on the part of any potential clients. She fervently wished Declan would prove to be the first step in such a plan. But that, of course, would depend on Simpkins.

As far as Beryl was concerned, Declan seemed exactly the sort of person to have wandering about the place. With his blue-black hair clinging to his head in soft waves and his sparkling dark blue eyes, he was as fine a specimen as any of Edwina's beloved plants. His posture was as straight as that of any trained soldier, and even with his shirt buttoned up to the neck, it was easy to see his muscular frame straining below the cloth. Unless he had an undisclosed back injury or respiratory weakness, she could see no reason he would not be an excellent choice, at least for handling heavy work, like grubbing about with a spade or shimmying up trees to lop off dead limbs.

"Have you done any gardening before?" Simpkins asked Declan.

"I know almost nothing about plants, but I've got a strong back and a willingness to learn," Declan said. "And truth be told, I need the job, and I'm not too proud to turn my hand to whatever would honestly make me the money that I need."

"Miss Beryl told me you had some difficulties with the magistrate. I like to drink as much as the next man, but I am not inclined to hire those with an ugly temper on account of it. What do you say to that?" Simpkins asked.

Declan stood even straighter. "I was not the one who started the altercation. But when I've been accused of things I haven't done, I find it impossible not to speak up for myself," Declan said.

"What exactly were you accused of?" Simpkins asked. He shot Beryl a significant glance. Then he cocked one bushy eyebrow up at her, as if concerned that she had not shared all she knew with him.

He was right to have thought so.

"It was just some nonsense about him being Irish," Beryl said.

"Is that right, young man?" Simpkins asked.

Declan shook his head. "I expect that me being Irish is what caused the accusation, but specifically, it was said that I was suspected of being the burglar that's been plaguing the village of late," Declan said, crossing his arms across his chest. Beryl noticed his biceps bulging beneath the thin fabric of his shirt. His arms would be well suited for trundling a wheelbarrow. But she could also see that they could easily cause damage if turned to more violent purposes.

"And are you the one responsible for those burglaries?" Simpkins asked.

"No, sir, I am not." Declan stared straight at Simpkins, as if daring him to accuse him.

Simpkins looked the younger man up and down once more. "I'm inclined to believe you, but if my instinct is incorrect, you will be dismissed without pay. Do you understand?" Simpkins asked.

"I'll give you no cause to be dissatisfied with my work."

Simpkins turned to Beryl. "It would be best if we don't mention the rumors to Miss Edwina. I can't see that being something she needs to know, if you catch my meaning."

Indeed, Beryl did catch Simpkins's meaning. She understood him completely. Despite Beryl's best efforts to influence her friend, Edwina remained ever so slightly a snob. She concerned herself more with her reputation than Beryl believed was good for her, and any whiff of scandal associated with her household would cause Edwina enormous discomfort.

In the time they had lived under the same roof, Edwina had softened on much of her thinking. The fact that Simpkins now resided at the Beeches and had one of the guest rooms assigned to him, rather than a space in the servants' quarters, was testament to how much Edwina had altered her stance on the lower classes of late. But there was no sense in troubling her for no reason. Edwina would benefit more than anyone else from the gardens being returned to their former glory, and Beryl saw no reason to give her any impediment to that pleasure.

"I certainly shan't be the one to tell her, and neither shall you," she said, turning to Declan.

"What shall I tell her if she asks why I want the money?" Declan asked. "After all, I have another employer already."

"Miss Edwina is far too much of a lady to go enquiring after other people's financial matters," Simpkins said. "If you don't mention it, she won't ask."

"Besides, very few people in Walmsley Parva could not do with a bit more jingle in their pockets," Beryl said. "I'm sure she will imagine you are simply another of them. If it comes up, you might mention sending money back home to your relatives. An aging mother would do admirably."

"Where shall we say that you met him?" Simpkins asked.

"Why don't we go ahead and play into the existing prejudices? I'll simply say we met at the pub," Beryl said.

"When can you start?" Simpkins asked.

"My job at the stables at Brightwell Farm takes up much of my time, but I could be here for at least a few hours a week starting tomorrow. Does that suit?"

"That will give me time to sort out plans for what to have you start with," Simpkins said. "I suggest you get to bed early tonight. Miss Edwina expects value for her money." With that, he dismissed the younger man, and Beryl waited until his retreating back had disappeared around the side of the house before turning to Simpkins.

"I noticed you did not tell him that you were his employer," Beryl said. "Why was that?"

"I would never embarrass Miss Edwina that way. The Beeches belongs to her, and she is the mistress of everything here. It wouldn't do to get above myself, now would it?" Simpkins said.

"That's very kind of you," Beryl said, placing her hand on Simpkins's grubby shirtsleeve. She noticed a bit of pink coloring his cheeks, below his scruffy whiskers.

The elderly gardener winked elaborately. "Besides, I'll get more work out of him if he thinks that we are both in the same boat."

Saturday evenings at the pub were usually lively affairs, and this one was no different. In fact, Beryl observed, there was a heightened degree of excitement in the air. A number of strangers sat amongst the regulars, and perhaps, she thought, they accounted for the unusual atmosphere at the Dove and Duck that evening. Beryl carried her large whiskey to her favorite table overlooking the street, where she settled in comfortably on the upholstered bench and observed the crowd swirling around her.

As was so often the case in Beryl's life, she was the only woman present, save for members of staff. Annie, the barmaid, a cheerful woman in her late thirties, stood behind the long wooden bar and handily rejected flirtatious advances without inflicting any real sense of rejection. Simpkins was amongst a crowd of local men waiting their turn for Annie to pull a pint for them from the vast assortment of choices on offer.

As far as Beryl could tell, Simpkins was in no hurry to have his order filled. On the contrary, he seemed engrossed in conversation with one of the newcomers. As she took an appreciative sip of the high-quality spirits, she reflected on her good fortune at finding such a comfortable place to land for the duration of Prohibition. Despite Beryl's love for her country and her willingness to repeatedly undertake highly secretive exploits on behalf of the federal government, she simply could not entertain the notion of regularly partaking of bathtub gin.

Even though she could see the allure of a speakeasy on occasion, there was no denying it was not something she wished to add to her schedule regularly. Perhaps, she thought with surprise, she had grown just a bit too old for such shenanigans. Or maybe she simply couldn't be bothered to get up to that sort of mischief when the trouble she could partake in as a private enquiry agent was ever so much more alluring. No matter the reason, she found it far more congenial to head to the local pub, where one could be assured of interesting company and spirits that would not leave you blinded or suffering from jake leg.

As she contemplated her good fortune, she watched Simpkins lead a far younger man towards her. As they wove between the tables, carefully holding their drinks aloft so as not to spill a drop, Beryl took the opportunity to observe the stranger. He had the fair hair and blue eyes of so many of his fellow countrymen. His cheeks were slightly rosy, which could, of course, be attributed to the drink. Of average height and slender frame, Beryl judged him to be a rather good-looking specimen. Unlike so many of his generation, he bore no scars upon his face, and he appeared to have all his limbs intact. But as they approached the table, Beryl thought she detected a slight limp.

Simpkins placed his glass on the table and eased into the chair next to Beryl's. He gestured for the stranger to join them.

"Mr. Faraday, allow me to present Miss Beryl Helliwell," Simpkins said with a wave of his gnarled hand.

"It's a pleasure to make your acquaintance, Miss Helliwell," the man said as he took a seat. "I've enjoyed reading about your exploits over the years."

"How very kind of you to say so," Beryl said.

The fact of the matter was there were few people in the English-speaking world who did not know of her adventures. She had made a name for herself for more than two decades in planes, hot-air balloons, and any sort of ground vehicle that could achieve high rates of speed. Newspapers across the globe had made a pretty packet by featuring her adventures on their front pages, and even newsreels had splashed her likeness across the silver screen on more than one occasion.

Despite the fact it had been many months since her last spectacular feat of daring, Beryl was gratified to know she had not yet faded from the public's consciousness. She was banking on the fact that her name held some sway, as this was one of the ways she felt she brought value to the fledgling Davenport and Helliwell, Private Enquiry Agents. As the pair of them still had little practical experience, Beryl felt they needed all the advantages they could muster.

"Mr. Faraday, are you by any chance related to our local magistrate?" Beryl asked.

"Please, call me Alan," he said. "Guilty as charged, I'm afraid." He turned to Simpkins.

"Don't go holding it against the lad, though," Simpkins said. The younger man flashed him a grateful smile.

"Gordon is my older brother. I'm here visiting him for Father's Day. He's my half brother, but he has always seemed more like a father, really. He took on the responsibility of my upbringing after our father died, when I was still quite young," Alan said.

Beryl tried to reconcile the pompous and prejudiced man she had met at the magistrates' court with the notion of him behaving paternally towards anyone. She had often found people to be far more complicated than they appeared on the surface. It would seem the magistrate was no different.

"I had the opportunity to meet your brother just yesterday," Beryl said.

"The opportunity being provided by Constable Gibbs," Simpkins said before taking a long tug on his pint of beer.

"Don't tell me you were brought up before the magistrate?" Alan said. "What was the charge, if you don't mind me asking?"

"Reckless driving, if you can believe it," Beryl said. The notion of it still stung her pride. "Fortunately, your brother was able to see the sense of dismissing the charges. He came around quite quickly to my way of thinking that if there's anyone in the entire village to be trusted with the safe operation of a motorcar, it is I."

"My brother may be occasionally zealous in the fulfillment of his duties, but I cannot imagine him failing to see the sense in your argument," Alan said. "And I hope I shall be able to persuade you that not everyone in the family is so difficult to get along with."

He leaned ever so slightly closer and gave her the sort of smile she was sure worked well on very young women with little experience in the world. She let her mind wander momentarily to a similarly flirtatious young man she had enjoyed a weekend with just before setting out for Walmsley Parva. Perhaps she would not mind getting to know at least one member of the Faraday family better, after all.

"Alan's visit isn't the only thing causing chatter in here this evening," Simpkins said.

"I thought I noticed something a bit fractious in the air," Beryl said. "Do tell."

"The census is on everyone's mind," Alan said. "That's the other reason I'm here this weekend. Gordon wanted me to be officially counted as a member of his household. He is rather old fashioned about such things."

"Are people upset about something as routine as a census?" Beryl asked.

"Some of them are. Many worry that the questions are an invasion into their privacy. They wonder what will happen to the information after they share it. A rather unsophisticated lot for the most part, I'd say, wouldn't you?" Alan said.

Beryl suddenly found his smile far less winning. If there was one thing she could not abide, it was a snob. Even though he might be almost a generation younger than his older brother, certain family traits appeared to be shared strongly between them. Perhaps it was her American upbringing, but Beryl simply found the entire class structure and its constraints in England utterly baffling.

Why one person felt superior to another simply as a result of their birth station was something she would never understand. Beryl always took great pleasure in rooting for the underdog. The harder someone had had to fight to reach the top, the more she found she admired them. She squinted at the young man and thought she could just make out the outline of a silver spoon sticking out of the corner of Alan Faraday's mouth. She vastly preferred Simpkins and his unpretentious manner to the arrogance of the younger man.

Still, it simply would not do to give offense where it was not necessary. Beryl made no bones about sharing her opinions or calling someone out on actions when she felt it necessary and in support of a greater good. This did not seem to be one of those occasions. Besides, people were more likely to share what they knew if they were not put on the defensive.

"Surely the amount of information being asked for is not all that much, is it?" Beryl said. "And there must be some sort of restriction on who sees it and when, isn't there?"

Alan nodded. "I think the biggest part of the concern is a growing distrust of the establishment. Nothing has been the same since the war, and with all the unrest on account of the strikers, I believe it simply feeds into the existing mood."

"In the States there's a lag time between when the census is taken and when the information is made public. Surely that's the same here," Beryl said.

"One hundred and one years," Simpkins said. "The government keeps the record sealed long enough for those who might be concerned about their privacy to have long since turned up their toes."

"That certainly seems like long enough to allow people to

feel comfortable answering a few questions," Beryl said. As someone who had lived a very public life, she was often surprised at how jealously many others guarded their privacy. She was far more concerned that no one would remember her in a few years' time than that they would still be talking about her more than a hundred years hence.

"A lot of folks here prefer to keep themselves to themselves. It's difficult to reconcile sharing any sort of personal information with that habit," Alan said.

"The census is not the only thing besides Alan's visit causing a bit of a ruckus this evening," Simpkins said.

"I thought the tone sounded more gossipy than theoretical," Beryl said.

"It's the burglaries that are really the topic of conversation. And the speculation as to who it might be that's been causing them," Simpkins said. He took a long sip of his beer, then wiped the foam from his face with the back of his hand. Beryl followed his gaze out across the crowded room. Knots of villagers clustered around the tables, the bar, and every spacing between. Most of them were speaking quite animatedly. She recognized many of the faces as belonging to men who had been in attendance at the magistrates' court the day before.

"My brother mentioned something about a recent spate of burglaries," Alan said. "I was quite surprised to hear something like that was going on in a quiet little backwater like Walmsley Parva."

Beryl felt Simpkins stiffen slightly beside her. Although it might be true that Walmsley Parva was an out-of-the-way, sleepy sort of place, Simpkins was no more inclined to like hearing it being disparaged than was Edwina. She gave Simpkins a wink, then turned her attention to Alan.

"Oh, I don't know about that. Most of the places I've been on my adventures would make Walmsley Parva look as busy as the center of London. It seems to me perhaps you are not all that well traveled if that's your evaluation." To take the sting out of her words, she flashed Alan one of her notoriously irresistible smiles and leaned slightly closer to him. "What did your brother have to say about the burglaries?"

Despite a flush of red creeping up Alan's neck, he managed to find his voice. "Gordon seems to think there's a gang of Irishmen most likely involved. A thoroughly bad lot, of course," Alan said.

"I see you haven't been to Ireland, either," Beryl said before turning to Simpkins once more. "Is that what you're hearing from your cronies, as well?"

"There have been rumblings that none of the mischief started before certain individuals arrived in town," Simpkins said. "But not everyone feels that way. There are always those ready to jump at the chance to accuse someone new, regardless of their background."

"But anti-Irish sentiment is running high in the village, isn't it?" Beryl said.

"That it is, miss. Speaking plainly, it's never been easy on the Irish here, but the recent events have only made it worse."

Ireland's desire for independence certainly was not making things easier on her citizens abroad. Neither was the fact that many of the more radical elements fighting for independence had aligned themselves with Germany during the war. In fact, the Germans had attempted to supply the Irish Republican Army with a shipment of arms during the war. Depending on whose side of things one stood on, one either rejoiced or was driven to despair by the arbitrary nature of what had happened next. The ship carrying the guns was wrecked far off the coast and what could have made a difference to the rebel cause sank to the bottom of the sea.

Beryl knew that the Germans were not the only ones interested in helping the Irish people gain their independence through any means necessary. There were numerous organizations in the States committed to assisting, as well. With the vast number of Irish immigrants who had settled in America, there was a strong base of support for Irish nationalism. There were even rumors of "arms for whiskey" routes being firmly established between the two countries ever since Prohibition had become a possibility.

"They've brought it on themselves, as far as I'm concerned," Alan said as he looked about the room.

Beryl noticed Alan's gaze landing squarely on the figure of Declan O'Shea. Simpkins seemed to notice the same and gave her a slight shake of his head. Beryl took this to mean that she should not mention their recent employment of the young Irishman. She wondered if Alan was in a position to make things more difficult for their new employee.

She couldn't help but notice that many of the men in the pub were giving him a wide berth. It was as if the noise in the pub tapered off to nothing as Declan's presence registered on the group's consciousness. Beryl could only guess that many of the pub's patrons had been gossiping ferociously about him and felt slightly chagrined when the subject of their conversation appeared in the flesh.

Declan seemed to notice it, too. In a loud, clear voice accented by the lilt of his home country, he ordered an Irish whiskey. Bill Nevins, the publican, poured him a glass, and Beryl was relieved to see he did not ask for payment before sliding it over to the young man. She would have hated to refrain from taking her trade to the Dove and Duck, especially as it was the only pub in town. But had the owner taken a notion to discriminate against her new employee based on idle gossip, she would not have been able to support him with her business, as much as it would have pained her to refrain from doing so. She drained her glass and pushed back her chair.

"Shall I fetch us another round?" she asked Simpkins, knowing he was never one to refuse. Without waiting for a response, she headed to the bar and for once found it remarkably un-crowded. She could feel the eyes of the entire pub on her as she stopped beside Declan and greeted him warmly.

"You can put Declan's whiskey on my tab," Beryl said in a voice loud enough for everyone in the room to hear.

Chapter 4

Edwina stared at the blank page in front of her. No matter how many times she rolled and unrolled the crisp white sheet of paper after aligning it perfectly under the roller of the typewriter, she could not seem to convince herself to settle down to the task at hand. Several weeks earlier, Beryl had taken it into her head to learn to type and had splashed out on a shiny new typewriting machine. Beryl had proven immovably inept in its use.

Whatever had possessed her friend to think she had the temperament to sit still behind a desk, diligently practicing the same keystrokes hour after hour until she had mastered them, Edwina could not fathom. Even though Beryl was certainly the sort to throw herself behind the wheel of anything mechanized, especially if it was known to go fast, she had very little patience for things that required a methodical application of effort.

Almost immediately, Beryl had lost interest in the typewriter. Even more quickly, she had forgotten why she had purchased it in the first place. Edwina had been surprised and rather put out when Beryl had suggested she was going to write a book advising other women on the fine art of adventure travel. She had implied that writing a book would be no more difficult than any of her other high jinks had proved to be. Edwina was not proud of it, but she had been secretly rather pleased when Beryl had suddenly stopped mentioning her plans to add the title of celebrated authoress to all her other claims to fame.

The truth of the matter was, Edwina had always cherished a secret desire to become a lady novelist. As much as she loved knitting and gardening, there was nothing she loved more than to lose herself in one of the books she borrowed from the Walmsley Parva Reading Room. The romance of the American Wild West set her heart aflutter every time she delved into the pages of a Zane Grey novel. She delighted in matching wits against murderers and other criminals in books by the recently acclaimed Agatha Christie.

Even old favorites, like those written by Sir Arthur Conan Doyle and melodramatic works by Charles Dickens and Elizabeth Gaskell, held her in their sway. Edwina had long desired the courage to put pen to paper herself, but during the long years of waiting hand and foot on her hypochondriac mother or doing her bit for the war effort, she had put such a cherished dream at the bottom of her to-do list.

But now she found there were no more excuses. As much as she was surprised to find it to be true, the self-confidence and assertiveness she was developing had caused her to reconsider many self-imposed barriers in her life. After all, if she could imagine herself being a lady detective, why could she not imagine all sorts of other things? So, without sharing her plans with anyone else, she had surreptitiously begun tapping out a novel of her own. She had not gotten to the stage where she felt comfortable sharing her plans with anyone else, however. So, her writing time was restricted to those periods when she was sure that other members of the household were not within hearing distance.

There were only so many hours in the day when she could convincingly state that she was working on client reports or pursuing business correspondence. Unfortunately, Beryl knew her far too well to be fooled into believing Edwina had taken up attending to personal correspondence on the typewriting machine. She had often remarked how much she valued writing letters in longhand to her far-flung friends and acquaintances. And sadly, their business interests were not so vast as to require much time devoted to them at the typewriter.

Instead she waited for opportunities to thump away with wild artistic abandon on the gleaming machine when both Simpkins and Beryl were not withindoors at the Beeches. Although the thick plaster and lath of the interior walls provided a great deal of privacy from one room to the next, there was something peculiarly noticeable about the tip-tapping sound of the machine keys clacking against the roller. Edwina did not even like to attempt to use the machine when she knew that Beddoes was nearby.

In fact, it had been one of the things about Simpkins's generous offer to employ a servant for the house to which Edwina had most objected. But as she had not wanted to say anything about her project, she hadn't been able to voice her concerns to either Simpkins or Beryl. Beddoes, however, was too good a servant to remark on anything she might have seen concerning Edwina. In fact, she seemed to enjoy siding with the one woman in the household she felt was worthy of her respect. Edwina doubted very much from the way Beddoes looked at Beryl that she would betray her secret to anyone.

Edwina had come home from Sunday morning church service that morning to discover that Beddoes had taken it upon herself to prepare the Sunday meal. And what a meal it had been. Not only was Beddoes what Beryl called a crackerjack of a housekeeper, but she was also a very fine cook. Not fine like one might expect from a French chef, but fine in the way that Edwina preferred. She knew exactly how to roast a joint and how to produce crispy fingerling potatoes and a sticky toffee pudding to finish off the meal. It was all very traditionally British, and it left Edwina feeling pampered in a way she had not realized she was missing until such a gift had been provided to her.

So it was that she could not even claim to be too tired from her efforts earlier in the day to work creatively. As she stared at the blank sheet of paper, Edwina had to confess her mind was simply not on the task at hand. Even though Beryl had made plans to go motoring with Michael and Nora Blackburn for the afternoon, and Simpkins was safely pottering about in the garden shed, ostensibly rooting cuttings for a new garden, Edwina could not find the words to plunk down. She pushed herself back from the desk and began pacing the room.

The fact of the matter was Edwina was still unsure of what to do concerning the census. Of all the things she might have imagined happening in her life, listing her jobbing gardener as a member of her household had never been one of them. Edwina was enormously grateful for the influx of cash Simpkins's investment in their fledgling private enquiry agency had provided. She also felt exceedingly uncomfortable to be beholden to him. The fact that he wished to be a silent partner and had been true to his word, never offering the smallest bit of interference unless he was directly asked for an opinion, only made her feel all the more ill at ease.

There were so many things about the Great War that one carried like an invisible rucksack of stones on one's back. Grief, an understanding of how cruel humanity could be, and vast numbers of persons missing from one's life were all part and parcel of what the conflict had brought. The common sight of otherwise healthy young men with missing limbs or missing parts of their faces had made one almost numbed to some of the strain left over from the war years. What was far more surprising, at least in Edwina's opinion, were the social changes that seemed to crop up afresh every time she turned around.

As she pondered the ways in which the world had changed, she caught a glimpse of her reflection out of the corner of her eye in the ornate gilt-framed mirror hanging above the fireplace. All her life she had worn her dark hair long and modestly pinned up. Recently, she had taken the drastic step of having it bobbed at Alma's House of Beauty. She was still not quite used to her own reflection or the way the ends of her hair tickled at the nape of her neck when she moved her head or her locks were caught by a sudden breeze.

But other changes, like Simpkins's new role in her life, were also on account of the shifting sand beneath the culture's feet. Or maybe it was the squelching mud of the trenches at the front that was more the cause of things. The lines had blurred, and the concept of who was better and who was not had become somewhat murky. Working side by side with other women from all stations of life to knit socks for the soldiers and to ration all manner of supplies in order to support the troops had leveled out the village in new ways. There was no denying that the lower classes had suffered and died for their country at least as frequently as the upper ones.

Perhaps what really bothered Edwina, she realized with a start, was her own hypocrisy. She was absolutely delighted with her freshly cropped hair. She burst with pride every time she thought about writing the occupation private enquiry agent next to her name on the census schedule. She even felt a maverick sort of thrill at sipping cocktails with Beryl over a game of cards rather than the cups of Horlicks her mother had preferred. What troubled her was how difficult it was to change her own long-held beliefs. She felt ashamed of her own bias, whilst simultaneously feeling completely beholden to it.

Her palm itched as she reached out for the census schedule once more. She had tucked it away in a drawer in her desk right after Terrence Crossley had taken his leave of her upon its delivery. She read through it once again. It very clearly asked for the names, ages, occupations, and relationships between the members of the household. It enquired after income, marital status, and religious affiliation. No matter how Edwina imagined filling it in, she would have to decide what to mark down about Simpkins.

Although he had been vehement in his insistence that he remain a silent partner, she felt uncomfortable about failing to mention his role as an investor in the enquiry agency. As the head of the household, Edwina was the one faced with the task of filling out the census schedule. Surely Simpkins would never know one way or the other how she had reported his occupation.

The more she thought about it, the more uncomfortable she became. Her stomach felt rather queasy, and she wished that she had not partaken so heartily of the roast joint and Yorkshire pudding so expertly turned out by the capable Beddoes. The food roiled in her stomach all the more as she considered that it was Simpkins's money that paid for a household treasure like Beddoes in the first place.

Not to mention that his connections had secured her as their employee. Heavens knew there was no such a creature available in Walmsley Parva. Simpkins had unearthed her from the village in which his aunt lived and had brought her posthaste to the Beeches before someone else could snatch her up.

With the strong sense of feeling she was damned if she did and damned if she didn't, Edwina bent over the census schedule and began to fill it out carefully with her least favorite fountain pen. As she stared down at her careful, prim handwriting, she fervently hoped no one would know its contents.

*   *   *

Beryl could not help but feel Edwina was uncharacteristically agitated. Despite her best efforts to jolly her friend along, Edwina remained stoically ill tempered. It was a relief when Edwina shut herself away in the morning room, with the excuse that she was set on replying to some business correspondence and totting up the expenses. Beryl expected to hear the keys of her new typewriter clattering away, as they so often did when Edwina made her excuses and secreted herself away at the machine.

It was just like Edwina, she thought, not to realize that her efforts to write a novel were not a secret. At least not from her. Beryl had to admit she had felt slightly chagrined when she realized how unsuited she was for the task of authorship herself. She had felt a slight sting of shameful remorse when she pondered the amount of money she had squandered on the gleaming typewriter. But all that had faded from her mind when she had stumbled upon a sheaf of used typing paper turned facedown on the morning-room desk.

Even though Beryl was not one to pry into her friend's correspondence, she had wondered if the cause of all the secretive typing was an alarming number of dunning notices from local tradesmen that had stacked up, which Edwina had been reluctant to mention. Upon flipping over the top sheet in the pile, she realized that what she had revealed was a manuscript under construction rather than an overdue bill from the butcher or the greengrocer.

As her gaze drifted over the neatly typed page, she felt a swell of pride at having had the good sense to spend money they didn't have on the typewriter. She carefully replaced the sheet, being sure to align it neatly with its fellows. Edwina was very exacting with the landscape of her desk. Almost as exacting as she was concerning the flower beds at the Beeches.

The fact that Edwina had not shared with Beryl her literary inclinations gave her pause, but then Beryl realized it was more a reflection of her friend's deeply cherished hopes than any rift that had sprung up between them. Edwina was reserved by nature, and anything that was truly important to her she would mull over for some time before sharing it. Rather than taking offense at Edwina's secrecy, Beryl simply found excuses to leave Edwina alone in the morning room for stretches of time every day. As she cocked her ear for the sounds of the typewriter, she wondered what could be troubling Edwina so greatly that she did not take advantage of her privacy in order to add a few pages to her work in progress.

Perhaps Edwina was simply out of sorts on account of a case of writer's block. Beryl, during her short stint of fancying herself as an author, had found that there was a vast difference between imagining a book written and actually constructing one. She could hardly blame Ed for experiencing a bit of a hitch in her get-along. In fact, Beryl was more surprised it had not happened before. Content that her friend's ill temper, as well as the silence of the typewriter, was no more serious than a temporary creative setback, she turned towards a long window overlooking the back garden of the Beeches.

Declan O'Shea stood with his back towards her, satisfyingly shirtless. As he bent over a garden bed with a spade grasped firmly in both hands, she took a moment to admire his efforts. It had been some time since her reporter friend Archie Harrison had been in town for a visit, and Beryl considered whether or not she might enjoy getting to know Declan a little better. Although she was considerably older than he, she was a woman of the world and thus likely had plenty of ways to offset any disadvantage her age might create. Just as she turned towards the hallway to fetch a hat, she heard Crumpet launch a furious spate of barking. He hurtled past her down the hallway and stood before the front door, his hackles raised.

Beryl admonished him to stand back and flung the door open. There on the stoop was the unwanted presence of Constable Doris Gibbs. Doris's cheeks were flushed, and her hair appeared matted down with perspiration beneath her uniform helmet. For just a moment, Beryl felt slightly sorry for the other woman. Then she remembered the incident with the dangerous-driving summons, and her feelings of empathy fled as quickly as they had appeared.

"What brings you by on such a warm afternoon, Constable?" Beryl asked, keeping her hand firmly upon the heavy oak door. She would not put it past the constable to insinuate herself into any perceivable gap.

Edwina, roused by the commotion Crumpet had caused, bustled down the hallway, a scowl imprinted upon her face. It was easy to see that Edwina was in no better mood now than she had been before closing herself off in the morning room. Beryl doubted very much her mood was likely to improve upon her spotting Doris Gibbs stationed on her front step.

"I'm here to question your employee," Constable Gibbs said.

"What is it that you think that Simpkins has done now?" Edwina asked, stepping towards the door and crossing her thin arms over her chest.

"Not Simpkins. The new one," the constable said.

"Why ever would you want to speak with Beddoes?" Edwina asked.

Beryl noticed Constable Gibbs's face flicker with irritation and a trace of confusion. Although she and Simpkins had not set out to keep the news of Declan's employment from Edwina, it occurred to her that they had failed to mention it. Edwina had been so touchy about the money Simpkins desperately wished to lavish upon the Beeches, and perhaps, if she admitted the truth to herself, Beryl would have to say she had hoped Declan would be able to prove his worth before Edwina got wind of his employment on the property. It was just like Constable Gibbs to complicate matters.

"I refer to an Irish laborer by the name of Declan O'Shea. It is my understanding that he is employed here as a gardener," Constable Gibbs said as she made an elaborate show of consulting a page in her notebook.

Beryl had to hand it to Edwina. She did a remarkable job of hiding her own ignorance on the subject of those employed at her property. Beryl marveled at the way Edwina's face betrayed none of the confusion and emotions that she knew must be simmering below the surface.

"And what cause do you have to come to my home to question him?" Edwina asked, her impeccable posture straightening to a painful degree.

"I need to speak with him concerning the burglaries that have been blighting the village. It seems to me it cannot possibly be a coincidence that they began at approximately the same time he arrived in Walmsley Parva," the constable said, snapping her notebook shut.

"Do you have any proof of his involvement in criminal activity?" Edwina asked.

"I am at the beginning stages of my investigation," the constable said, attempting to step into the house. "I require an interview with him in order to further my enquiries."

"I'm afraid you're out of luck, Constable. I have not set eyes on him today and very much doubt he is on the premises. I suggest that you search for him elsewhere and, should you choose to return, that you have more to go on than gossip likely gleaned at the Dove and Duck," Edwina said before firmly shutting the door in the constable's face.

Edwina turned towards Beryl. She lowered her voice to a whisper, as if she feared the constable still stood on the other side of the door, straining her ears. "Do you have something you ought to have told me?" she asked.

"I'm afraid I simply forgot to mention that Simpkins took it upon himself to hire an under-gardener," Beryl said.

"He did what?" Edwina said.

"It isn't all his fault. In fact, I would have to say it is almost entirely mine," Beryl said, taking Edwina by the elbow and guiding her down the hallway and towards the back door. "I met Declan at the magistrates' court."

"He's a criminal." Edwina's voice sounded shrill and unlady-like. "I thought that Constable Gibbs was simply being her usual annoying self. If I had known he was already a convicted criminal, I might not have been so forceful in my defense of him."

"His only real crime is that he was born an Irishman," Beryl said. She pointed out the window to the spot where Simpkins stood handing young plants to his assistant. The younger man bent over the freshly turned earth and gently tucked the bit of green into a waiting hole in the ground.

"Then why was he at the magistrates' court?" Edwina asked. Her tone was frosty, and Beryl noticed her arms were still folded tightly across her chest. "It is not actually a crime to be Irish, as well you know."

"It might as well be from what I've been seeing and hearing about the village and in the magistrates' court."

"What was he charged with?" Edwina asked.

"Disorderly conduct and public drunkenness," Beryl said. There seemed to be no point in softening the news. Edwina was sure to find out, anyway.

"And you thought it would be a good idea to hire him?" Edwina asked. Crumpet capered about her feet, as if agitated by his mistress's tone of voice. Edwina did not even seem to notice her faithful little companion.

"He needed money in a hurry to pay off the heavy fine the magistrate levied on him, and I thought Simpkins could use some help, so I recommended him as a gardening assistant," Beryl said. The two women turned once more towards the window and watched as Declan gently placed a second plant and then a third into the prepared bed. Simpkins seemed to sense them staring and turned towards the window. The wide smile that had played across his face flitted away as he caught sight of Edwina.

"What sort of disorderly conduct?" Edwina said, her tone slightly softening.

"There was a bit of a dustup outside the pub, and even though several people were involved, Declan was the one the constable charged with disorderly conduct. I believe it was his accent that swayed her decision as to who to arrest," Beryl said.

"Was anyone injured in the fray?" Edwina asked, unfolding her arms.

"Not to my knowledge," Beryl said. "I think she simply allowed her own prejudices to get the better of her."

"Do you think he's inclined to drink to excess?" Edwina asked. "I'm not sure he could earn his wages if trying to do so whilst under the influence."

Beryl was not sure how to answer. The fact that Simpkins was so often inebriated had completely failed to attract Edwina's notice. If he had been able to maintain his position as head gardener at the Beeches for as long as he had, as pickled as he so often was, Beryl did not feel Declan would have any difficulty fulfilling his duties. On the other hand, she did not wish to lie to her friend.

"I am quite certain he is fully capable of performing his duties to the level to which you are accustomed," Beryl said.

Edwina raised one dark eyebrow. "That's hardly the most ringing of endorsements," she said, directing her gaze towards Simpkins. "I am unconvinced that this hiring decision was a good one. I do wish the pair of you had consulted with me before offering a stranger employment. And I'm not entirely convinced that the magistrate was in error in finding this young man guilty. After all, shouldn't he take his duties to uphold the law quite seriously?"

"Well, of course he ought to. The question is whether or not he does," Beryl said. Edwina was practical and clear eyed about many things. But her willingness to automatically allow those in authority to receive the benefit of the doubt was an area in which Beryl found her friend to be surprisingly naïve. Perhaps it was Beryl's own globe-trotting that made her believe that no matter where in the world one found oneself, those in power were regularly the most inclined towards nefarious behavior. After all, they so often had the most to lose.

Or perhaps it was the fact that as an American, she did not have any automatic allegiances to the government of the United Kingdom. She was able to see it as a system filled primarily by human beings and thus likely to be subject to character flaws of all sorts. The local magistrate exemplified the worst sort of person in power, in Beryl's opinion. She had noted over the years that those with the smallest amount of clout to wield often did it with the most enthusiasm.

"I do wonder if we would be best served by paying him for his work today and dismissing him from further service," Edwina said.

"We are in the business of finding out the truth and looking for facts, no matter the surface impressions. It would not reflect well upon our business if it were to be said, and with cause, that we did not apply the same sort of rigorous evaluation to our own lives as we did to those of our clients and those connected to their cases," Beryl said.

Out of the corner of her eye, she watched as Edwina's brows pulled closer together. Edwina remained focused on the pair of gardeners bent over their work. Declan brushed the dirt from his hands on the legs of his trousers and straightened. He took a step backwards and revealed a tidy band of freshly planted flowers. Edwina cocked her head to one side, then turned towards Beryl.

"I suppose we could give him the benefit of the doubt for an additional few days. Still, I think it would be best if we did a little bit of looking around into his background," Edwina said.

"I would say that's more than fair. And in an effort to meet you partway, I shall ask Simpkins to give Declan the rest of the afternoon off in order to allow the constable to ask any questions of him she may have. If she truly has some proof about wrongdoing, it will be out of our hands as to whether or not he is employable," Beryl said.

"I hope it comes to nothing. That garden bed hasn't looked so tidy since before the war began," Edwina said. "Still, I'd like to speak with the magistrate myself. The accusations Constable Gibbs raised are very serious indeed. And I am quite sure you are aware that offering employment at the Beeches is tantamount to vouching for his character. If we continue to employ him and he is in fact the one responsible for the burglaries, we are putting the rest of the village at risk through our example."

"You fetch your hat while I speak to Simpkins. We will head to the magistrate's house right away."

"Just promise me you don't plan to drive too fast. You certainly don't need to be stopped for excessive speed on the way to the magistrate's home," Edwina said.

Beryl was as good as her word, Edwina was relieved to notice. Although they arrived at the magistrate's house in good time, Beryl had proceeded sedately, at least for Beryl. She had even slowed down as they rounded the bend and proceeded along the gravel drive up to the magistrate's house, Groveton Hall. Unlike her usual style of screeching to a halt in billows of dust, she simply eased off the accelerator and slowed to a stop.

Edwina wondered what had gotten into her friend, until her eyes landed on the front door of the house before them.

It was an enormous structure. Unlike so many other large houses in the surrounding area, the magistrate's home had remained, at least on the outside, in fine fettle. The tiled roof showed no patchy spots of baldness; the mellow grey stones making up the exterior walls held fast together, without the smallest sign of crumbling. Bright white paint clung closely to the window casements. The four enormous chimneys extending skyward did so with impeccable posture and smoothly fitted joins in the brickwork. Even the shrubbery ringing the house and flanking the front door was neatly clipped into pleasing geometrical shapes.

But the glossy black front door stood open.

"That doesn't seem the sort of thing a careful man like the magistrate would allow, now does it?" Beryl said.

Edwina shook her head. "Although I like to think of Walmsley Parva as the sort of place where one does not need to lock one's doors, we still do make a habit of closing them. For one thing, leaving them open provides an opportunity for any manner of creature to enter."

"That's just what I was thinking about. What sort of creature might have entered?" Beryl said, reaching for her door handle. Despite the warmth of the day, Beryl wore driving gloves, which, Edwina noted, her friend did not remove as she stepped towards the house. Edwina hurried after her, and the pair of them cautiously mounted the front steps. Edwina was alarmed to notice her friend slipping her hand into a pocket of her linen dress.

Unless she missed her guess, Beryl had brought along her pistol. Why she would have done such a thing, Edwina did not like to consider. She knew that her friend had not been pleased with her treatment at the magistrates' court, but she did not think Beryl had been driven to seek a violent confrontation as a result of their interaction. Another thought occurred to her. Had Beryl taken up the habit of simply carrying her pistol wherever she went? Or had the burglaries in Walmsley Parva caused her to be more cautious than was her habit?

Beryl pressed the door open wide enough to pass through the entrance. Reluctantly, Edwina followed.

"I really think we ought to knock," Edwina whispered as she tugged at Beryl's sleeve.

"We don't know if there is someone in here that shouldn't be. I wouldn't wish to scare them off before we have a chance to identify them," Beryl said.

"We absolutely do know that there are at least two people in here that ought not be," Edwina said.

Beryl placed a gloved finger to her lips and then beckoned for Edwina to follow her.

They cautiously stepped forward, despite Edwina's misgivings. As they crept along the hallway, Edwina strained her ears for any sounds that would indicate someone was at home, authorized or not. The only sounds she could hear were the slight tapping noises of their own hard-soled shoes upon the marble tiled floor. The walls of the hallway were hung with gloomy oil paintings featuring heavy-jowled middle-aged men and dour-looking women stiffly posed against dark interior backgrounds.

Edwina wondered if they were actual relations of the magistrate or if they were paintings he had purchased to replace more valued ones that had been sold off to make ends meet. With economic distress so widely felt, the ownership of a fine property like the magistrate's was no indication of any real wealth. In fact, a large property could be considered far more of a liability than any form of asset. Edwina chided herself for her suspicious thoughts as they crept quietly along the hallway.

As her eyes became more accustomed to the gloom of the darkly paneled interior, Edwina suddenly became aware of signs of disorder. The hall table stood slightly askew, and a bowl of waxed fruit had tumbled onto the floor. Beryl stopped short and pulled her hand from her pocket. To her horror, Edwina saw that she had been right to wonder about the pistol. On the left side of the hallway, a door stood open. Cautiously, they stepped through it and at once encountered a room that had been completely ransacked.

The room seemed to be a sort of library. Books had been flung from the shelves lining the walls and were scattered upon the floor. A vase made of some sort of blue and white porcelain lay dashed in jagged pieces upon the hearth. Drawers of a Queen Anne–style secretary desk stood open, and the papers that had been within spilled over the edges of the open drawers.

"Do you think whoever did it is still here?" Edwina asked quietly.

"I think we had better check the rest of the house," Beryl said.

Edwina nodded, and they methodically turned their attention to the door on the opposite side of the hallway. Beyond it lay a small parlor, which, Edwina guessed, would be used as a morning room, as it faced east and let in the early light. It also bore signs of pilfering. Drawers had been left similarly flung open, and Edwina could see evidence of items having been taken from the mantelpiece. Whilst she would not say the surface of the mantel was dusty, her discerning eye noticed distinct circles of cleanliness where bric-a-brac had recently stood. At the far side of the room, a dusty-rose drapery billowed in the breeze.

Edwina crossed the room and pulled back the drape to reveal a French door, which stood open and led to a stone terrace dotted with plant pots and adorned with wrought-iron seating.

"This may be the way the burglar escaped," Beryl said as she stepped up next to Edwina and squinted out across the rolling fields beyond the house. "There is no sign of whoever it was now, though."

"I think we should make sure there is no one at home and then telephone for Constable Gibbs," Edwina said.

"You know she will only accuse us of having burgled the place ourselves," Beryl said.

"Someone is sure to have seen us heading this way. She will hear about our involvement whether we tell her or not. Surely it would be best to simply get it over with sooner rather than later," Edwina said.

"I'm sure you are speaking sense, but I do find that woman tiresome. We shall do as you propose just as soon as we have finished having a good look around," Beryl said, pointing her pistol towards the ceiling with one hand and motioning Edwina to follow her with the other.

They slipped back out of the room and headed for a doorway at the end of the hall. Beryl wrapped her strong fingers around the doorknob and pressed the door open with a creak. Edwina once again thought of the fact that Beryl had left her gloves on despite the warmth of the day. Given the troubles they had so frequently had with Constable Gibbs, not leaving their fingerprints seemed to be a wise decision. Although she absolutely intended to own up to their presence on the property, she did not wish to give the constable any fuel for her interrogation.

Edwina followed Beryl and found herself blinking in the bright light of the room in which they stood. A glass dome served as a roof suspended at least two stories above their heads. The space was completely bathed in light, and the scent of fragrant blossoms filled the air. Edwina looked for the source of the smell and noticed a tall plant stand holding an enormous urn filled with pure white lilies. Potted palm trees stood majestically on either side of a grand staircase. Edwina's heart hammered in her chest. Just beyond one of the enormous blue-and-white porcelain pots, she caught a glimpse of what appeared to be the sole of a rather large man's shoe.

She touched Beryl's arm, and her friend nodded as if she had also seen the foot. Together they approached the base of the enormous staircase. There, sprawled inelegantly across the floor, his neck at an altogether unwholesome angle, lay the motionless body of the magistrate.

Chapter 5

Beryl stepped forward, crouched down, and pulled off one of her gloves. The magistrate had not been an attractive man the last time she had seen him, at least not to her eyes. The tumble down the stairs had not improved his looks. Even though his head was twisted at an awkward angle, his eyes were open and seemed to be staring up at her blankly. A trickle of blood had partially dried on his forehead, just above his bushy left eyebrow.

She held the back of her hand right below his nose and waited, to no avail, to feel the warm, moist exhalation on her skin. Although she did not hold out hope that anything beside a decent burial could be done for him, she reached inside his collar and laid two fingers along the side of his neck. Just as she suspected, he had no more pulse than he had breath.

"He's a goner, I'm afraid," Beryl said, standing once more. "It looks as if he broke his neck when he fell down the stairs."

"Do you think that he discovered the intruder and lost his footing as he gave chase?" Edwina asked.

"Either that or the intruder pushed him down the stairs as he made his escape. Either way, it can't have been a very good way to go. That look on his face is one I won't soon forget," Beryl said.

"Although I hate to say it, we really must telephone for Constable Gibbs at once," Edwina said.

Even though Beryl was in agreement with her friend that the authorities should be contacted eventually, she was not prepared to do so with any degree of haste. If there was one thing she had learned over the past few weeks, it was that Constable Gibbs was vigilant in carrying out her duties but was not always likely to come to the right conclusion. Beryl put far more faith in her own abilities and those of Edwina as far as the fine art of detecting was concerned than in those of Doris Gibbs. She felt they owed it to the public to do a bit of snooping before turning things over to the police.

After all, they were private enquiry agents and, as such, were certainly capable of adding to the investigation no matter what the police might think about their involvement. They could hardly help it if they were the first ones to appear at the scene of a crime. The least they could do was to give a hand while the trail was still warm.

"I agree that the constable must be informed, but I suggest we do a bit of poking around on our own to ascertain that no one else has been injured before we raise a hue and cry. If we wait down here for her to arrive, someone might be expiring in another part of the home, and we wouldn't want to be responsible for that, now would we?" Beryl asked.

She always found it more expedient to appeal to Edwina's altruistic side than to reason with her in some other way. To her relief, Edwina flicked her gaze up the imposing stairway, nodded, and began to mount the steps with vigor.

At the top of the stairs, they made the decision to part company for expediency's sake. Edwina turned to the left, and

Beryl to the right. Room after room yielded nothing more distressing than the same sort of untidiness they had seen in the rooms on the first floor. Although, it might be fair to say that the condition of one of the rooms might have had nothing whatsoever to do with an intruder.

As Beryl stood in a large and airy room papered in yellow rosebuds and bunches of violets, she thought it likely the room's inhabitant was simply untidy by nature. Stockings and frocks lay strewn about the window seat and the end of the bed. A pair of shoes appeared to have been kicked off in front of an overstuffed chair. The dressing table was littered with sweets wrappers, clumps of honey-colored hair pulled from a brush, and a thick dusting of face powder. Beryl would have been surprised if a maid had been allowed into the room in some time. Windrows of dust crept along the skirting boards.

On the whole, the room reminded her of her own when she was a young woman. It put her in mind of those unhappy holidays when she had left boarding school and returned to her parents' home for what always seemed to be interminably long stays. As she spotted Edwina exiting another room along the hall, her heart gave a slight squeeze. Even in the midst of a crisis, she was acutely aware of how much her life had improved since coming to Walmsley Parva.

Her many admirers would likely be surprised to hear that she had come to value a quiet life in the country far more than the one she had led gallivanting about the globe. The truth of the matter was that even though Beryl had always delighted in racing about the globe, breaking one land speed record after another, and meeting interesting locals wherever she went, be they brandishing swords or inviting her to a banquet, she had never had an adventure quite like the one she had recently shared with Edwina.

Starting a business of her own with an equally enthusiastic

friend had proved to be the sort of challenge that only became more interesting over time. Even though it could not be said that either of them was an expert in the art of detection, at least as of yet, she felt they were progressing nicely, and felt no compunction whatsoever in advancing their expertise whenever possible. Although Edwina might still feel hesitant about advertising herself and Beryl as professionals, Beryl felt no such qualms. After all, how did one become a private enquiry agent if not through trial and error? It wasn't as though there was any clear path set down for the profession in which they found themselves engaged.

Edwina joined her at the door to the room, and Beryl was quite certain she heard a decided tut-tut from her friend. She knew that Edwina did not hold with messy bedrooms. After all, Beryl had been the recipient of such understated admonishments herself from time to time.

"I've spotted no sign of any intruder still lingering about the house," Edwina said. "Have you found anything?"

"Nothing that you wouldn't expect to see in a home that had been recently burgled," Beryl said.

"In the case of this room, I'm not sure that one would be able to tell," Edwina said, pointing at the sight of the unmade bed.

There was nothing more for them to gain by prowling about, Beryl decided. "I believe it's time to do our civic duty and telephone Constable Gibbs," she said.

With that, she and Edwina descended the wide grand staircase with deliberate care. As they did so, Beryl noticed Edwina averting her eyes from Mr. Faraday's body. It suddenly occurred to her to wonder how his demise might impact her own court case. Then she considered how it might impact the cases of everyone else.

Would Declan still be required to pay the fine levied against him? And who would ensure that he did so? Even though it appeared that the magistrate had tripped down the stairs, Beryl couldn't help but wonder if there was more to his death than first met the eye. She felt it best to keep her thoughts to herself until after they were safely away. Edwina truly looked rather green about the gills.

Constable Doris Gibbs arrived with her usual air of officialdom hovering about her person like a cloud of gnats. Considering how unlikely it was that the constable would appreciate finding them inside the house and how Edwina had eagerly acquiesced to Beryl's suggestion to wait outside, the constable found them standing under the shade of a spreading oak tree. Above their heads a pair of squirrels chattered and frisked, but Constable Gibbs did an admirable job of drowning out their cheerful sounds as she approached.

"Why am I not surprised to find the two of you in the presence of a dead body?" Constable Gibbs said. Edwina felt the implication was rather unfair. Generally, she prided herself on her ability to hold her tongue, but she could feel a wave of indignation roiling up from within her, and before she knew it, it had spilled out from between her lips.

"And why am I not surprised that you haven't solved the burglaries in time to prevent such an unfortunate death? One might begin to wonder more about negligence on your part than unfortunate coincidences on ours," Edwina said.

She felt rather than saw Beryl give her a glance from the side. Usually, if someone was to be going on the offensive, it was Beryl. Edwina allowed her gaze to dart towards her friend, and she saw a look of admiration stamped upon Beryl's features. She glanced back at the constable, who did not seem anywhere near as pleased.

"My investigation into the burglaries was considerably hindered by your attitude towards me questioning your employee. I don't think it would be remiss to imply that you and Miss Helliwell are in part responsible for what happened here," the constable said, widening her stance.

"I think the person we should be looking to blame is the burglar, rather than each other," Beryl said.

It seemed quite strange for Beryl to be the voice of reason in any confrontation. Edwina had always thought of herself as the one destined to play that role. But if a rash of burglaries could break out in tranquil Walmsley Parva, then she supposed anything was within the realm of possibility. She wondered if she was well on her way to becoming a cantankerous old maid. She found the thought did not shock or distress her as much as it might have done before Beryl's arrival some months before. After all, a successful businesswoman could not always prioritize the niceties over expediencies.

"I'm beginning to wonder if I should be looking at the two of you as possible suspects in the burglaries," the constable said.

"Does that mean you would not like to take our statement concerning what we found inside?" Edwina asked.

"Certainly not. It means I will be all the more careful to take down everything you say in great detail," the constable said, pulling a small notepad from a pocket in her uniform jacket and retrieving a pencil from behind her ear. "Let's start with what gave you the notion to enter the house unbidden."

"A sense of duty, of course," Edwina said. "After all, with such a rash of burglaries sweeping through the village, entirely unchecked by the constabulary, we felt it wise to investigate when we arrived to find the front door flung open, just as you see it now." Edwina gestured towards the front of the house, where they had left the door just as they had found it.

"What brought you here in the first place? Did you have an

appointment with the magistrate or with Mrs. Faraday?" the constable asked.

"I had offered to allow the magistrate to take my automobile out for a test run," Beryl said.

Edwina was always impressed by Beryl's ability to make up utter nonsense completely on the spot. Certainly, it would not have done Declan any good for them to have admitted to the constable that they were at the scene of the crime to enquire after evidence against him concerning the burglaries. She was not sure she would have been able to invent something so quickly herself. Her skills at lying tended to lean towards the detection of them rather than the creation thereof.

"So, you had an appointment with the magistrate? I suppose his wife will be able to confirm that when I speak with her," the constable said, scribbling Beryl's response furiously in her notebook.

"I have no idea what the magistrate does or does not confide to his wife. But after the way he shamelessly made overtures towards me when I drove him back here at his insistence after my court appearance on Friday, I should not be one bit surprised that he had failed to mention it. Based on his behavior, I would not say that he was the most faithful of husbands," Beryl said.

Edwina was pleased to see the constable's jaw flap open and then snap shut. She held her pencil above her notebook, as if debating whether or not to record Beryl's response. Apparently, she did not wish to keep a record of insinuations against the dead man, as she simply tapped up and down on the page with the tip of the pencil and moved along her line of questioning.

"How did you come to find him?" the constable said.

"When we saw that the door was open, we called out to ask if anyone was within," Edwina said. "When no one answered, we decided to investigate because, as I said, the door left hanging open gave us concern for the home's inhabitants." She turned towards Beryl, as if to confirm her statement. Beryl nodded vigorously.

"That's right. After calling out at the threshold, we entered the home and began to make a search. In the first room we entered, we found signs of disturbance, which caused us to feel even more concerned for any members of the household. We progressed along the entry hallway, checking the rooms on either side," Beryl said.

"When did you find the body?" the constable asked.

"We found the magistrate at the base of the formal staircase. At first glance, it appeared he had accidentally fallen and broken his neck," Beryl said.

"You said, 'At first glance.' Was there something that made you think his neck was not broken?" the constable asked.

"I meant rather that the question was if he had accidentally fallen. It did occur to me that perhaps he had been pushed," Beryl said.

"You think that perhaps the burglar deliberately shoved him down the stairs?" the constable asked.

"I think that he could have ended up dead on the floor at the bottom of the stairs in several different ways, and I would not want to make assumptions as to which way that happened before more investigation takes place," Beryl said.

"Exactly how much investigating did you do?" the constable said.

"Whatever do you mean, Constable?" Beryl asked.

"I mean, did you disturb the crime scene in any way by poking your noses where they don't belong?" the constable said.

"I can assure you we know better than to disarrange the evidence," Edwina said. "I can't see that this is any way for you to be treating people who are only trying to assist."

The constable made a harrumphing noise and turned, towards the house. Beryl and Edwina started to follow.

"I don't expect I will be needing your assistance," the constable said.

"I seem to recall that our assistance has benefited you a great deal recently," Edwina said. "I can't see why you should be so resistant to it now."

"You have your line of work, and I will say, Edwina, you have done a fine job of it. But no one has hired you to investigate the burglaries, or anything else lately, as far as I know. And might I remind you that one of your employees is the prime suspect in this case?" the constable said.

"I should think that means that we have an even greater reason to wish to get to the bottom of it," Beryl said.

"What it means is that you have a clear conflict of interest. I want you to put any notion of involving yourselves in this matter right out of your heads. In a very real manner of speaking, the magistrate is a law enforcement official, and that makes this case hit close to home for me," Constable Gibbs said. "I cannot have the two of you poking your noses in and making any cracks for solicitors when the case comes to trial."

"That's assuming you get to the bottom of who did it in order for it to come to trial," Edwina said. She took a step forward, as if she would accompany the constable into the house. Beryl reached out and took her by the arm and held her back.

"I entirely see your point, Constable," Beryl said. "You know where to find us if you have any other questions you need answered."

Constable Gibbs squinted at them, as if not quite sure they weren't determined to make mischief, despite Beryl's words. "Very sensible of you, Miss Helliwell. I'm sure I'll be able to locate you at the Beeches should I have more questions for you later." With that, she turned her back upon them and stomped towards the house.

"You can't possibly intend to leave the matter entirely in her hands, can you?" Edwina asked.

"Certainly not. But as she says, we haven't a client, and so we cannot pursue this case head-on. I suggest we return home and ponder how best to assist Declan. I think it very likely he is going to need us before the day is out."

Chapter 6

After such a trying day, there was only one thing for it. Beryl set to work at the drinks table in the parlor as soon as they returned to the Beeches. In five minutes flat she had chipped a quantity of ice and mixed up a gin fizz for Edwina and a martini for herself. Edwina primly perched on the settee and took a delicate sip of her fortifying beverage. Beryl flung herself into one of the wingback chairs and thrust her feet upon the ottoman. She swirled her olives about the bottom of her glass as she considered the problem before them.

"You know things don't look good for Declan, don't you?" Edwina said. She plucked her knitting from her knitting basket placed nearby on the floor and set to work on a half-finished sock.

Beryl often wondered just how many hand-knitted items any one village could require. Perhaps, she thought idly, Edwina never had ramped down from the quantities demanded by the war years. Hand-knitting socks for the soldiers had been considered a patriotic duty at the time. Beryl wondered why her friend never tired of her hobby. Edwina had said it helped her to think, but Beryl couldn't see how that could possibly be the case.

"I agree that his position has not improved since this morning, when the constable first came with questions for him," Beryl said. "But I don't know that it has worsened substantially."

Edwina looked up from her knitting and arched an eyebrow. "Surely you must see that the magistrate coming to harm has upped the ante in the case considerably," she said.

"I can't see that it's made any sort of a change to the circumstances whatsoever. In fact, our refusal to dismiss him from our service makes it all the more unlikely that he was the one involved," Beryl said.

"How do you figure that?" Edwina asked.

"If Declan was the one running around committing all these burglaries, he would not have needed to take the job here at the Beeches. He would have been able to sell off the items he had stolen and pay for his court fine with the proceeds," Beryl said before taking a sip of her martini. It was just the way she liked it, like an Arctic winter, extremely cold and very dry.

"I don't think one thing necessarily eliminates the other," Edwina said. "We have no idea what his expenses are overall. Perhaps he was already in need of money before the fine was levied. For all we know, he has a wife and thirteen children somewhere that require his support. Or perhaps an elderly set of parents who entirely rely upon him for their financial support."

"Those are only guesses, though, aren't they?" Beryl said.

"I suppose it might be possible that the two incidents are in no way connected," Edwina said.

"What do you mean?" Beryl said.

"I mean that what we know for certain is that there was a burglary at the magistrate's house and that the magistrate died.

That does not mean that one thing caused the other," Edwina said.

"So, you think that perhaps he simply fell accidentally to his death?" Beryl said. "If that's the case, then it might have nothing to do with Declan whatsoever."

"Not necessarily," Edwina said. "He might have gone to the magistrate's house with no intention of robbing him but rather with the intention of confronting him."

"Are you suggesting that Declan set out to harm the magistrate and that the burglary was simply a separate incident?" Beryl asked.

"I think it's something to consider. After all, his reputation was being seriously damaged by the magistrate's accusations. Considering how little proof anyone seems to have had of the identity of the burglar, I can easily imagine Declan feeling well and truly put out about the situation," Edwina said.

Beryl took another sip of her drink and stared up at the ceiling, pondering what her friend had said. As much as she did not like to consider the possibility that the handsome young Irishman had been involved, she had to admit Edwina raised an interesting point.

"Declan is a bit hotheaded, I'll admit, but I find it hard to imagine him taking the risk of going to the magistrate's home. Surely someone would have seen him. How could he have known that no one would be there with the magistrate when he arrived? It would have been a terrible risk. Especially for someone like Declan, generally assumed to be of poor character already," Beryl said.

"But if he is as much of a hothead as you're saying, then surely he might have lost his temper and headed over to confront the magistrate without thinking things through," Edwina said. "After all, he wouldn't be the first person to do something so foolish, now would he?"

"Still, it seems a tremendous risk. And besides, what's the

likelihood that there would be a burglary and a death in the same location at the same time without them being connected?" Beryl said.

"We have no idea when the burglary happened or when his death occurred. There is every possibility that these things did not happen at the same time but had enough time between them to allow them to be completely separate incidents," Edwina said.

"I hope these are the sort of questions that Constable Gibbs is asking herself. Still, if they did occur at similar times, it's possible that there might be a witness to what happened," Beryl said.

"A witness to his death?" Edwina asked, dropping her knitting into her lap and fixing her entire attention upon Beryl.

"It's possible that whoever was burgling the house saw the magistrate fall and fled from the scene with the knowledge of what happened," Beryl said.

"That would make the necessity of solving this crime even greater," Edwina said. "I still think Constable Gibbs would be well served to involve us in the investigation."

"We can't force her to allow us to assist, but we can make some discreet enquiries of our own," Beryl said. "In fact, I think we owe it to the entire village to do so, don't you?"

"We at least owe it to ourselves. After what we saw at the magistrate's house today, I can tell you for certain I am even more convinced than before that I need assurance Declan was not involved in any criminality before I permit him to continue to work here at the Beeches. Even without the death of the magistrate, I have absolutely no desire to allow someone who is a thief to become familiarized with my home in any way," Edwina said.

"Where do you suppose we should begin? Do you think we ought to question Declan?" Beryl asked.

"I think it might be wise to take a more roundabout approach. Perhaps we should make a few enquiries around the village as to who seems to have any idea who might be responsible," Edwina said.

"Surely Prudence Rathbone and Minnie Mumford will have an opinion on the matter," Beryl said. "Although I would not be one bit surprised if both of them feel that Declan is the one responsible."

"One cannot get away from the fact that the burglaries did not start up until after he arrived in Walmsley Parva," Edwina said.

"That may be just a coincidence," Beryl said. "After all, all sorts of things have started to happen in Walmsley Parva since I arrived."

"That fact had not escaped my notice," Edwina said, picking up her knitting once more.

Beryl waved her hand dismissively. "Declan is not the only new person in the village, though, is he?"

"Who else are you thinking of investigating?" Edwina asked.

"What about Beddoes?" Beryl asked.

"Beddoes? *Our* Beddoes?"

"I should think it more accurate to call her *your* Beddoes. She doesn't seem to care for me in the least."

"I don't think the fact that she is almost singularly immune to your charms makes her more likely to be a burglar," Edwina said. Beryl was quite sure she heard a twinge of amusement in Edwina's voice.

"You know, something's just occurred to me," Beryl said.

"What's that?" Edwina asked.

"Are we absolutely certain no harm has come to other members of the magistrate's family?" Beryl asked. "They might have been well away from home when the incident took place."

"But then again, they might have been at home and were witnesses themselves to what occurred. Surely you don't think they have come to harm themselves, do you?" Edwina said.

"I certainly hope that it's an angle to the situation that the constable is investigating. Who makes up his household exactly?" Beryl asked.

"The magistrate has a wife and a son from that marriage. I believe the boy has a governess and that the magistrate has an adolescent stepdaughter from a previous marriage," Edwina said. "They also employ a married couple as domestic servants. I've forgotten their names."

"There's also the magistrate's brother," Beryl said. "I met him at the pub on Saturday night."

"That's very interesting. I had no idea that Alan was in town. Did he say what brought him to Walmsley Parva?" Edwina said, putting down her knitting once more.

"He said something about wishing to pass Father's Day with his older brother and also that the magistrate had mentioned he wanted him at the family home on the night of the census taking," Beryl said. "Why is it interesting?"

"I seem to remember hearing that there was something of a rift between the brothers a while back. Alan has not been in Walmsley Parva for some time, and frankly, given the intractable nature of the magistrate, I did not think a reconciliation between the two would be easily reached."

"He seemed perfectly pleased to be here to me when I met him," Beryl said. "He said that his brother was like a father to him and that he was glad to accommodate his wishes."

"It is true that there was an age difference of a good many years between the brothers. I suppose Alan could have looked upon his brother as a sort of surrogate father from that standpoint," Edwina said.

Beryl could not help notice the note of hesitation in her friend's voice. "You don't sound very convinced by the report of Alan's devotion."

"It isn't that I think Alan untrustworthy, per se, but rather that his brother would have made the sort of father figure it would be difficult to feel kindly towards. He wasn't a man to inspire affection," Edwina said. She took another sip from her glass and stretched her tiny feet out onto the ottoman across from Beryl's own. "Did Alan mention anything else whilst you were chatting to him at the pub?"

"He seemed very interested in the burglaries when the conversation turned to them."

"Did he happen to say anything about his brother's opinion on the likely perpetrator in the crimes?"

"He confided that his brother had mentioned the burglaries and that he thought there was a roving band of Irishmen likely responsible for the crime spree. I am sorry to report that young Alan seemed to share his older brother's feelings on the Irish." Just remembering the incident left a bad taste in Beryl's mouth. Luckily the remedy for that was at hand. She took another sip of her martini, then lifted an olive from her glass and popped it into her mouth.

"I am quite sure the sentiment in the Dove and Duck leaned more to Alan's way of thinking than your own," Edwina said.

"It was quite clear that Declan did not have much support in the room when I was there, apart from my own and that of Simpkins. It never fails to amaze me how much can be gleaned about the hearts and minds of the population just by allowing them to get a word in edgewise."

"I think tomorrow we ought to go into the village and do some shopping. I am sure that we will hear much more about it if we spend a little bit of time perusing the shops along the high street," Edwina said.

"As you wish," Beryl said. "Shall I turn on the wireless? I think we could both use a bit of a distraction from the events of the day before we turn in for the night."

Beryl still lay sprawled beneath a white cotton sheet in her bed, a satin mask covering her eyes, when she heard a knock upon the door. She lifted the mask and creaked one eye open as she called out, "Come in."

Beddoes, the newly hired domestic servant, pushed open the door and stood in the threshold with an excited look upon her face. "I'm ever so sorry to disturb you, miss, what with you needing your beauty sleep and all," she said.

Beryl thought she detected a note of sarcasm in the maid's voice. It had not escaped her attention that Beddoes did not hold her in high regard. In fact, she was well aware of the other woman's disdain. Beryl did not know exactly what she had done to offend their new employee, but she was unwilling to mention it. After all, Edwina was absolutely thrilled to have household help of such high caliber, and Beryl was well aware what sort of effort it had taken to install her at the Beeches. She was certainly going to do nothing to endanger the arrangement. So rather than be offended, Beryl made a point to look on the situation as amusing.

She propped up on one elbow. "Thank you for your concern, Beddoes. I'm sure that there must be something important for you to knock at the door."

"Miss Edwina has requested your presence as quickly as possible in the morning room."

"May I ask why?" Beryl asked.

"She awaits you there with a caller," Beddoes said. "It's an official-looking gentleman with a worried look on his face."

"If you had to hazard a guess, what would you say was the nature of his business?" Beryl asked, swinging her feet over the side of the bed and slipping into a pair of marabou-trimmed slippers. Beddoes looked askance.

"I'm sure I could not say, miss. It's not my place to make assumptions," the maid said, pointedly looking up and down Beryl's statuesque frame, which was covered in a frothy nightgown.

"Are you certain you couldn't hazard a guess as to whether

or not he might be a client?" Beryl asked, gathering a dressing gown around her and stepping towards her wardrobe.

"He did not say so to me, and I would not like it to be said that I listened in at doorways," Beddoes said. With that, she stepped back out into the hallway and yanked the door shut with a bang.

Beryl flung open the doors of her wardrobe and looked inside. A worried-looking gentleman at the crack of dawn suggested a client indeed. Although she was determined not to keep Edwina waiting alone with a stranger any longer than she must, Beryl knew the value of making an effort with her appearance. Much of her success in life came down to the fact that she had combined adventure and glamour in one irresistible package. She had no reason to suspect that the strategy that had served her so well as a celebrated aviatrix and race-car driver would not also be a winning combination for a private enquiry agent.

She selected an emerald-green pair of silk trousers and a white tunic covered in jewel-toned embroidery. She slid her feet into a pair of blue satin slippers before brushing her platinum-blond bobbed hair into place. A bit of powder, carefully applied red lipstick, and a spritz of perfume completed her ensemble. In under five minutes she felt ready to take on whatever the day might throw at her. Especially if the something was a new case.

Beryl rather hoped that it was. Even though it had been only a couple of weeks since their last investigation came to a satisfactory close, Beryl found that her appetite for a new adventure was enormous. She was surprised at how she had not felt her enthusiasm for their fledgling business dimming in any way. Over the past few years, she had become rather downhearted about her inability to remain enthusiastic about any of her earlier passions. Race-car driving, aviation, and even, to some extent, handsome men did not keep her attention as they once had.

Truth be told, before she had turned up in Walmsley Parva,

on Edwina's doorstep, the previous autumn, she had been feeling decidedly at loose ends. In fact, she had not felt quite like herself at all. Even though she had not shared that burden with anyone, even Edwina, she had been rather concerned about a growing sense of ennui.

So, it had been with a great deal of relief that she had discovered her lightheartedness returning just as soon as they had found themselves in the thick of a criminal investigation. Although she could not say that she was happy to have discovered the magistrate dead at the base of his own staircase, she did not find it to be the sort of thing that drained her of energy. In fact, she found it was exactly the sort of circumstance that charged her batteries.

As she tripped lightly down the stairs, she reminded herself that she did not wish to end up like the magistrate, nor did she wish to arrive in the parlor out of breath and perspiring. She slowed her steps and carefully placed one satin-clad foot in front of the other. After arriving just outside the morning room door, she paused in order to listen to what was being said inside.

From within she could hear Edwina's soothing alto voice engaging a stranger in general pleasantries. Even through the thick oak door, Beryl could distinguish some tension in the visitor's response. His low voice sounded clipped and strained. When she was certain there would be nothing to gain by delaying her entrance into the room, she squared her shoulders and turned the doorknob.

Edwina released a quiet sigh of relief. She had feared it would take Beryl much longer to appear in the morning room than it had. Although Edwina was adept at making conversation and sticking to expected avenues of idle chitchat, she was not yet confident in her role as a private enquiry agent. To her, it seemed they were still at the "bluff and bluster" stage, and

Beryl was ever so much better at that than was she. Had the gentleman caller come to discuss fund-raising for a local charitable organization or to seek advice on how to divide his dahlia tubers, Edwina would have felt up to the task of entertaining him on her own for the rest of the morning. As it was, she had felt a desperate need for the unbridled optimism her business partner provided.

She had worried with each passing moment she had spent alone with their potential client that their chances of retaining him were growing slimmer and slimmer. Although, he did seem to be quite desperate, despite his admirable attempt at hiding that fact. Edwina had often seen that sort of look on the faces of young men as they gave their loved ones a final embrace before boarding a train out of the village and on to whatever the fates had planned for them during the war years. She hoped that whatever was troubling their caller did not involve stakes quite as high as the ones the soldiers had met.

Beryl swept into the room, looking exuberant and stylish. Edwina never failed to admire the way her partner made the best of an entrance. She strode directly toward their caller and thrust out her right hand. The gentleman sprang to his feet and took Beryl's outstretched hand in his own.

"I'm so sorry to have kept you waiting. I was up very late last night on a matter of great importance and slept in rather late as a result. I do hope I have not caused you a terrible inconvenience," Beryl said.

"It's a pleasure to meet you, Miss Helliwell," the man said. "Allow me to introduce myself. My name is Gerald Melton, and I would not have dreamed of imposing upon you two ladies at such an early hour, and without an appointment, had not the need been extremely urgent."

Beryl nodded and gestured that Mr. Melton should take his seat once more. She took her usual seat in the morning room near to Edwina and crossed one long leg over the other. Edwina often thought that Beryl favored trousers for their shock value, but she also felt that they accommodated Beryl's inclination to behave in unladylike ways with far more grace than any sort of dress or skirt would provide. It occurred to Edwina that Beryl was matching their visitor's own posture. Perhaps that was part of her ability to charm, Edwina thought to herself. She promised herself to pay more attention to such things during quiet periods.

"Mr. Melton wished to wait to discuss the reason for his visit until you were able to join us," Edwina said. "Now that you've arrived, I'm sure he has something he would like to get off his chest." She smiled encouragingly towards their visitor.

"I find the whole matter so distressing, I do not wish to go over it more than once. I am going to need to have your promise of complete and utter discretion before I proceed to tell you the purpose of my visit," Mr. Melton said.

"We understand completely," Edwina said.

"You can rest assured that both Miss Davenport and I are the souls of discretion. We would not have remained in this business or any of the others we have undertaken were we not capable of honoring the privacy of others," Beryl said.

"I wish to impress upon you that I am here as a matter of national security," Mr. Melton said. "I do hope you comprehend the magnitude of that responsibility."

"I can promise you, Mr. Melton, we do. In fact, as concerns the war years, Edwina and I have many secrets even from each other," Beryl said, exchanging a significant look with her partner.

Whilst Edwina had always suspected that her friend had been remarkably busy during the war years, the fact remained that neither of them had discussed it. It was not just a matter of honoring secrets. It was simply the way things were done. Or not done. One did not pry into what would likely prove painful for others. Edwina did not know anyone in Walmsley Parva who had not been touched by tragedy during the war years. Even those who had remained at home had been daily reminded of the possibility of enemy invasion. The loss of loved ones, the threat of hunger and a lack of basic supplies, the very unraveling of society itself in so many everyday ways had had a profound impact on each and every one of them.

For someone like Beryl, whom Edwina suspected of spending time either in the service of her own government or in the service of the king, the horrors she had seen could have been even more wounding. In Edwina's opinion, it did no one any good to dwell on troubles that had already passed. There were more than enough for any given day, and it only made things more difficult to heap one's plate with leftovers. The gentleman before them served as a reminder that each day had plenty of troubles of its own. She returned Beryl's gaze and nodded.

"Indeed, that is the case, sir. In addition to all our other qualifications, I would mention that I was raised by a solicitor in a small country village. I can't imagine better training for discretion than that," Edwina said.

Mr. Melton appeared appeased and reassured. He leaned forward and rubbed his palms against his knees. Edwina wondered if he was perspiring. She wondered once more if they would be up to whatever task he was about to set before them.

"I'm here to hire you to investigate a theft," Mr. Melton said.

Edwina could feel Beryl shoot her a quick glance. With a paying client, they would have a sterling excuse for investigating the rash of burglaries. Constable Gibbs could not accuse them of being busybodies if someone had hired them to investigate, could she? Still, the constable would not welcome their interference in an active investigation. In fact, she would take it as criticism of her capabilities. At the very least Edwina felt it right to point out the police were aware of the problem.

"Our local constable, Doris Gibbs, is actively investigating the spate of burglaries currently plaguing our village. Have you taken your concerns to her?" Edwina said.

"This is not a matter I wish to discuss with the constabulary," Mr. Melton said.

"Is it a matter of some delicacy?" Beryl asked.

"Although I provided you with my name, I did not mention my occupation. I am the district registrar," he said. "So, yes, you could say the matter is a delicate one, and a matter to be embarked upon with discretion."

"Are you here about something to do with the census?" Edwina said.

Icy fingers seemed to clutch at her chest. She wondered if she had already been found out for what she had written on the census schedule. She felt the back of her neck begin to burn, as it always did when she was worried or embarrassed. Although she felt an undeniable amount of freedom in having recently bobbed her hair, she did miss how her longer locks had more adequately covered that telling part of her neck. Still, she was grateful that it was not something their visitor could see.

"That's it precisely. In fact, I am here at the request of the registrar-general," he said.

Edwina noticed his prominent Adam's apple bobbing deeply in his throat. She felt her nervousness spread, and her stomach began to turn over queasily. Beryl simply shifted slightly in her seat whilst keeping her attention trained on their visitor.

"I think you should tell us all about it," Beryl said. "You mentioned national security. I assume that whatever was taken is more important than a pair of candlesticks or a few pound notes."

Beryl had made a good point. Edwina was not self-aggrandizing enough to believe that any inaccuracies she had put down on her census schedule would constitute a matter of national security. Something in the matter-of-fact quality of Beryl's tone soothed Edwina's nerves ever so slightly. Whatever was about to be revealed was something she would be able to live down if Beryl would stand by her.

"This was no ordinary burglary," Mr. Melton said. He lowered his voice and leaned forward. He paused to look around the room, as if to assure himself that they were in fact not about to be overheard, before continuing. "I'm very sorry to say that the census schedules for your village have been stolen."

Edwina's mind reeled. Her heart thudded in her chest, and she felt her palms grow clammy. Was nothing sacred? What ever could a burglar have wanted with the schedules?

"That still does not explain to me why you could not ask for assistance from Constable Gibbs," Beryl said. "There is every likelihood that this crime is connected to the ones she is already investigating."

"I don't wish to take the information to the constable, because she is required to investigate in a way that is entirely aboveboard. There would be a record of her investigation, and rightly so. However, it is in the best interest of the public that nothing about this come to light," Mr. Melton said. He looked at Edwina, and she nodded.

"Privacy concerns," she said.

Mr. Melton nodded vigorously. "That's it exactly. We already needed to delay the census by two months in order to have any hope that the public would consent to participate across the board. Can you imagine what will happen if news of this theft gets out?"

"I should think it would be fodder for growing anti-government sentiment," Edwina said.

"That's it exactly. The Triple Alliance has been able to agitate for their cause without anything as worrisome as this taking place. News of this sort of a breach would give them all the more reason to stir up anti-government furor," Mr. Melton said.

Edwina was not so sure that she agreed with his statement that the Triple Alliance, an organization of British trade unions, did not have just cause for feeling aggrieved. Although she had not always been so broad minded, a case that had taken them into a neighboring coal village had influenced her worldview considerably in recent weeks. After considering the conditions under which the miners operated, Edwina had been surprised to see how much she sided with their concerns.

The Triple Alliance was made up of members from the coal, transportation, and railway industries who pledged mutual support for strikes proposed by any of the groups. The fear of a general strike rippled through the country, and its specter was never far from the minds of many who bothered to read the newspapers. Their grievances were many and extended to promises not kept once an armistice was declared.

So many soldiers, who had been promised a country worthy of them upon their return, had instead encountered a record-breaking unemployment rate and governmental heavy-handedness in forcing unwilling workers back into mine shafts and other duties they no longer wished to fulfill at wages incapable of feeding their families. Edwina felt their grievances were, by and large, justified. Members of those unions would certainly benefit from the panic that would ensue from highly sensitive documents like the census schedules going missing.

"So, you wish for us to recover the missing census schedules?" Beryl said.

"I wish for you to recover the schedules, identify the thief, and report your findings as soon as possible and only to myself or those persons I authorize," Mr. Melton said.

"In order to conduct an investigation, we generally need to be able to say a bit about our reason for asking questions," Beryl said.

"Well, in this case you will need to go about your business without revealing anything of our conversation here this morning," Mr. Melton said. "It is absolutely vital that you keep this entirely secret."

"I assume that we would be able to discuss the case with the census taker, Terrence Crossley," Edwina said.

"Well, yes. You would be able to speak with Terrence. After

all, he's the one who reported the theft to me in the first place," Mr. Melton said grudgingly. "But besides Mr. Crossley, you must not mention it to anyone. Not anyone at all. Do I have your word?" he asked, leaning forward.

Beryl leaned back in her chair and drummed her fingers on its wooden arms. Edwina thought Beryl looked as though she had all the time in the world to come to a decision. Mr. Melton's agitation appeared to grow as the second hand of the clock on the mantelpiece ticked loudly in the quiet room.

"This will make the investigation far more difficult than our usual undertaking. And the urgency with which a solution must be found adds to the complexity," Beryl said. "Wouldn't you agree, Edwina?"

Beryl turned her bright blue eyes towards Edwina, who realized what her friend was trying to convey. She felt a moral obligation to support His Majesty's government in a fair and honorable way. Edwina also felt the conflicting obligation to pursue their business with professional zeal. The subject of money always made her writhe with discomfort. She was very grateful for Beryl's utter lack of scruples on that topic.

Her friend was like all the other Americans that she had encountered. None of them seemed remotely abashed at trumpeting their financial interests to everyone within earshot. They brazenly haggled over the prices of goods and services and proudly proclaimed how much or how little they had paid for either. Edwina was happy to play along and allow Beryl to take the lead on any financial negotiations they had with their clients.

"It does seem a unique case," Edwina said, not wishing to contribute more than that to the conversation.

"We will, of course, be required to charge you our discretionary expedited rate." Beryl reached for a piece of paper and a pen from the desk beside her. Edwina's face blanched as she read the number Beryl wrote down on the paper before passing it to Mr. Melton. "This would be our daily rate, plus expenses."

Mr. Melton gave the number a cursory glance and nodded. "Of course. I assume you need a retainer to begin. I also have a copy of the list here for you of all the households Mr. Crossley was hired to visit." He reached inside his jacket pocket and withdrew a chequebook and an envelope. "Shall we say the rate for two days' worth of investigation, plus an additional twenty-five pounds to cover expenses?" he asked, holding a pen above a blank cheque.

Edwina felt a bit dizzy at such a sum before reminding herself that her jobbing gardener, Simpkins, had far more money than that tucked away in his sock drawer after having received a substantial inheritance.

"Yes, that will do nicely for now. We will be in touch if we require you to add to your retainer," Beryl said.

"Is there anything else you require of me to get the investigation under way?" Mr. Melton asked.

"We simply ask that you inform Mr. Crossley that we are authorized to investigate on your behalf. It would be very distressing if he refused to cooperate," Beryl said.

"There isn't a chance that you suspect Mr. Crossley of being the one to have taken them himself?" Edwina said.

"I very much doubt that's the case," Mr. Melton said. "Although his personal habits are not strictly those of which I approve, he came highly recommended by the local magistrate."

"Have you had any threats or rumors circulating that would have led you to suspect something like this could occur?" Beryl asked.

"Not a one. Although, I suppose it's possible that a member of the Triple Alliance has stolen the census schedules in order to bring about exactly the kind of excuse for a general strike that we have all been concerned with of late," Mr. Melton said.

"Do you think that's really likely?" Beryl asked.

"I don't think any of this is likely, but it's gone ahead and happened, anyway," Mr. Melton said. "And I would think that the Triple Alliance would have the greatest reason for taking them of anyone. Didn't you have some strike agitation happening nearby recently?"

"One of our most recent cases did involve an attempt to unionize a local coal mine," Edwina said. "But the mine has shut down since, and I have heard nothing of other unionizing activities being attempted."

"Walmsley Parva is not exactly a hotbed of industry," Beryl said. "Yes, the train runs through, and so transportation is involved, but for the most part, our residents are made up of those involved in agriculture and also the merchant classes."

"I do not think you should discount the possibility that members of a union could have been involved. They need not live in Walmsley Parva or even nearby to have targeted this place to serve their purposes as far as the census goes. In fact, it might just be ideal. Who would expect something like that to occur in such a sleepy village?" Mr. Melton asked.

"We will certainly add that to our lines of enquiry," Edwina said, pushing back her chair and getting to her feet. She came around the side of the desk and extended her hand to Mr. Melton. She still did not feel entirely comfortable with the businesslike act of shaking hands, but she felt that with time she would grow accustomed to it. It did seem an effective way to signal that an interview was at its conclusion. Mr. Melton bid his good-byes, and Edwina saw him to the door. She hurried back to the morning room and gave her full attention to Beryl.

"And to think just yesterday we were looking for some reason to justify our involvement in the investigations of the magistrate's death and the burglaries," Edwina said.

"I'm not sure that this helps us with that in any way," Beryl said.

"Why is that?" Edwina said.

"Because we can't tell Constable Gibbs anything about it," Beryl said.

"So we're right back where we started, then," Edwina said.

"Right back where we started as far as Constable Gibbs is concerned. But we have a rather large cheque to deposit in the bank and a person who desperately needs to be questioned. We have a new client, so as far as I can see, all is right in the world," Beryl said.

"I think, Beryl, that when we have a new client, it's absolutely a signal that all is most assuredly not right in the world," Edwina said.

"I suppose it depends on how you look at it. I'll wait for you out in the automobile while you fetch your hat," Beryl said with a wide smile.

Chapter 7

Beryl felt electrified with enthusiasm. Nothing set her heart aflutter like all the possibilities laid out in front of her at the beginning of an investigation. Once things were well and truly under way, they often became a bit muddied, tangled, and frustrating. But at the very beginning, the case seemed simply to glitter like rhinestones in a sunbeam.

Combining her eager anticipation for the adventures ahead with the delights of conducting her motorcar at high rates of speed made her actually feel glad to have been awakened at such an ungodly hour. The fact that the client had insisted the case be solved posthaste made her feel even more reckless than usual as she put her car through its paces. It wasn't until she heard a terrified squeak escape from Edwina that she realized how quickly she had been going.

She immediately slowed her pace. Not only did she have Edwina to consider, but it also occurred to her that she would not wish to cause speculation as to the urgency of their mission. In a small village like Walmsley Parva, it was hard to keep secret what one had for breakfast, let alone an investigation into a private matter. In fact, Beryl was not at all certain how they would manage to pull that off, despite the fact that she would not in any way worry about keeping her own lips sealed. Or those of Edwina.

But still, other members of the village were not so inclined to mind their own business. Beryl had deliberately chosen to take a route that kept them off the high street and thus away from the prying eyes of Postmistress Prudence Rathbone and tea shop proprietress Minnie Mumford. It could justifiably be said that those two women alone kept the rumor mill in business in the village. If they were to have any chance of honoring their commitment to Mr. Melton, they would need to utterly refrain from piquing those troublesome ladies' formidable curiosity.

Beryl pulled to a stop in front of a slightly ramshackle white stone cottage. As she exited the vehicle, she took stock of the building in front of her. The thatched roof was in dire need of repair, and Beryl was quite certain that had they happened to have called on a rainy day, she would have found the resident placing buckets and pans under leaks in the roof. Three windowpanes were cracked on the front side of the cottage alone. The door knocker hung askew amid rough curls of flaking paint. Beryl and Edwina had not mounted the front steps before the cottage door flung open and a dismal and anxious-looking man stood before them.

Even though Beryl did not suffer the ill effects of over-imbibing herself to any degree, she had spent enough time with those that did to recognize the signs. Terrence Crossley's eyes were bloodshot, and his face looked slack. He held the door open with one hand, and the other he placed protectively at his stomach. Beryl wondered if he had a chronic problem with drink or if he had tried to drown his sorrows upon discovering the census schedules had been stolen. She made an effort to pitch her voice low when she noticed him wincing at a passing birdcall.

"Whatever you're selling, I'm not buying it," the man said.

"Mr. Terrence Crossley, I presume?" Beryl said.

"Who wants to know?" he said. "Wait, don't I recognize you?" He turned to Edwina.

"You dropped some census schedules at my house, the Beeches, late last week," Edwina said.

Beryl noticed a flicker of pain pass over Mr. Crossley's features when the words *census schedules* penetrated his addled brain.

"Oh yes, I seem to remember now. What brings you by this morning?" he asked.

"We've been employed by the district registrar to get to the bottom of your problem," Edwina said.

Mr. Crossley looked up and down the country lane before taking a step backwards. He beckoned them inside and shut the door firmly behind them.

Beryl was no great housekeeper, but even she felt the cottage could use some attention from the starchy Beddoes. Even Beryl's own inadequate ministrations would not go amiss. Everywhere her gaze landed, she spotted dust or dirt or an item simply needing to be put away. She could feel Edwina's disdain as Mr. Crossley led them to the sitting room.

Beryl never minded sitting down on a straw mat, a grassy verge, or even on a sandy spot in the middle of the desert. She felt far less inclined to take her chances with one of the chairs in Mr. Crossley's sitting room. She happened to like her trousers. She had not expected it would be advisable to dress as though going on an expedition simply to pay a call at a local cottage.

Edwina, thankfully, kept any chiding thoughts to herself and settled gently onto the seat indicated. She crossed her ankles neatly, then pulled out her trusty notebook and matching tiny pencil. Beryl had to admire the stoicism with which her friend undertook her duties, despite the circumstances.

"Mr. Melton has told us that you reported to him first thing this morning that the census schedules had been stolen. When did you discover their absence?" Edwina asked.

"Just before I rang him, I had awakened with the great need to use the convenience," Mr. Crossley said, with a faint blush reaching his greyish face, "and as it takes me outside and into the back garden, I passed by my bicycle."

"Your bicycle?" Edwina asked.

"That's right, my bicycle. Which is where the problem first occurred to me," Mr. Crossley said.

Edwina made a notation in her notebook, and as she did so, Beryl thought she noticed a flicker of discomfort cross Mr. Crossley's face. As someone associated so closely with the halls of officialdom, Beryl had to ask herself why he would be uncomfortable with his version of events being taken down in writing. Was there more to Mr. Crossley than first met the eye?

"It was as I was returning from my trip to the little house that I paid attention to my bicycle. I use it on my rounds in order to reach the far edges of the village more efficiently. As a matter of fact, some form of conveyance was a requirement for securing the job as a census taker," Mr. Crossley said.

Beryl could imagine that it might well be a job requirement to have some way to perform the required duties besides on foot. The population of Walmsley Parva was small, but the acreage covered by the little village would take quite some time to traverse on foot. There was a great deal of land put to agricultural use, and it tended to spread things out more than the average person might assume. She had often been grateful for her prized cherry-red Rolls-Royce Silver Ghost when she and Edwina had found themselves in need of interviewing suspects or chasing down bits of information in the course of their investigations.

If she had not won her automobile in a card game several months earlier, she supposed she would have had to purchase a bicycle herself. Edwina already had one, which she regularly used. In fact, for reasons Beryl could not comprehend, Edwina seemed to prefer to use her bicycle whenever possible.

"Does your bicycle have something to do with the theft of the census schedules?" Edwina said.

Beryl thought she detected a note of impatience slipping into her friend's voice. She wondered if Edwina had been amongst those people who felt uncomfortable with the idea of sharing private information in the census. It was unlike her friend to be impatient or ill tempered with a suspect, let alone a client. Not that Mr. Crossley was their client, per se, but they needed his cooperation in order to at least make a start on unraveling the mystery. She found herself in the unlikely position of being the one to add a soothing voice to the interview.

"I'm sure it would be best to let Mr. Crossley tell his story in his own way, Edwina," Beryl said, bestowing one of her sparkling smiles on the miserable man.

Edwina simply pursed her lips and looked down at her notebook. Beryl thought it likely she would need to apologize later for embarrassing her partner in front of a virtual stranger. Still, they were on the case, and niceties could not always be observed. Especially when expediency was required, as it was in this case.

"When I looked at my bicycle, I didn't see the large sack that I used to carry the census schedules strapped onto the back. That's when it occurred to me that I couldn't remember having taken them inside when I arrived home the night before," Mr. Crossley said.

"What did you do next?" Beryl asked, leaning forward.

"I stood there staring at my bicycle, asking myself when the last time I had seen them was," Mr. Crossley said.

"And when was the last time you remember seeing the schedules?" Edwina said, lifting her eyes from her notebook.

"Are you going to have to tell this to Mr. Melton?" Mr. Crossley said. "I really need this job."

He looked from Beryl to Edwina and back again, his lower lip wobbling slightly as he did so. Beryl had the dreadful suspicion that he might burst into tears. This would not endear him to Edwina. Beryl had found that a brisk tone of voice generally helped to buck up the troops. The worst possible thing she could do was to speak to him gently or kindly. Edwina seemed to feel the same approach was required.

"I'm sure you must realize that our obligation is to king and country first in a matter such as this. After that, we report to the district registrar. Consideration of your employment is the very least of our concerns. Should you find yourself capable of helping us to discover what has happened to such sensitive documents, we will, of course, report that fact in a favorable light to Mr. Melton," Edwina said, giving him one of her starchiest stares.

Mr. Crossley looked as though he had been spoken to firmly by his nanny. As though he had been admonished for nibbling his toast away from the crusts and leaving his egg yolks on his plate. But his lip had ceased its wobbling, and he simply bobbed his head before continuing with his version of events.

"Of course, I understand. I shouldn't wonder if they would sack me after what's happened," Mr. Crossley said.

"You might help yourself by telling us where you last remember seeing the bag of census schedules," Beryl said.

"As it happens, the last time I remember clearly seeing the sack was on the back of my bicycle when I parked it in Walmsley Parva late last evening," Mr. Crossley said.

"And where did you park it exactly?" Beryl asked. There was a glint in Edwina's eyes she did not quite like the look of.

"I regret to say I left it leaned up against the wall of the Dove and Duck," Mr. Crossley said. His eyes drifted towards the floor, and he seemed to find his toe caps fascinating. Beryl thought she detected a bead of sweat trickling down his forehead.

"Which wall?" Beryl asked.

"The one on the side of the building, in that little alleyway between the pub and the cheesemonger," Mr. Crossley said quietly.

"You mean to say that you left sensitive private documents unattended on the back of a bicycle in a darkened alleyway next to a public house?" Edwina said.

Beryl was reminded of their days back at Miss DuPont's Finishing School for Young Ladies. Edwina had not been one of the first girls that one noticed. She had always been rather quiet and had basically abided by the rules. At least those rules that she had thought made sense. Beryl had noticed Edwina never got in trouble for those she broke, either. But now and again, something had struck Edwina as completely and utterly senseless, outrageous, or morally dubious.

Truth be told, the first time Beryl had ever really paid any attention to Edwina was the first time she had heard her raising her voice. Her tone had been almost identical to the one she was using on Terrence Crossley. The incident had involved an older girl who was a notorious bully. Beryl had happened upon a confrontation between Edwina and Veronica DeLisle one afternoon halfway through her first term at the school.

Edwina and Veronica had stood in the center of a ring of other girls. The confrontation had taken place in a large dormitory space, where one of the smallest and least prepossessing girls, Mary Winters, sat huddled, weeping silently on one of the iron bedsteads at the edge of the room.

Veronica, the spoilt sole daughter of an American shipping magnate, had spent weeks making sly digs and comments about Mary Winters. Edwina had finally had enough of it and had called her out in front of the rest of the dormitory of young women. There had simply been something so authoritative in her tone that all the other young women had backed away and had left Veronica on her own to face the icy dragon that lurked inside Edwina's rather diminutive chest.

Although she had not felt any remorse at seeing Veronica DeLisle put neatly in her place for her cruelty towards her fellow student, Beryl did not see that it was in their best interest to allow her friend to unleash the same sort of righteous indignation on Mr. Crossley.

"I'm sure that Mr. Crossley felt that in a village as peaceful and law abiding as Walmsley Parva, no harm would come to his property," Beryl said.

"But that's just it. It wasn't his property, was it? It belongs to the rest of us and, one could argue, to His Majesty," Edwina said. Beryl tried to signal to Edwina with her eyebrows that she was getting out of hand, but her friend simply ignored her and pushed on. "I don't suppose you had stopped by the pub to collect the census schedule from the proprietor, now had you?"

Mr. Crossley looked over at Beryl, as if to ask what his chances were of using that excuse for his irresponsible behavior. With Edwina's well-established ability to ferret out lies, Beryl didn't fancy his chances. She gave her head the slightest of shakes, and he swallowed dryly.

"No, Miss Davenport, I was there as a patron, not as a public servant," he said.

"Well, there's nothing to be done about it now besides to get to the truth. What time were you at the Dove and Duck?" Edwina asked.

"I suppose I arrived at about five thirty in the evening," Mr. Crossley said.

"And what time do you suppose that you left?" Beryl asked.

"That I don't rightly know," Mr. Crossley said. "I'm not really much of a drinker usually, and I believe I may have miscalculated my capacity for strong spirits. Very little of the evening remains clear to me as I try to think back on it now."

"So, you don't remember what time you left the Dove and Duck. Do you know if it was prior to closing time or if they had to turn you out after last call?" Beryl asked.

"I don't know. I seem to remember someone placing a firm hand under my arm and steering me out the door, but I don't know if that was because I had become unsociable, had run out of the means to pay for my drinks, or if the pub was closing," Mr. Crossley said.

"Do you remember if the sack was on the back of the bicycle when you exited the pub?" Edwina asked.

"I don't remember even riding the bicycle all the way back to this cottage," Mr. Crossley said.

"I should think that a large sack of census schedules might be quite heavy. Do you remember if it took extra effort to peddle your way home?" Beryl asked.

"As I said, I don't remember it at all. If I had to hazard a guess, I would say that everything seemed to take an extra effort last night. But I cannot possibly tell you if the bag was still there when I cycled home or if it had already been taken," Mr. Crossley said.

"So, you may have cycled all the way back here with it strapped to the back and taken it inside with you or set it somewhere for safekeeping, mightn't you have?" Edwina said with a note of hopefulness creeping into her voice for the first time during their visit.

"I thought of that as soon as I realized there was nothing on the back of the bicycle," Mr. Crossley said. "In fact, it was with a sense of sheer terror that I ran about the cottage, searching for the bag, as soon as I noticed it was not on the back of my bicycle."

"Is that when you decided to telephone to the district registrar?" Beryl asked.

"It was indeed. The worst telephone call I've ever had to place in my lifetime. I've never liked the blasted thing, anyway. Delivering bad news through it makes me like it even less."

Beryl had heard the same thing from any number of people. Edwina did not seem to particularly enjoy using the telephone if it was possible for her to communicate in some other way. Beryl had noticed that her friend was willing to answer it but did not seem to enjoy doing so. In fact, one of the ways in which Simpkins had convinced her to accept the presence of Beddoes and his financial assistance in doing so was a rather convincing argument he had made for Beddoes's impeccable phone manners.

Edwina had positively lit up at the notion that she would no longer need to attend to the telephone. When questioned about it, Edwina had said she was never quite certain if she was interrupting someone at an inopportune time when she telephoned. She had said that it made her feel presumptuous to do so and that she gravely disliked the notion that she could not see the face of the person with whom she was speaking. It seemed as though Mr. Crossley and Edwina had at least one thing in common.

"So, it would not be of any use for us to look over the cottage with you once more, would it?" Beryl said.

"I assure you there is nothing here for you to see. I would certainly not have put myself through the difficulty of relaying such a terrible bit of news to my employer if it had not been completely necessary. I assure you I made an entirely thorough search."

"It's not such a very large cottage that I expect it would be difficult to search it yourself thoroughly, anyway," Beryl said.

"I would still like to see the bicycle, in order to best describe it to anyone we question about having seen it yesterday," Edwina said, getting to her feet and snapping her notebook shut. Mr. Crossley rose and ushered the two ladies to the door.

He led them around the side of the cottage. The path beneath their feet was simply one created by footsteps passing between the door and the convenience located in a small shed at the back of the garden. No one had lavished the sort of care on the cottage that Beryl had become accustomed to noticing about the village.

No flowering plants made an effort to brighten up the property, nor were there any spots of earth put to good use for the production of food. Even the grass did not grow robustly. A large tree with a leafy canopy thrust most of the back garden into shadow. A ginger cat lay sunning itself in one of the few spots where light penetrated through the leaves. It blinked twice at them, then stretched and sauntered over to sniff delicately at Edwina's stocking-clad legs.

Leaning against the wall of the back side of the cottage was a black bicycle with gleaming chrome trim. For a man so desperately in need of a job, Mr. Crossley certainly had a fine-looking specimen of a bicycle. Edwina leaned over it for a thorough inspection. On the back of the bicycle Mr. Crossley had rigged up a sort of platform made of a wooden board and some wire to attach it. She assumed that must be how he had carried a heavy sack.

"Is this where you left the sack?" Edwina asked.

"Yes, it is," Mr. Crossley said.

"How did you attach the sack to the platform?" Edwina asked, pointing at the flat board in front of her.

"I used a stout bit of rope and lashed it down onto the platform," Mr. Crossley said.

"Is there any possibility that you might have not tied it down quite as firmly as you thought?" Beryl said, an idea dawning on her as she spoke.

"Are you suggesting that the bag simply fell off the back of the bicycle?" Edwina asked.

"I think it makes as much sense to assume it could have fallen off by accident as it does to think that someone would have deliberately stolen a bag of census schedules," Beryl said.

"Did you check the route between your cottage and the village?" Edwina asked.

Mr. Crossley shook his head slowly. "No, it did not occur to me to do so. I thoroughly investigated the cottage, and when I found it missing, I simply assumed someone had stolen it," he said.

"I bet that means that Mr. Melton did not make an effort to search for it, either," Beryl said. She turned to Edwina, who nodded.

"He certainly did not mention any such search to us when he asked us to look into the matter," Edwina said.

"I don't suppose you remember which route you took to come home last night, do you?" Beryl asked.

"I'm sorry, no, I don't. I would guess that I took the same route I generally take back from the village. If one is having difficulty finding one's way, it seems that relying upon the familiar would make the most sense," he said.

"And which route is that?" Edwina asked.

"If I'm coming back to the cottage from the center of the village, I generally travel along the Dunstable Road. It's the most direct route, and by the time I am finished up for the day, I'm generally not looking to add any more miles on my bicycle. I expect that would be the most logical place to look," he said.

"We shall do so right away," Edwina said. "I'm sure I don't need to remind you to keep this information to yourself. As Mr. Melton expressed to us this morning, it is a matter of national security."

"Mr. Melton turned the air blue making that clear to me when I first telephoned. There is no need to remind me, I assure you," Mr. Melton said.

"I don't suppose you'd care to accompany us as we go in search of your missing bag?" Edwina said.

Mr. Crossley placed a broad hand over his stomach. "Motorcars always make me feel a bit queasy, and my stomach is rocky enough this morning without it finding itself under duress."

If there was one thing Beryl did not particularly like, it was the idea of anything marring the beautiful leather interior of her automobile. Although she was more than willing to put the car through its paces, and even to brush aside the idea of a crumpled fender or a dent in one of the side panels as a result of enthusiastic driving, she felt there was no excuse for the interior to look anything but pristine. She was on no account prepared to allow a hungover public servant to sully her prize possession. She took Edwina by the arm and steered her back towards the front of the cottage and beat a hasty retreat, leaving Mr. Crossley to recede in the rearview mirror.

Chapter 8

There was no other word for it, Edwina thought to herself. She was fuming. Nothing about Mr. Crossley and his reasons for having lost the bag of census schedules produced any feelings of empathy on her part. For him to be so utterly irresponsible made her so angry, she wasn't sure she could quite remember how to breathe. Just the very fact that he generally took the Dunstable Road on his way back to his cottage caused her to feel irritated. Of all the places to have to search for missing items, the Dunstable Road was particularly disagreeable.

Both sides of the winding road were lined with overgrown hedgerows. Here and there piles of sticks and gullies provided even more challenges to the prospect of quickly scanning the area for signs of human debris. Although Edwina could rightly say that on occasion Beryl's driving made her feel quite motion sick, she couldn't imagine shirking her duty to her fledgling business or to her fellow citizens by claiming she could not assist with the search on account of it as Mr. Crossley had done. How such a man had ever acquired a post like that of census taker, she could not imagine. She made a mental note to ask Mr.

Melton how Mr. Crossley had come to be hired the very first time she had an opportunity to do so.

Beryl, however, seemed to be in her element poking through ditches and scrambling over low stone walls, assisted by a sturdy stick and a cheerful attitude. Edwina supposed Beryl didn't mind, as her private information was being recorded by someone else's government. Not that Beryl seemed to think much should be considered private. She lived her life like an open book and seemed to seek celebrity at every opportunity.

During the years between the time when they had been at finishing school together and when Beryl had turned up unexpectedly at the end of Edwina's driveway last autumn, Edwina had kept track of her famous friend through her infrequent letters and her ongoing presence in newspapers, in magazine articles, and even on film reels. Edwina thought it likely that Beryl would have had the details of her census information printed for all the world to see without a second thought.

Edwina had to admit to herself that not only was she irritated with Mr. Crossley, but she was somewhat miffed at her friend, as well. Beryl did not seem to take into consideration how distressed the average person would be knowing their details were available for all the world to see should the census schedules fall into the wrong hands. Edwina also had no desire to plod through every thicket and hedgerow between Mr. Crossley's cottage and the high street of Walmsley Parva. It did her disposition no good as she considered that there were at least three other ways he might have taken on his inebriated journey home.

She was bent over, poking at a pile of leaves and twigs, when she heard a motorcar slow to a stop beside her. Nora Blackburn, of Blackburn's Garage, leaned her head through the window, an enquiring look upon her face.

"Edwina, whatever are you up to?" Nora asked.

Edwina looked down at her once pristine business attire. She prided herself on looking professional every morning, when she awoke. It was a habit that had served her well that morning, when Mr. Melton had unexpectedly arrived at the Beeches, insisting upon speaking with private enquiry agents. In their rush to interrogate Terrence Crossley, it had not occurred to her to change into clothing more suitable for roaming about the countryside on a top secret scavenger hunt. She could not have foreseen the damage that would be done to her shoes, her stockings, and even to her second-best hat. Now she was forced to think of a likely story to tell Nora.

Edwina was not in the habit of lying, and she particularly disliked telling fibs to those people whose company she valued. Nora was one such person, and she found herself feeling even more irritated than she had been before Nora had slowed down to make her enquiries.

"I've lost a scarf, you see," she said. "You know the way that Beryl drives. It was such a nice day that we had the top down on the motorcar when we went out for a drive, and the wind simply blew it right off my neck."

"Would you like me to get out and help you to look?" Nora said. The young woman had such an eager and open face that Edwina felt doubly sorry for lying to her.

"Oh, that won't be necessary, but thank you so much for offering. Beryl is over there giving me a hand, and I'm sure that if it's possible to find what we're looking for, the two of us will manage it before long," Edwina said.

Nora did not look entirely convinced, but she gave a wave of her hand and drove off, leaving a cloud of dust behind her. Beryl appeared at Edwina's side as the car rounded the corner and slipped out of sight.

"Was that Nora Blackburn?" Beryl said.

"Yes. She stopped to offer to help look for whatever was missing," Edwina said. "I found myself in the unenviable position of having to lie to her."

"It's all part of our business, Ed," Beryl said. "Have you found anything?"

"Not a sausage," Edwina said. "I haven't seen signs of anything worth noting along through here at all, besides the odd sweets wrapper and an empty bottle of beer. But nothing that looks at all like a bag or even signs of recent disturbance. Even the wrapper that I found seems to be ages old. How about you?"

"Not a thing. Shall we drive on and check a little farther up the road?" Beryl asked.

Edwina nodded, and the two climbed back into the motorcar. Nothing else that unfolded that afternoon did anything to improve Edwina's mood. She was more disheartened than ever by the time they reached the village. She had come to realize that the average motorist or passerby gave no thought whatsoever to the impact upon the countryside of simply tossing one's leavings along the roadside. Truly, it was monstrous how unpleasant the highways and byways of her little village had become. She had never noticed before how thoughtless some people could be.

It did not help her mood that she and Beryl had agreed they would be remiss if they did not make at least a cursory attempt at searching for the bag along the other routes Mr. Crossley might have taken home in his drunken stupor. It was well past lunchtime when they decided he had been correct in his assessment that the bag had been stolen rather than simply lost off the back of a jouncing bicycle. Hot, thirsty, and thoroughly disgruntled, the two of them clambered back into the motorcar and made their way towards the Beeches.

"I suppose that leaves us with the next logical step," Beryl said, looking as though she had not spent hours poking through the undergrowth.

In fact, if anything, Beryl seemed cheered by their activity. Edwina thought how much her friend must have been missing her life of adventure poking about the brush in the back reaches of exotic locations, if a ramble through the hedgerows on the outskirts of Walmsley Parva left her looking so revitalized. It was with pain that she wondered if Beryl was going to be able to live a quiet life in the country for the long term. Still, she had no time for such worries at present. There were far more pressing things that needed her attention.

"And which step would that be exactly?" Edwina said.

"I think we need to start with the last location Mr. Crossley remembers being at," Beryl said. She looked over at the Dove and Duck. They had pulled to a stop across the street from the pub, and although she was not pleased to agree, Edwina knew that her friend was right to make such a suggestion. However, she could not imagine presenting herself on the high street looking so bedraggled. She would never consider heading into town wearing her gardening clothes. She was afraid she looked a far sight worse at present than she did after an afternoon planting and weeding in her beds.

"You think we should go in and speak with Bill, don't you?" Edwina said.

Bill Nevins, whilst a taciturn man, would be likely to know approximately how long Mr. Crossley had been in his establishment the evening before. With a sense of dread, Edwina reached for the door handle of the motorcar and prepared to exit. She felt Beryl's restraining hand on her arm.

"If discretion concerning the case is of the utmost importance, I don't believe it's in our best interest to make a spectacle of ourselves by looking like this in the high street," Beryl said. "I suggest we head back to the Beeches and ask Simpkins if he knows anything about Mr. Crossley's visit to the pub last night. I am quite certain he spent the evening there, as he almost always does."

Edwina had never felt quite so grateful for her gardener's disreputable habits in her life. She leaned back against the leather seat and felt some of her irritation melt away.

"An excellent idea," she said.

* * *

Although Simpkins had managed to convince Edwina to accept his help in paying the wages necessary to acquire a domestic servant to help with the housekeeping, he had not managed to warm her to the notion of also employing a cook. If the matter had been left up to Beryl, she would have vastly preferred to hire someone to assist with food preparation than to dust the bookshelves and sweep the floors. As far as Beryl could see, a body had to eat, but it made little difference to survival if one plumped the pillows or made the beds. Beryl herself was unable to be relied upon not to inflict food poisoning upon others should she be in charge of the kitchen. The extent of her culinary skills consisted of a fine array of cocktail recipes and the ability to open a tin of baked beans.

With their new responsibilities as enquiry agents, Edwina often did not spend as much time tending to kitchen duties as she had done in the past. Beryl did not concern herself particularly with such things, but she knew that Edwina felt there were standards to be upheld. As soon as they pulled to a stop in front of the Beeches, Edwina hurried out of the automobile and straight on to the scullery.

As Beryl followed her down the long hallway towards the back of the house, she noticed a savory smell already drifted through the air. Unlike herself, Simpkins was a dab hand in the kitchen. He had turned towards assisting with such duties with regularity of late. Beryl was not always entirely sure what she was being served when he placed plates of food in front of her, but she had made it a lifelong habit not to make careful enquiries about such things. Given the locations in which she had spent much of her time, and the hosts with whom she had spent it, it would not have done to be perceived to be fussy about her food. One never knew if one's host might become violent if offended.

Besides, she applied the same philosophy to her eating habits as she did to any new ventures in life, never assuming she would not like a thing until she tried it. Despite this, she had been inordinately relieved when Edwina had explained that toad-in-the-hole was not in any way a dish that featured amphibians. Beryl had on occasion encountered local delicacies that relied upon reptiles and amphibians as a main ingredient, but she could not honestly say she had ever enjoyed the experience. Still, if it came down to a choice between survival and its alternative, Beryl voted for survival every time. After all, her mouth was only one small part of her existence.

But it didn't smell as though she was likely to be disappointed on any front with whatever it was that Simpkins was preparing. His newfound wealth and access to the culinary delights of Colonel Kimberly's Condiment Company had broadened his culinary offerings considerably. Despite the fact that she had often seen him so attired, it always gave Beryl a bit of a chuckle to enter the kitchen and find a grizzled Simpkins adorned in one of Edwina's frilly aprons. She supposed if their domestic arrangements were to continue as they had been for the past few weeks, it would be wise for him to acquire an apron all his own. Although she thought that suggesting such might be opening a tin of worms that no one wished to stare down into.

Simpkins's continuing presence at the Beeches as a member of the household had taken some getting used to. She knew that the arrangement weighed on Edwina's mind, and she knew that Simpkins was aware that it might be a somewhat precarious arrangement, as well. She wondered idly if his willingness to launch himself into the domestic responsibilities breach had something to do with his desire to remain in residence.

She expected that his life before moving into a guest room at the back of the house had been quite a lonely one. For many years Simpkins had been a widower, and with the recent loss of his brother-in-law, he was quite alone in the world. She supposed his long years of living without a woman in the house explained his skills in the kitchen. He looked up and pointed a wooden spoon at them as she and Edwina entered the kitchen.

"It's a good job this meal didn't have to be served straight out of the oven, like one of them fancy French puffy-egg dishes," Simpkins said. "I thought you were only going to be gone for a little while. What time do you call this then?"

"We are on a new case," Edwina said. "We were unexpectedly detained."

"A new case, you say. Why don't you sit down and take a load off? It looks like it must be something out of the ordinary for the two of you to be so rumpled looking," he said, wiping his hands on the apron.

Beryl would have to agree that Simpkins's assessment was accurate. The two of them looked like they had been off on a two-day tramp through jungle underbrush. Her trousers were stained, and her hands were grubby. Edwina's shoes would be lucky to be salvaged. After months of drought conditions, the rains had returned, and Edwina seemed to have found at least one muddy hollow to have wandered into.

"If the luncheon will last a moment more, and even if it won't, I must freshen up," Edwina said.

Beryl expected Edwina to head to her bedroom to change her entire outfit, but instead her diminutive friend simply turned towards the kitchen sink and turned on the taps. Beryl joined her at the sink for a thorough scrubbing, and within two minutes' time, they were both seated at the kitchen table, with plates of rice and some sort of sauced poultry in front of them. Beryl leaned in and inhaled the steaming fragrant scent wafting off her plate. She recognized the scent of the spices as something similar to that of a dish she had once enjoyed on a trek through India.

"What have you whipped up for us this time?" Beryl asked. Out of the corner of her eye, she noticed Edwina moving the food around ever so slightly with her fork to inspect it.

"It's something called a curry. I have all those jars and bottles of samples from Colonel Kimberly's. They came with a recipe booklet, so I thought I would give one a try. What do you think?" Simpkins asked as he sat at the table to join them.

Beryl raised her fork to her lips and sampled a bite of the deep yellow sauce, chicken, and rice. Like most of Simpkins's concoctions, it was surprisingly delicious. It was not, however, suited for eating with a fork. She seemed to remember an entirely different manner of consumption when she had visited a family in their home during her journey to India.

"It's absolutely delicious. This is exactly the sort of thing English cuisine could use to perk it right up," Beryl said. "But I do think we'll do better with spoons." She shoved back her chair and fetched three of them from a drawer in the butler's pantry. She handed one to Edwina, who flashed her a look of gratitude. Although Edwina might be willing to get grubby out traipsing through the underbrush, following clues, she was not likely to endure the humiliation of dribbling her food down the front of her blouse.

Beryl noticed Simpkins trying not to betray his interest in Edwina's reaction. He always did seem to be desirous of her approval for his creative efforts. Or maybe it was just that he was concerned about her overall health. Unlike Beryl, she did tend to have trouble keeping on weight, and when at all agitated, she lost her appetite entirely. Perhaps it was not that Simpkins had an interest in praise, but rather he was taking notes as to the things that would be most likely to coerce Edwina into eating.

"Simpkins, you've outdone yourself," Edwina said after swallowing a bite. "Is this something you have come up with yourself, or was this sauce already concocted and bottled up as an offering from Colonel Kimberly's product line?"

"It's really a mixture of this and that from several different bottles and jars. I added one or two adjustments to the recipe they sent, but I can't take credit for any sort of genius on this front," Simpkins said before a wide smile spread across his face as he watched Edwina tuck her spoon into her dish for a second bite.

"I think you would be wise to share those adjustments with whoever is in charge of product development at Colonel Kimberly's. I can see how a line of foodstuffs that are already assembled in jars would make good sense for working women. Not everyone has someone in the kitchen taking care of things whilst they're out working, do they?" Edwina said.

"You might be on to something there. I'll be sure to bring it up at the next board meeting," Simpkins said.

It was amusing to consider Simpkins sitting in the conference room of the Colonel Kimberly's headquarters in London, his hobnailed boots stretched out beneath the long varnished table ringed by men in three-piece suits. Beryl had accompanied him, as had Edwina, on his first trip into London to meet with the company. It had been an experience Beryl would never forget. And although Simpkins had been an unorthodox head of the company in the few short weeks since he took up the position, he had taken his responsibilities seriously.

Part of their trip to the London headquarters of the company had involved a visit to the factory where the products were made, at Simpkins's insistence. Even though he had seemed quite out of place in the boardroom, he had easily struck up conversations with factory workers. With his gap-toothed smile and his childlike interest in the workings of the factory, he had charmed his employees to a surprising degree. Even the ladies in the office who handled the bookkeeping and correspondence had seemed to feel he was a breath of fresh air.

But it was his stop at the recipe-development kitchen that had been the highlight of their visit. He had carefully sampled each and every new recipe under consideration and had given thorough and thoughtful feedback. He had struck up a lively correspondence with the condiment creator in chief, and the Beeches had benefited greatly from his new connection. Beryl had been wondering just how long she would be able to endure meals consisting of fried eggs, plain roasted chickens, and innumerable iterations of potatoes.

Although she was always willing to eat what was placed before her, if forced to admit the truth, she would say there were certainly other cuisines in the world she would prefer to be stuck with. Now and again while staring down at a plate of mushy peas, she would cast her mind back to a different sort of meal entirely that she had enjoyed in China or one she had partaken of in Italy.

"It certainly beats grabbing a pie down at the pub," Beryl said.

"Speaking of the pub, Simpkins, we have a question for you concerning the new case," Edwina said.

"You haven't said exactly which case it is," Simpkins said.

Edwina and Beryl looked significantly at each other. Even though they had promised not to disclose the nature of their case to anyone besides the census taker, they had not discussed the fact that their little private enquiry agency had in fact admitted a one-third partner. Such a thing had not come up before, and Beryl felt it wise to let Edwina take the lead in this decision. She shrugged her shoulders and turned her attention back to her bowl of curry.

"This is one of those times when it's important that the silent part of 'silent partner' be strictly adhered to. Are you quite certain you can do that?" Edwina said, laying down her spoon.

Simpkins nodded. "Did you know that I am one of the three people in the world who know the exact recipe for Colonel Kimberly's piccalilli?" he asked. "I expect if I can be entrusted with a secret like that, I can hold my tongue with the details of the case."

"I just wanted to impress upon you that we have given our

word not to discuss it, and we need you to provide yours, as well," Edwina said. "I know you have good judgment on such matters."

"Well, what is it, then?" Simpkins asked. "Beddoes said this morning that a rather het up gentleman had appeared at the crack of dawn, demanding to see you two."

"In a nutshell, the census schedules for all of Walmsley Parva have been stolen," Beryl said. She felt it was best to get things out in the open as quickly as possible. Besides, she had noticed that when speaking with Simpkins, getting to the point was always a better choice than dawdling.

"Stolen, you say? Do you think that's part of the burglaries that have been going on?" Simpkins asked.

"We honestly don't know at this point. We just know that it's imperative that we recover them and that we do so without anyone finding out they have gone missing," Beryl said.

"They're worried about a general strike, aren't they?" Simpkins said.

"The district registrar did mention that it would be likely to cause a widespread disturbance if this news got out," Edwina said.

"So, what is it you wanted to ask me about? I don't know anything about the burglaries. If I did, I would have already told you," Simpkins said.

"We wanted to ask if you remember seeing Terrence Crossley at the pub last night," Beryl said.

"Does that have to do with the theft?" Simpkins said. "Does he think someone from the Dove and Duck stole them?"

"The fact of the matter is he can't seem to remember exactly when they went missing. He remembers being at the Dove and Duck, but he doesn't remember if the bag of census schedules was on the back of his bicycle when he left to head home or if it had already gone missing at that point," Edwina said.

"What we wondered was, do you know what time he left,

did you see anyone acting suspiciously, and do you remember seeing his bicycle?" Beryl said.

Simpkins leaned back in his chair with a creak and stared up at the ceiling. He scratched his greying stubble with a gnarled finger for a moment and then turned his gaze from one woman to the other.

"I remember Terrence Crossley being at the pub, because he was calling a bit of attention to himself. I don't think he's much of a drinker under ordinary circumstances, and he had gotten a little bit merry on not very much cider," Simpkins said.

"Was he there until the pub closed?" Beryl asked.

"I wasn't there until closing time myself, but I believe he was still there when I left," Simpkins said. "I don't remember seeing a bag, which would've been out of place inside the Dove and Duck, that evening."

"Did you see his bicycle when you left?" Edwina asked.

"I can't say that I did. Where was it supposedly left?" Simpkins asked.

"He said he propped it up on the wall between the pub and the cheesemonger," Edwina said. "He claims to have left the sack of census schedules tied to a board on the back of the bicycle when he went inside."

"What a damn fool. Excuse my language," Simpkins said.

"That's exactly what Edwina thought," Beryl said. "Did you see it?"

"That would have been going in the opposite direction. I walked home coming up the high street, not going down it, so even if the bag was still there when I left, I wouldn't have seen it. I'm sorry I can't be more help," Simpkins said.

"Do you remember anyone else behaving strangely?" Edwina asked.

"To be honest with you, Miss Edwina, the clientele at the Dove and Duck often acts a bit strangely. Last night there was a lively dart game that had the dander up for a lot of the lads."

"Do you remember any gossip about the magistrate's death?" Beryl asked.

"Do you think that the census-schedule theft is connected to what happened to old Faraday?" Simpkins asked.

"It's far too early to assume they are connected or not connected. I was just wondering if it was a topic of conversation," Beryl said.

"It was mentioned for sure. I'd have to say that there weren't many mourners there at the pub last night," Simpkins said.

"So, Mr. Faraday wasn't a particularly popular man amongst his neighbors?" Beryl asked.

"No, he was not. A lot of the men who frequent the pub had often found themselves frequenting his magistrates' court, as well. There was some idle talk about who could possibly have done away with the old coot."

Beryl thought it rich that Simpkins was calling anyone else old. Gordon Faraday had to have been at least ten years younger than Simpkins. And she guessed it likely his liver had been in far better condition. Still, she did not wish to dissuade Simpkins from sharing what he knew by insulting him.

"Did anyone share an opinion about who they thought might have killed him, if he was not someone who met with an accident?" Edwina asked.

"The general consensus was that our new under-gardener might've had a hand in what happened to him," Simpkins said.

"Do you think that was the case?" Beryl asked.

"I think it's always easiest to blame things on outsiders and newcomers. There were at least a half dozen men in the pub last night that had as good a reason as Declan O'Shea to want the magistrate belowground instead of above it," Simpkins said. "I can tell you that nobody was pointing a finger specifically at anybody besides him, though."

"It sounds as though we're going to need to speak to Bill Nevins down at the pub," Beryl said.

"I think that's a job best left to you," Edwina said. She dabbed gently at the corners of her mouth with her napkin before pushing back her chair. "Thank you for the meal, Simpkins. Now, if you'll excuse me, I'm going to go and run a hot bath."

Chapter 9

Edwina felt a little guilty about having a bath after luncheon. It was simply not the right time of day to do such a thing. The entire day felt poorly arranged. It did feel good, however, to remove the dirt from underneath her fingernails and to thoroughly rinse the muck from her arms and her face. And, she confessed, it was lovely to have someone else in the house to draw the bath for her.

Beddoes was well trained enough to not even look askance when her mistress had enquired if it was possible that there was enough hot water for a bath at this unorthodox time of day. The maid had simply nodded and set about taking care of things. Edwina felt all the more grateful for the assistance when she discovered her freshly cleaned and polished shoes placed in front of her wardrobe in her bedroom after leaving the bathroom.

She dressed quickly in a lightweight day dress that would prove suitable for whatever the afternoon might have in store for her. Edwina had learned quickly that one never knew what could happen when she and Beryl were on a case. As that very day had proved, it was best to be prepared to receive callers, to head straight into the village, or even to go beating through the hedgerows in search of clues.

She hoped that she might be able to spend a little time that afternoon at the typewriter. She had spent her time poking about through the underbrush not only searching for Terrence Crossley's lost bag but also turning over in her mind what might happen next in her novel. In that way, at least, the time spent grubbing about that morning had not been a complete waste.

Humming quietly to herself as she tripped down the stairs and along the passageway towards the morning room, she felt the eager anticipation that a stolen hour for her novel always elicited. But before she rolled a crisp blank sheet of typewriter paper beneath the roller bar of the gleaming Remington portable, she heard a sharp rap at the door. After a moment Beddoes poked her head in and announced a visitor had arrived.

"Thank you, Beddoes. Please show whoever it is in," Edwina said.

"I thought you would want to know, miss, that Constable Gibbs has come to pay a call on the under-gardener. She did not actually come to the door," Beddoes said.

Edwina thought she noticed a flicker of criticism pass over the other woman's face. She was quite certain Beddoes did not approve of the police skulking about and certainly not if they did so without having announced themselves properly by coming to the front door. Edwina could not agree more. She pushed back her chair and went to the long window at the far end of the room. There, near the goldfish pond, stood Constable Gibbs and Declan. Even from a distance it was clear that her new employee did not look as though the conversation suited him.

"Thank you, Beddoes. I'll see to this myself," Edwina said.

She headed out the door of the morning room and down the hallway, then paused to grab a wide-brimmed hat from the hall tree. It would never do to allow Constable Gibbs to think she had provoked Edwina into hurrying. Besides, Edwina took a bit of pride in her complexion and had no intention of spoiling it for anyone, least of all for a new under-gardener and the local constable. She was about to whistle for Crumpet when he appeared at her feet and pranced around them in eager anticipation of a romp outside. She opened the front door, and he jetted out past her. She was gratified to hear him release a long series of barks as he rounded the side of the house in the direction Edwina knew the constable would be found.

Edwina followed sedately, observing the constable and Declan as she approached. Declan's body language was growing more and more hostile with each step she took. Constable Gibbs's looked much as usual. That is to say, she always looked somewhat hostile. Despite the fact that he towered over the police officer, Constable Gibbs appeared to be holding her own. The square set of her shoulders and her hands propped into fists upon her hips made her appear to take up far more space than was actually the case. Whilst Edwina did not enjoy the constable's company, she did admire the way the woman had managed to hold on to her job even after the men had returned from the war. It was a commentary on her tenacity as well as her capability that she had done so.

Edwina called to Crumpet just before he reached the pair at the goldfish pond. She did not want her dog to make a habit of nipping at the police officer's heels.

"Constable Gibbs, what brings you by again today?" Edwina called out.

"I told you I would be back to ask your employee some questions if I felt that the situation merited it. I'm sorry to say that it does," Constable Gibbs said.

"What has changed since yesterday that you wish to speak with him?" Edwina said. She felt a cold finger of dread creep up her spine as she considered the fact that the constable was likely there in connection with the magistrate's death.

"I am still investigating the series of burglaries. But now that there has been an unexplained death, it's all the more urgent that I get to the bottom of things before anyone else is hurt," Constable Gibbs said.

"You're not trying to pin what happened to the magistrate on me, are you?" Declan O'Shea asked.

"I am not interested in blaming anyone for a crime they did not commit. But I am here to ask you about your whereabouts yesterday, at the time the magistrate's house was being broken into," the constable said.

Edwina would be interested in knowing where the young man had been at that time, as well. Although she generally trusted Beryl's judgment, she was not completely convinced that it had been wise to hire the young man in the first place. The timing of his arrival and that of the commencement of the spate of burglaries undeniably overlapped. And he had proven to have an easily provoked disposition.

"I don't know what time his house was being broken into, so I couldn't possibly tell you where I was, now could I?" Declan said. "You're not going to trick me like that."

"Why don't you just go ahead and tell me where you were all of yesterday afternoon?" the constable said.

"After I left here, I went straight back to the stables. I mucked out a few stalls and polished some of the tack. For the rest of the afternoon, I was in my room up above the horses, and I stayed there until I went to the pub in the evening," Declan said.

"Can anyone vouch for you?" Constable Gibbs asked.

"You mean, did anyone see me, and can this person verify my whereabouts?" Declan asked.

"That's exactly what I meant," the constable said.

"Not unless you can take down a witness statement from the horses," Declan said. "We weren't scheduled for any riding lessons yesterday, and nobody stopped by unannounced whilst I was there, either."

"So no one can confirm that you were where you say you were all of yesterday afternoon?" Constable Gibbs said.

"I guess that is what I'm saying," Declan said. "But you're not going to be able to find anyone who says they saw me anywhere else, either, I can promise you that."

"You can be certain I will make it my business to find out if you are lying about not being at the magistrate's property," Constable Gibbs said. "The stakes in the case are considerably higher now."

"Are you accusing me of having had a hand in what happened to the magistrate?" Declan asked. For a fleeting moment, Edwina thought he was about to strike Constable Gibbs with the heavy iron digging fork he clutched in his broad hands.

"That is exactly what I am accusing you of doing. If you thought you had trouble with the law when he levied a fine against you, it is nothing compared to the trouble you are facing as a suspect in his untimely death," Constable Gibbs said.

"Are you arresting him?" Edwina asked, taking a step forward to lay a restraining hand on the young man's arm.

"Let's just say I want to speak to him in a more formal setting. Declan O'Shea, you will accompany me to the police station. I'm sure Miss Davenport can get by without you this afternoon. After all, she has only recently found the means to pay for staff, so she shan't feel much sting in your loss, I shouldn't think," the constable said. Constable Gibbs pointed towards the street side of the property, and for a second, Edwina wondered if Declan would attempt to run. Instead, he turned to her with a pleading look in his eyes.

"I didn't do anything wrong, miss. I want to hire you and

Miss Helliwell to take my case. I don't have any money to pay you, but I'll work without wages here at the Beeches for however long it takes to pay it off," he said as Constable Gibbs stepped forward and reached for his arm. "Please, get to the bottom of this before it is too late for me."

Beryl pulled up in front of the Beeches just in time to see Constable Gibbs escorting Declan off the property. Her first thought was to go after them and make enquiries. Her second was that he was likely in no real danger at the moment and provoking Constable Gibbs so early in an investigation would do no one any good, not even the young man about to be interrogated. She slid out from behind the wheel of her automobile and slammed the door behind her with a little more force than was necessary.

Beryl was not one to entertain prejudice against other people based on their nationality. If anything, her roaming about the world had confirmed to her that people were pretty much the same wherever one went. Some were dark, some were pale, some were kind, and some were cruel. It seemed that those things had very little to do with the place in which they were raised or the parents to whom they had been born. In the town in which her parents resided, there was a decided prejudice towards anyone who was not of Anglo-Saxon descent.

Upon her entrance into the wider world, Beryl had been amused to discover how highly regarded were all things French by parties more sophisticated than the small mill town in which she had been raised. During her childhood there had been a persistent prejudice against the French-Canadian population working in the mills, and it had surprised and delighted Beryl to find that such things were not true everywhere that she went.

It was disheartening, however, after so many truly tragic things had occurred during the war years to find that something so trivial as someone's background still seemed to matter so much, especially to those in power. Although, it could be argued that Constable Gibbs was not someone who wielded a great deal of power. In Beryl's experience, oftentimes those with only a little bit of power were the most likely to try to use it, especially against those with even less than their own. She supposed it was a way to get one's foot onto the ladder of success, but it always gave her pause when she had to deal with such individuals.

She pushed open the door to the Beeches and hurried along the hallway. She could hear the faint clacking sound of the Remington portable typewriter echoing through the house. She followed the sound to the morning room and pushed open the door. She felt no need to knock as the space was a joint office space she shared with Edwina, but when she noticed Edwina hastily rolling a sheet of typewriter paper from the machine and tucking it away in a desk, Beryl wondered if she should be more respectful of her friend's privacy. Certainly, Edwina looked abashed about something.

Beryl thought about teasing her about whatever she might have been up to, but then thought better of it. One of the things she had learned during her many journeys with small parties was that respecting privacy was one of the best ways to keep morale at its peak. Edwina was used to living on her own and had never complained about Beryl's presence in her home. Beryl did not wish to give her any cause to do so and wisely kept her inquisitiveness, at least on the subject of secretive documents, to herself.

"I just saw Constable Gibbs leading off our new undergardener," Beryl said in an effort to lead the conversation in a direction wholly unconnected to Edwina's typing. She noticed her friend's shoulders creeping back down away from her ears and congratulated herself on making the right decision.

"She is taking him in for official questioning in connection with the crimes at the magistrate's house," Edwina said.

"I suppose that was bound to happen sooner or later, wasn't it?" Beryl said. "What with the attitude towards the manner in which the magistrate died."

"I think that if someone is responsible for the magistrate's death, there are few suspects that seem more likely than Declan O'Shea," Edwina said. "The poor young man seems rather desperate."

"I suppose he must be. I think it unlikely that he will get the same sort of fair investigation from Constable Gibbs that a local young man might."

"I would say he agrees with you. I expect that's why he attempted to hire us as she was leading him away," Edwina said.

"Did he now?" Beryl said, sitting down in one of the shabby but comfortable chairs flanking the fireplace.

"Yes, he did. He offered to work here at the Beeches for free until he could pay off our fee," Edwina said. "I'm afraid that did very little to convince me of his innocence."

"This is an honorable enough thing to do. And one that is typical, is it not? I should think that in a small community such as this one, bartering for goods and services is often the done thing," Beryl said.

"I thought the sole reason he needed this job for pay was to pay off his fine levied by the magistrate. How does he suddenly have no need of the money we would pay him?" Edwina asked.

"I suppose he thinks that if he faces the hangman's noose, a fine for brawling in front of the pub is of very little consequence. I doubt very much the local court will go after any of his far-off relatives to pay it off after he's been hanged, don't you?" Beryl asked.

"That's one explanation. But you have to consider that there might just be another," Edwina said, tapping her small fingers on the desk in front of her.

Beryl had often noticed that when Edwina did not have her

knitting, she tended to fidget. Perhaps that was why she turned out such a high volume of woolen items. There was something far more ladylike about using restless energy to produce handcrafts than there was in shifting and shuffling about in one's seat like a small boy in a pew at church.

Beryl never had such problems herself. When she was moving, she was moving somewhere. When she was sitting still, she sat completely still. Many was the time she had surprised local guides with her ability to remain perfectly motionless in the bush while waiting for large game to pass by. Edwina would never be able to sit still quietly enough for anything interesting at all to show up at the local watering hole.

"And what do you suggest that is?" Beryl said.

"It's possible that he has already found a way to get ahold of the money he needs and that he no longer requires our wages to pay off his fine."

"Do you really think that Declan is the burglar?" Beryl said.

"I don't know who the burglar is. But I don't feel convinced of his innocence. And before you get on your high horse and say it's because he's Irish, I hope you will do me the favor of considering that you may be just as inclined to believe him innocent because he's Irish as others are to believe him guilty for the same reason," Edwina said.

Beryl traced the worn brocade pattern on the arm of her chair with a long index finger. There was something to be said for Edwina's insight. Perhaps she had been too quick to defend him as a matter of habit. She always did root for the underdog. The truth of the matter was that she did not know enough about his character to suggest whether or not he made a likely suspect. She knew nothing of his history or even what had brought him to the village. It occurred to her that she was not behaving as a professional investigator and had allowed emotion to sway her as much as she had berated the villagers of Walmsley Parva for doing the same.

"Thank you for helping me to see sense. Of course, you're right that we need to investigate this in a completely open-minded way," Beryl said. "Did you refuse to take his case?" she asked. "If you did, I would completely understand."

"I didn't respond one way or the other. Constable Gibbs dragged him off before I could formulate a response. Besides, I wished to consult with you before making a decision. It seems like the sort of thing we should decide together."

"We do already have a client, and one that will take most of our efforts if we are to determine what happened before word leaks out that the census schedules have gone missing," Beryl said. "I'm not sure we will have enough time and energy left over to devote to his troubles."

"It seems to me that the two cases could well be linked. Walmsley Parva has never been the sort of place where one worried about locking one's doors. Somehow it seems unlikely to me that there would suddenly be two sets of thieves running about the village," Edwina said.

"Are you suggesting that we fold an investigation into the burglaries in general into our specific enquiry into the census-schedule theft?" Beryl asked. "That would cover investigating Declan at the same time, wouldn't it?"

"It would include him in the investigation, but not necessarily as our client. We could focus our investigation solely on the truth of the matter," Edwina said.

"So, if he's guilty, we won't keep that from Constable Gibbs or from the district registrar, right?" Beryl said.

"Exactly. We will follow the investigation wherever it leads, and if it leads to Declan so be it. If it takes us somewhere else, we will help to exonerate him," Edwina said.

"So, what's next?" Beryl asked.

Edwina looked up at the mantel clock.

"I propose that you change into something more suitable for

paying a condolence call and that we motor on over to pay our respects to Mrs. Faraday," Edwina said. "She may be able to give us some more information about the exact timing of the burglary. Perhaps that will help us to have a better idea if Declan was involved."

"I'll be back in a tick," Beryl said.

Chapter 10

Mrs. Deirdre Faraday was a good number of years younger than her husband. Not quite so young to have caused a scandal, but young enough to have caused tongues to wag when he had first brought her to the family home and installed her as the lady of the house. Seeing her now seated in the strong light of a south-facing window, Edwina realized she was perhaps not quite as young as she first appeared. As the light played against Mrs. Faraday's fair skin, Edwina noticed a network of fine lines tracing the edges of her eyes. There was a slight softening below her chin and a gathering of skin on her neck, which gave away her age. Edwina was shocked to think that Mrs. Faraday was likely only a very few years her junior.

She was a remarkably pretty woman. Perhaps that was part of the reason she appeared so youthful. Her eyes were a deep royal blue, and her golden-blond hair fell in soft waves around her heart-shaped face. Even though she showed signs of tremendous strain in her face and her posture, it was clear to see why rumors about her had swirled through the village when she had first arrived on Gordon Faraday's arm.

"It is very kind of you to call on me," Mrs. Faraday said. "I think it very brave of you to return here after what must have been such an upsetting incident the last time." Mrs. Faraday's gaze flicked towards the doorway. Edwina had noticed that the room in which Mrs. Faraday received them was positioned almost directly opposite the spot where her husband's body had been discovered.

"It was the very least we could do after such a tragic accident," Beryl said. "I'm sure you were far more shocked than we were."

"I never imagined when I left that morning that I would never see Gordon alive again," Mrs. Faraday said as she dabbed at the corner of her eye with a lace-trimmed hanky.

"I'm sure it was very distressing indeed," Edwina said. "I suppose it was just an ordinary day before the incident occurred, was it?"

"Entirely ordinary. That's one of the things that makes it feel so unreal. I had made plans to go off for the day, as had the children, like one so often does. If I had had any idea such an accident would befall him, I would have insisted that Gordon accompany me," Mrs. Faraday said.

"Were you off on some sort of adventure that he did not wish to join?" Beryl asked.

Mrs. Faraday nodded. "I love to go on long rambles through the countryside. I was forever trying to get Gordon to take more exercise. The doctor had recommended he lose at least a stone, and I thought it would do him a world of good. In fact, I had asked him to join me one last time just before I went out the door," she said.

"But he was not interested?" Edwina asked.

"He said he had no intention of traipsing about the countryside with no purpose whatsoever. He felt that my pastime was a waste of time and that it would be far better for me to spend my time on something more likely to raise his stature in the community," Mrs. Faraday said.

"What sort of thing did he have in mind?" Beryl asked.

"The Women's Institute was something he mentioned quite frequently. He also suggested I join the local bell ringers or offer to supervise the girl guides if I was so interested in spending time out of doors. He simply couldn't see the point of enjoying a bit of solitude in nature," Mrs. Faraday said. "But I've always felt that if one lived in the country, one should enjoy it. Otherwise why not live in town?"

Edwina could entirely see Mrs. Faraday's point. She loved rambling about the countryside herself with Crumpet at her side and her trusty camera dangling from its leather strap around her neck. Her mother had been no more approving of such things than it sounded like Mr. Faraday had been. One did not like to speak ill of the dead, but nothing she had heard about the magistrate had caused her to feel remorse over his sudden demise beyond that of common decency towards any fellow creature.

"So, Mr. Faraday was here alone all that morning?" Beryl said.

"He was, as far as I know. At least none of the family were here, nor was Nanny Meechum. My stepdaughter, Monica, had planned to go for a ride on her horse, which we keep stabled out at Brightwell Farm. And my son, Timothy, and his nanny were off to the shops for some shopping they needed to do," Mrs. Faraday said.

"I understand that your brother-in-law has been staying with you," Edwina said. "Had he left by then to return to his own home?"

"No. As a matter of fact, Alan is here still," Mrs. Faraday said. "Of course, he would want to remain with the family after such a tragedy. I've come to quite rely upon him since it happened. He is so very good at practical things."

"It's a shame he was not here with his brother when the burglary took place," Edwina said. "He might have been able to prevent whatever happened."

"Yes, it is a great pity. The poor boy is entirely consumed with guilt over what happened. He keeps saying over and over that if he had not been so insistent on going out himself, this might not have happened," Mrs. Faraday said. "I've said to him it's only natural that he would want to get out for a bit of fresh air now and again. He has always loved to fish."

"So, he was off fishing then?" Beryl asked.

"Yes, he was. Fishing is a lifelong hobby of his. He claims that he never has as good luck anywhere else as he does down at the mill pond at the edge of the village," Mrs. Faraday said. "Although I don't know if he will ever pick up his rod and reel again after what happened."

"There were no servants here, either, when we arrived," Edwina said.

"We have only Nanny and two in-house servants now," Mrs. Faraday said. She turned towards Edwina. "You know how difficult it is to keep help in the country."

Edwina nodded. "We've been very lucky to have recently acquired help of our own," Edwina said.

"You certainly are. Our help is a married couple, and they insist upon having the same day off. It is rather inconvenient, but with things being as they are, I was willing to acquiesce to their request," Mrs. Faraday said. "Mr. and Mrs. Breen are superior sorts of servants, so I am happy to make the concessions necessary to keep them in my employ."

"The day of the tragedy was the Breens' day off?" Edwina asked.

"Unfortunately, yes. That is the same day they have off every week, so there was nothing unusual in it at all," Mrs. Faraday said.

Edwina caught Beryl's gaze and arched an eyebrow significantly. Was it possible that the burglar knew the family schedule?

"Do you know if anyone else knew about your household

arrangements, especially in terms of your servants' day off?" Edwina asked.

"I suppose anyone might have known. It's the sort of thing one chats to others about in idle conversation. You know what it's like at parties and gatherings. Everyone with any size house whatsoever is always bemoaning the fact that they can't seem to keep servants. Days off, services rendered, and pay rates are topics of conversation at almost every luncheon, bridge party, and dinner gathering I attend," Mrs. Faraday said.

"I suppose the servants might have mentioned to someone that they had a certain day off, as well," Beryl said.

"Of course they did. Servants gossip even more readily than the rest of us do. The fact that we allowed the two of them to have the same day off would be considered quite the coup, I'm sure. I expect they were boasting about it to their social set as soon as their request was granted," Mrs. Faraday said.

Edwina thought Mrs. Faraday made a fair point. Anytime a member of the serving class was able to garner a concession from an employer, it was considered a triumph. Even though the serving class preferred to work for those they felt were, in fact, their betters, it did raise their estimation amongst their peers to have negotiated for the best possible concessions as regarded the terms of their employment. Edwina thought it likely that the schedule the Faraday servants adhered to was widely known throughout the village.

She was a little surprised that she had not already heard of it herself, although she supposed that Beddoes was not as well connected as some of the other servants in the village, as she was so new to town. And she was a superior sort of woman, one who likely would not find it appropriate to carry tales to her employer.

"Were you the first one of the household to return to Groveton Hall?" Edwina asked.

"I am relieved to say that I was. I would not have wanted one of the children to arrive here and find their father. Or to discover that the police had been called," Mrs. Faraday said.

"When we were here, we noticed that there were many signs of disturbance in the house, at least along the first-floor hallway," Beryl said. "I hope your losses were not very great in terms of the burglary, as well as the loss of your husband."

"We did lose several things of considerable value," Mrs. Faraday said. "A number of pieces of silver and, I'm sorry to say, quite a few items of jewelry from my dressing table were taken."

"Have you had the chance to look over things thoroughly in order to give a complete list to Constable Gibbs?" Edwina asked. "It would not be surprising if you have not had the presence of mind or the time, given what has befallen your husband, to turn your attention to smaller matters."

"It may sound a bit coldhearted, but checking the house over for stolen items has given me something to distract myself with since my husband's death," Mrs. Faraday said. "And I feel it likely to be of use in the investigation if I am able to provide Constable Gibbs with a complete list of what has gone missing."

Edwina nodded. "I'm quite certain that it would be very useful for her to know what to look for should a suspect come to her attention. If she could connect some of the stolen items to a suspect, it might well make a case."

"Besides your jewelry and the silver, was there anything else taken?" Beryl asked.

"Yes. A toy aeroplane that belongs to my son was also stolen," Mrs. Faraday said.

"A toy aeroplane? Is it valuable?" Beryl asked.

"It is to my son, but I can't imagine that it has any economic value. It holds a great deal of sentimental worth. It is one of his most prized possessions, and he has been rather distressed by its loss," Mrs. Faraday said.

"Can you think of any reason why anyone would want to take it?" Beryl asked.

"I suppose it just caught the burglar's eye. Perhaps he or she has a small child to give it to. Although I do think it was rather unkind," Mrs. Faraday said.

"What an odd thing to take," Edwina said.

"My poor son has been quite inconsolable ever since we discovered its loss," Mrs. Faraday said.

"The timing certainly couldn't have been worse, could it?" Edwina said. "After the loss of his father, to find that he did not have his favorite toy seems doubly cruel."

Edwina kept her eyes trained on Mrs. Faraday's face as she spoke. After her own dealings with Mr. Faraday, she could not imagine him being a particularly beloved father. There was every possibility that young Master Faraday had not keenly felt a sense of loss upon his father's demise. In fact, it would not surprise her in the least to hear that the child was as relieved as could be at the removal of the unpleasant and blustery man from his daily life.

"Of course, he's terribly distressed by the entire situation. The poor boy keeps having nightmares," Mrs. Faraday said. "It's taken considerable effort on the part of both Nanny and me to calm him down in the night."

"Was anything stolen from your brother-in-law or from your stepdaughter?" Beryl asked.

"Monica claims she also lost some small pieces of jewelry. Being still quite young, she does not have much of real value, although she did have a pair of sapphire earrings she had inherited. They belonged to her mother and are important to her, I believe."

"And what about Alan?" Edwina asked.

"I believe Alan mentioned some cuff links going missing, as well as a pocket watch and a cigar cutter," Mrs. Faraday said. "As he does not actually live here, Alan did not have as many possessions on site that could have been taken."

Beryl glanced over at Edwina and shifted slightly in her chair. Edwina took that as a sign that her friend felt that it was time to take their leave. Edwina could not agree more. It did not do to infringe upon the privacy of the bereaved for longer than was absolutely necessary. If there was one thing that everyone had gotten quite good at during the war years, it was paying condolence calls. Between the deaths overseas and the vast numbers of civilians lost to the flu epidemic, it had seemed a week could not go by without some sort of tragedy befalling someone at least loosely connected to the village.

"We are very sorry for your loss and do not wish to take up any more of your time. Please do let us know if we can assist you in any way," Edwina said, getting to her feet.

Mrs. Faraday nodded wearily and thanked them for calling as she showed them to the door.

Once they were safely back inside the motorcar and away from earshot, Edwina turned towards Beryl.

"What do you think of the grieving widow?" Beryl asked.

"I think she seems much as I would expect her to. I doubt very much that anyone would be overwhelmed with grief at the loss of a husband like Gordon Faraday," Edwina said.

"I would have to agree. She looked shocked more than saddened. And no matter how you feel about the deceased, there is always a great deal of tedious minutiae to take care of in the event of a death," Beryl said. "I don't envy her in the least."

"Nor do I. And it can't be easy to suddenly find oneself left to finish raising a son on one's own," Edwina said.

"And she has a stepdaughter, as well, correct?" Beryl said.

"Yes, Monica Billington," Edwina said. "It seems quite cruel for her to have lost so many parents at such a young age."

"What do you mean by 'so many'?" Beryl asked.

"Monica Billington is not only Mrs. Faraday's stepdaughter but Mr. Faraday's, as well. Her natural mother married Mr. Faraday after Monica's father died," Edwina said. "When she died, Mr. Faraday continued to act as her stepfather and guardian over the past several years."

"I wonder how well she has taken this latest turn of events," Beryl said. "Although considering his temperament, perhaps she will not feel the loss too keenly."

"I've never heard very much about the relationship between Monica and her father, but I suppose it likely that somebody has. I expect we should speak to her ourselves, if we can track her down," Edwina said.

"It shouldn't be too difficult. We know that she likes to go riding at Brightwell Farm," Beryl said.

"You know, her stepmother said something that troubles me just a bit about young Monica," Edwina said. "Did you notice that?"

"You mean when she spoke about the items Monica lost in the burglary?" Beryl asked.

"Exactly. She said Monica *claimed* to have lost them. It makes me wonder if Mrs. Faraday does not entirely trust her stepdaughter to tell the truth."

"I wondered the same thing. Which does make one think about what else the young lady might be inclined to lie about," Beryl said.

"I think we need to put her on our list of people to interview as soon as possible," Edwina said.

"I feel as though our visit to the Faraday home has brought up more questions than answers," Beryl said. "I doubt it has brought us any closer to finding the census schedules."

"What do you think we ought to do next?" Edwina asked.

"I think one of us would do well to take a closer look at Brightwell Farm. I think we should do a little poking around over there to see if anyone can vouch for Declan being on the premises when he claims to have been there," Beryl said. "If we could find an alibi for him, then we could at least remove him from our list of burglary suspects. At least for the Faraday burglary."

"Would you like to go, or shall I?" Edwina said.

"If you don't mind, I think I would prefer for you to be the one to lead the investigation into Declan's guilt or innocence," Beryl said. "I realize that I have not been as rigorous in my scrutiny of him as I should be, and I think you would be most likely to notice anything amiss with an open mind."

"That suits me quite well. Whilst I'm there, I shall order a load of manure to be delivered to the Beeches. Simpkins was saying something just the other day about wanting to acquire some, and I know that's where he prefers to purchase it," Edwina said.

"I'll drop you off on my way back to the Beeches. Will you be able to make your way home from there on foot?" Beryl asked.

Edwina looked out at the bright blue sky. She could think of nothing she would like more than a ramble along the country lanes. But she wasn't going to make the mistake of rattling around the countryside ill shod once again.

"I think it would be best for you to motor back to the Beeches. I'll change my clothing there and collect my bicycle. It's a perfect day to go for a ride, but I don't wish to put Beddoes out a second time in the footwear department," Edwina said. "We are just as lucky to have her as Mrs. Faraday is to have Mr. and Mrs. Breen. I'm not sure she will remain in our employ for much longer if I keep turning up with shoes in the same state as I did this morning."

Beryl nodded, then turned over the engine and started down the driveway.

Edwina had been right to change her clothing. She was especially grateful for the change to her footwear. The sort of shoes best suited to paying condolence calls were not the same sort one preferred for cycling or for stomping about through a farmyard. As Edwina coasted to a stop in front of a large, tidy barn, she wondered if she had been mistaken in not choosing to wear Wellington boots. Even though the day was warm and dry, there was a great deal of muck everywhere her gaze landed.

To her left, a half dozen horses cavorted in a spacious paddock. The sound of their whinnying carried over on the breeze. She was glad she had decided to leave Crumpet at home. As much as she could generally rely upon him to be well behaved, her little terrier was inclined to excitability in the presence of horses. He could easily have darted under the fencing enclosing the paddock and caused quite a ruction. She was not at all certain that the horses would have enjoyed his company as much as he would have theirs.

She had been to Brightwell Farm several times over the years on exactly the same sort of errand she was planning to use to explain her presence now. Generally, Simpkins asked her to order a load of manure every autumn, but this past year he had refrained from doing so. As she recalled that time, she felt a blush spread to her cheeks. Simpkins must have avoided making the request because he knew that she could have ill afforded even something as inexpensive as a load of manure. When Edwina thought back to those unpleasant days, she felt all the more grateful for the life she was living now.

Between the influx of cash that Simpkins's investment in their business had provided and the fact that Beryl was sharing the household expenses, Edwina felt far more comfortable. That was not to say she felt prosperous in any way whatsoever. But rather, she felt as though there was a bit of wiggle room in the budget and that perhaps things might just be looking up. She gave herself permission to dream for a moment of the day when she could well afford to order any number of carts of fertilizer for her beloved gardens.

She leaned her bicycle against a small outbuilding and gave a passing thought to Mr. Crossley and the theft that had occurred off the back of his. She looked around, but having seen no one nearby, she assumed her bicycle would be safe where she left it.

What was the world coming to, she wondered, if a bicycle in Walmsley Parva might be at risk of being stolen?

She headed for the stables. A large door stood open, and she stepped into the cool, dark space. The pungent smell of horses, hay, and leather filled her nostrils. She heard a noise at the back of the building and followed it. A man in his late fifties, with a broad back and salt-and-pepper hair, stood in a stall, applying a stiff brush to a chestnut-colored horse. He looked up as she approached.

"Good afternoon, Miss Davenport. What brings you by?" Jim Johnson said. The owner of Brightwell Farm was always a pleasant man to deal with. His two rosy cheeks reminded Edwina of polished apples, and she always found it a wonder that the horses didn't nip at them.

"I wondered if you still had any aged manure as top dressing for the gardens available? I never seemed to have gotten around to ordering any this past autumn," Edwina said.

"I'm sure we still have at least one cart's worth. Did you need more than that?" he asked.

"I shall have to be satisfied with whatever you've got on hand. The fault is my own that I was so delayed in ordering it," Edwina said.

"Follow me round the back of the barn, and I'll take a look at what there is," he said, wiping his hands on his trousers and giving the horse a final pat on its gleaming flank.

Edwina followed him out a door at the back of the building and found herself squinting in the bright sunshine. She hurried along, trying to match his long strides as he hustled towards an enclosure built against the far end of the barn. Mr. Johnson lifted a stout iron latch and pulled open the wooden door.

"What do you think? Will that do?" he asked, gesturing inside. Edwina was pleased to see several wheelbarrows full of crumbling fertilizer. If they did not need to sack Declan, she could foresee him spending the rest of the week getting it worked into various garden beds around her property.

"That will be perfect. Would you be able to have it delivered by tomorrow?" Edwina asked.

"I can have Declan take it out to you. I understand he's been picking up some extra hours at the Beeches when he's not needed here," Mr. Johnson said. "So, I assume he knows the way."

"I would appreciate it if you would allow him to do so," Edwina said. "I hope his employment at the Beeches is in no way hampering his duties here."

"Declan is a hard worker. He manages to get it all fitted in without any trouble," Mr. Johnson said. "He's a dab hand with the horses, too, is that boy."

"So, you are satisfied with his work?" Edwina asked.

"Absolutely. He just seems to have a knack for handling the horses, and like I said, he's a hard worker. I never have to light a fire under him to get things done. Has he been working out at the Beeches?" Mr. Johnson said.

"Simpkins seems very satisfied with his willingness to work and to learn. He was very up front about the fact that he has little experience in garden matters, but he seems to be a fast learner," Edwina said.

"I'm glad to hear it. I understand he's been having a bit of trouble in town," Mr. Johnson said.

"You heard about the trouble with Constable Gibbs?" Edwina asked.

"I'm afraid that I did."

"Did it give you pause about continuing to employ him?" Edwina asked.

"It's hard enough to get any help, let alone good help. As far as I'm concerned, some of the best horse handlers there are come from Ireland. I'm lucky to have him," Mr. Johnson said.

"But what about the possibility he had something to do with the thefts in the village?" Edwina asked.

"He seems to be a very conscientious young man so I don't believe it. And I would be shocked if he had anything to do with something criminal. Besides, he's so busy working here and now for you at the Beeches that I can't imagine him having time to get into any sort of mischief," Mr. Johnson said.

"Things have gotten even more difficult for him since Mr. Faraday was found dead," Edwina said.

"That was right nasty, wasn't it?" Mr. Johnson said. "I heard the magistrate fell down the stairs and broke his neck. Are people spreading rumors that Declan was involved with that, too?"

"I know only that the constable is concerned that Mr. Faraday could have died as a result of a confrontation with whoever was burgling his house. Since Declan is her prime suspect in the burglaries, it has made things more difficult for him," Edwina said.

"That young man just can't seem to catch a break. I heard about the fine levied against him by the magistrates' court for nothing more than a bit of high spirits," Mr. Johnson said.

"But that's just made things more suspicious when it comes to the magistrate's death," Edwina said.

"I wish there was something I could do for the poor lad," Mr. Johnson said. "Like I said, he's been a valued employee."

"It might help if you could remember if he was here when some of the burglaries took place. Has Constable Gibbs been out to ask you about it?" she asked.

"As a matter of fact, she was here not long ago. I can tell you the same thing I told her," Mr. Johnson said.

"Which was?" Edwina asked.

"I wish I could tell anyone that I had seen Declan during the time in question, but I have to tell the truth. I didn't see him at all."

"Not at all during that entire time span of yesterday morning?" Edwina asked.

"Not at all. I had gone over to look at a foal in Pershing

Magna and was gone the better part of the day. What I can say is that when I returned here to the farm, all his duties had been performed," Mr. Johnson said.

"Which duties were those?" Edwina asked.

"Feeding and watering the horses and mucking out the stalls," Mr. Johnson said.

"How many horses do you have here on the property right now?" Edwina asked.

"We have twenty-six. It would've taken him quite a while to do all that," Mr. Johnson said.

"But you said you were gone all day, didn't you?" Edwina said. "Would that work have taken him all day?"

"Honestly, no, it would not have done. He could have fed, watered, and mucked out in the morning and had the rest of the afternoon free," he said.

"Or he could have done it in the afternoon, before you returned, couldn't he?" Edwina asked.

"I doubt very much he would've let the horses be hungry or thirsty. It's just not in his character to allow them to suffer like that," Mr. Johnson said.

"Suppose he had fed and watered them and then left the property. He could have returned later and mucked out the stalls, couldn't he?" Edwina said.

Mr. Johnson looked out across the field, at where the horses were cavorting in the paddock. He looked back at Edwina and nodded slowly.

"It's not the way we usually do things, but I suppose if you had a good reason to leave the property, that would be the way you would do it. All I can say is what I had expected him to do was done when I returned. I can't say more than that," Mr. Johnson said.

"Is there anyone else here on the property that might have seen him?" Edwina asked.

"It's just the missus and me that live here full-time, since the boys are gone."

Edwina wished she had not had to ask such an insensitive question. Mr. and Mrs. Johnson were amongst those unfortunate couples who had lost all three of their sons to the front. One by one by one, each of the boys—whom they had expected to carry on the farm in their old age—had been lost to enemy fire. Edwina wondered if Mr. Johnson's openheartedness towards Declan might be caused in part by his longing to fill the void left by his own children. It would not be the first time she had met someone who was replacing their loss with a stranger. One of the uglier sides of the aftermath of the war was how many people found it easy to take advantage of the grief of others. Still, the question did have to be asked.

"So, Declan is the only employee at Brightwell Farm at present?" Edwina asked.

"He is. You know how it is with agricultural labor now. It seems that all the young men who might still be able bodied have decided to leave the countryside and seek jobs in the cities. I never thought it would come to this," he said, shaking his head as he looked around.

"You give riding lessons here, as well, don't you?" Edwina asked.

"My wife does that, for the most part, although Declan has offered to pitch in a few times, and he's good at that, as well. At least with the customers who aren't put off by his accent."

"Did you have any riding lessons scheduled for that day? Could any of the riders have seen him?" Edwina asked.

"I'm afraid not. We had no one scheduled that day because I wanted to take the missus with me over to see that foal. My wife has a good eye for horseflesh, and I value her opinion," Mr. Johnson said. "Besides, we never take any lessons that day. With so many things that need doing around the farm, and with not so many people with money to spend on riding lessons, it makes good sense not to offer lessons every day."

"You also board horses for people who don't take lessons, don't you?" Edwina asked.

"Yes, we do. That's the majority of our business," Mr. Johnson said.

"Could any of the people who stable their horses here have simply dropped by, or do they need to schedule times to visit?" Edwina asked.

"I don't promise that one of us will be in attendance to help them with something, but those who board here are always welcome to have access to their own animals," Mr. Johnson said.

"Do you have a list of names of the people that board their horses here that you could provide me?" Edwina asked.

"Absolutely. I'd be happy to share the names with you, since it's not particularly private information. But why would you want it?" he asked.

"Declan has asked my business partner, Miss Helliwell, and me to look into the allegations against him. I said that I would do what I could to help establish his alibi for the time of the magistrate's death," Edwina said.

"Anything I can do to help Declan out is fine with me," Mr. Johnson said. "Follow me into the office, and I'll get you that list."

They traipsed into the barn, and Mr. Johnson led Edwina to a small room near the front that she had been in many times before, ordering manure or making a payment. The office smelled like the rest of the stable, but because it had a door, there were fewer bits of straw littering the floor or every available surface.

Mr. Johnson took a seat in a creaky chair behind a battered wooden desk. He opened a drawer and pulled out a large leather ledger and plunked it down in front of him. He turned the pages with a callused hand until he arrived at one marked *June* on the top of the page.

"If you can wait a few minutes, I will copy this out for you," he said.

"I wouldn't want you to go to any trouble, since I interrupted your work," Edwina said. "I'd be happy to let you get back to what you are doing and copy the names down myself."

"That would be most helpful. I have four more horses to attend to before I'll call it an afternoon," Mr. Johnson said. "If you'll just put the ledger back into the drawer when you're finished, I'll get back to what I was doing."

With that, he left the office, and Edwina took up his seat behind the desk. She pulled her small notepad from her pocket and began carefully copying the list into it. There were quite a number of familiar names amongst the boarders at Brightwell Farm. Just as Mrs. Faraday had said, her stepdaughter, Monica, stabled her horse, Dartmouth, there. Edwina copied her name into the notepad and hurried to finish the list.

She glanced at the door to be sure she was not being watched and then quietly turned the pages back. Monica Billington had been stabling her horse at the farm for the past three years. But contrary to what Mrs. Faraday had said, it seemed that the bill for the month of June had not been paid. In fact, there was a note written in the same hand as the rest of the ledger to check in with the Faradays about paying the fee.

Edwina wondered what could be the cause for the delay. As she carefully checked the rest of the ledger, there were no other notations about a payment from the Faraday household being in arrears. All the rest of the payments had been made on a timely basis. Edwina wondered what might have happened to have caused the change. Were the Faradays experiencing the same sort of financial difficulties that troubled so much of the rest of the country?

Had Monica decided she no longer wished to board her horse at Brightwell Farm? Did she have somewhere else she wanted to take it? Or had she decided she no longer wished to own a horse? Edwina thought it strange that Mrs. Faraday had not seemed to show any discomfort when she had mentioned the horse being stabled at Brightwell Farm. In fact, she had mentioned it so casually that Edwina had to wonder if Mrs. Faraday knew that the bill was in arrears. She carefully closed the ledger after making a notation of the dates upon which payments had been made in the past. She slid it back into its drawer and exited the office.

Standing in the passageway flanked by horse stalls, she wondered which stall held Monica's horse, Dartmouth. As she wandered down the center of the stable, she paused at each stall and read the name written on a piece of slate attached with a twist of wire to each door. She located the stall with the horse's name on it, but there was no animal within. She wondered if Dartmouth had been amongst the horses she had seen gamboling about the paddock.

Just as she was about to exit the rear of the stable to bid her good-byes to Mr. Johnson, she noticed a stairwell tucked into a corner on the right side of the back door. The stable was built with two stories, and she wondered if there was finished space up above or if it was a storage area. Checking over her shoulder to be sure she was not seen, she carefully mounted the stairs and found a door at the top. She lifted the latch and swung it open as quietly as she could. She peeked her head around the door and discovered a tidy small bedchamber.

This must be where Declan bedded down for the night. An iron bedstead, a small chest of drawers, and a washstand holding a basin and pitcher stood in plain sight. There was a small wardrobe pressed against the back wall and a single cane-bottom chair near the window overlooking the distant fields. The bed had been neatly made and was covered with a thin woolen blanket and topped with an even thinner pillow. Everything looked tidy and also very spare.

If Edwina was forced to guess who inhabited the room, she would be hard pressed to do so judging by its contents. The only personal item that could be seen from her position in the doorway was a leather-bound book centered on the bed. Edwina squinted at the spine but did not see a title. Perhaps it was a diary or journal. Just as she was about to enter the room to inspect it more closely, she caught sight of Mr. Johnson striding across the field towards the back side of the stable. She had no reason to be snooping about his property, and she did not wish to cause a rift with the best supplier of soil amendments in the village. After a final glance at the book, she hurried down the back stairs before Mr. Johnson could find her.

Chapter 11

Edwina slipped out into the sunshine before Mr. Johnson had a chance to enter the stable. She thanked him for his list of horse boarders once more.

"One of them has just arrived. I didn't expect to see Miss Billington today," Mr. Johnson said.

"I shall be glad to speak with her. Miss Helliwell and I stopped in at Groveton Hall this morning to pay a condolence call, but Miss Billington was not at home when we were there. This would give me the opportunity to pay my respects, however informally," Edwina said.

She left Mr. Johnson to trundle a barrow into the stable and made her way around the side of the building to the large paddock holding the horses. A young woman and a small boy stood with their backs to Edwina. The boy was leaning into the paddock over one of the lower railings, a clump of wildflowers clutched in his hand. He was trying to coax one of the horses to come and inspect them. Edwina imagined he wished to pat the horse and was using the vegetation as an enticement.

Edwina had seen Monica Billington in the village on many

occasions. She was a pretty young woman with honey-colored hair and a quick smile. Her reputation was that of a forthright young woman who sometimes put up the backs of more traditionally minded elders. Edwina remembered a particularly memorable incident in Prudence Rathbone's shop. Monica had expressed support for women entering the professions.

Whilst Prudence Rathbone was a businesswoman herself, she had not seemed to share Monica's sentiment that women should be permitted to follow whichever career might interest them. Prudence had looked quite shocked at Monica's suggestion that women ought to be allowed into the combat branches of the military. Edwina had found the suggestion rather startling but had not felt, as Prudence had seemed to, that it revealed a moral failing in the younger woman.

The small boy with her, Timothy Faraday, was less well known to Edwina. He was blond like his mother, with fair skin and legs still chubby enough to make her think of babyhood. He certainly looked too young to have lost his father, but the same could be said for so many other children across the kingdom. As she approached the pair, one of the horses started to head in her direction, and this caused the young people's attention to turn around.

"Good afternoon," Edwina said. "What a fine day to be out in the countryside."

"Anything would be better than being stuck inside the house right about now," Monica said. She lowered her voice and took a step away from her younger brother. "My stepmother asked me to take Timothy out for the afternoon. He has been particularly affected by what has happened."

"Please allow me to offer my condolences, my dear," Edwina said. "I'm sure Mr. Faraday's death has been very shocking for you all."

"It was rather. Gordon was the sort of man one simply expected to go on troubling those around him forever," Monica said. "The idea that one minute he was there and the next minute he was gone is simply unfathomable."

"I'm sure you are all very grieved about it," Edwina said.

"I wouldn't go so far as to say that. In fact, it would be true to say that he was the sort of man who inspired grief whenever he arrived rather than when he took his leave. I, for one, shan't miss him a jot," Monica said.

Edwina felt rather startled. Although she was used to the cavalier attitude so many young people had about death, it still seemed to be particularly surprising to hear the sentiments uttered so matter-of-factly. However, it might make things far easier for the investigation if everyone was as forthright concerning their true feelings as Monica seemed to be.

"Your stepmother seemed as though she will miss him," Edwina said. "My business partner, Miss Helliwell, and I called on her this morning to pay our condolences. She looked as though she had been through a very difficult couple of days."

"Well, it's different for Deirdre, of course. She chose to marry him. I did not choose to have him in my life. I simply got saddled with the experience," Monica said. "Unlike this poor little tyke, who never knew anything different."

"I'm sure your brother will miss him in his own way," Edwina said.

"He was going to miss him no matter what. Gordon had decided to send him off to boarding school for the next term, so I don't suppose it will make an awful lot of difference in Timmy's daily life if the old grump is dead or not. He would have seen him only on the school holidays, anyway, from now on," Monica said.

"Timothy seems rather young to be sent away to boarding school. How old is he?" Edwina asked.

"He just turned six. In fact, Gordon made the announcement on his birthday. He said that he headed off to boarding school at age five and that it was high time that Timothy did the same."

Monica looked over at her younger brother and shook her head slowly.

Edwina would not have guessed that Timothy was six years old. Whilst she did know that many members of the well-to-do sent their children off to boarding schools at a very young age, she had always found the practice heart wrenching. Even though she did not admit so out loud and did not permit herself to dwell upon it, the fact of the matter remained that Edwina had always regretted not having children of her own.

Her mother had been exceedingly demanding both of Edwina and of any sort of suitor her daughter might attract. She had outright discouraged Edwina from participating in the sorts of normal activities a young woman might in order to encounter eligible young men. By the time the war years had broken out, Edwina had gotten to be too old to be a viable potential bride. And now, with so many far younger women spending their lives as spinsters, there was very little chance Edwina herself would marry. Given that she had longed for a family of her own, the notion that those who were so blessed as to have one would deliberately and callously send their child away to be raised by strangers seemed almost like a divine prank.

In addition to her own feelings on the matter, Edwina was quite certain a boy like Timothy would find it difficult to navigate the environment such schools fostered. No boy as quiet as he appeared to be, and as small as he was for his age, would find it easy to survive the inevitable bullying from older pupils. Her friend local solicitor Charles Jarvis had been one such a boy. On several occasions he had confided to Edwina how harrowing he had found his years spent away at boarding school. It was with a pang that she recalled the look on his face as he had shared with her one particularly unpleasant memory involving a cherished stuffed toy and an improvised guillotine.

"Monica, which one am I going to ride?" Timothy said, pulling away from the fencing and turning towards the women.

Edwina's heart squeezed in her chest as she noticed the rounded cheeks of his babylike face. "I like that brown one." He held out a chubby hand and pointed with a grass-stained finger towards a shiny brown mare with a black mane and silky tail.

"We shall have to see what Mrs. Johnson has to say about it. She's the one who takes care of the riding lessons," Monica said.

"Are you starting riding lessons, Timothy?" Edwina asked.

"Mummy said I could," Timothy said, looking up at his stepsister for approval.

Monica nodded down at him and reached out to take him by the hand. "That's right. She did. That's one of the reasons I decided to bring Timmy out here today, when Deirdre suggested I take him out for some air. Since he's not going to be attending boarding school in the new term, she wanted to make sure that he had plenty of activities to keep him busy," Monica said. "Isn't that right, Timmy?"

The little cherub nodded his head and pulled on Monica's arm. "I would rather play with my aeroplane," he said.

"He lost his favorite toy during the burglary and has not been able to get it out of his mind since," Monica said.

"Are you sure it was stolen, or could it have simply been misplaced?" Edwina asked.

"Timmy and I were playing a game where one of us hid it and the other tried to find it. Weren't we, Timmy?" Monica turned to the boy.

"That's right. I was very clever and put it in a silver box Father kept on his desk. Monica didn't find it before the burglar stole it." Timothy's lower lip wobbled as he spoke.

"It's okay, Timmy. I expect you will love riding even more than playing with your plane. Shall we go see if Mrs. Johnson can fit you in for a lesson this week?" Monica said.

"Please don't let me keep you," Edwina said. "It was nice to see you, Miss Billington. Good luck with your lessons, Timothy."

Edwina watched as the two young people headed for the door of the stable. She could see Mr. Johnson, silhouetted in the doorway, watching their approach. She had to wonder if Mr. Faraday's death was not a good thing for at least one member of his family. Certainly, the change in plans for Timothy's attendance at boarding school would suggest that Mrs. Faraday had not agreed with her husband on the subject. Or at least, it had caused a delay in the plans. The children's presence at the farm raised another question, Edwina realized. If the Faraday family was in arrears with their horse-boarding fees, how were they suddenly able to pay for riding lessons for young Timothy?

Unlike Edwina, Beryl had absolutely no reluctance towards using the telephone. In fact, she often found herself feeling irritated with Beddoes, who managed to beat her to the device almost every time it rang. Beddoes always seemed to give her a critical glance should Beryl decide to answer the instrument herself.

Although she did not like to complain, Beryl could not help but suspect that Beddoes was not impressed with her. In fact, it was only after Beddoes could not locate Edwina that she condescended to alert Beryl to the fact that there was a telephone call from their client Mr. Melton.

Beryl waited until Beddoes took herself and her feather duster off to the dining room before turning her attention to the instrument. It wasn't that she did not trust Beddoes to be discreet. But rather she did not wish for her to have the satisfaction of knowing what Beryl knew. Beryl felt slightly petty about her own attitude towards their domestic help, but she told herself one could not be too careful when it came to client confidentiality.

"Good afternoon, Mr. Melton. How may I help you?" Beryl said.

"I'm calling to ask about your progress with the case," Mr. Melton said.

"Are you sure this is something you wish to discuss on the telephone?" Beryl asked. "Even though I am quite certain our operators here in Walmsley Parva are above listening in, I find some conversations are best conducted in person."

Beryl thought no such thing whatsoever. In fact, recently she had had good reason to know that telephone operators were not always the most trustworthy of characters. She hoped that whoever might be listening in from the telephone office in the center of the village might feel ashamed enough to remove her headset. Beryl made it a policy never to discuss any private matters on the telephone. She had seen enough distressing results of thoughtless, loose-lipped conversations throughout the war to know better than to participate in one herself.

"I am aware there is a risk in telephoning. I will trust that each of us can speak in such a way as to eliminate concern. As time is of the essence, I wish to enquire as to whether or not you have made any progress," Mr. Melton said.

"We met with the party you requested immediately upon your departure from our offices," Beryl said. "We have made a cursory evaluation of the circumstances and a physical investigation of the route taken by said individual."

"Is that all?" Mr. Melton said.

Beryl was quite certain she heard rising panic in their client's voice. She wished that Edwina had been there to answer the telephone in her stead. Edwina was ever so much better at soothing unhappy clients than was she. Beryl thought it had a great deal to do with the fact that Edwina was inclined to worry about things herself. Beryl simply could not imagine spending her time and energy dreaming up unpleasant circumstances that might never occur. Worrying was the sort of thing she almost never did. Thus, she was not particularly well prepared to assist others with their own habit of doing so.

Edwina, on the other hand, was a champion worrier. Her fertile imagination was able to concoct the most unlikely and unpleasant scenarios out of the smallest hint of trouble. She would be the perfect person to respectfully tut-tut into the telephone. However, Edwina was still nowhere to be seen. Beryl wondered if she ought to head off to Brightwell Farm in the automobile to collect her friend. Even though she did not like to do it, it was possible to attach Edwina's bicycle to the back of the car.

"We have been making enquiries into the location of various persons of interest at the time of the incident," Beryl said.

"Have you come to any conclusions?" Mr. Melton said.

"No, sir. But I would remind you that it is early days," Beryl said.

"We don't have *days*. Early or otherwise," Mr. Melton said. "I thought I had impressed upon you both the urgency of this matter and a need for its swift resolution."

"You have made it rather difficult, considering you require such complete secrecy. At present we are working on the possibility that your case is connected to another. Unfortunately, we are not able to make any swift progress into that line of enquiry, because you have insisted we hold our cards so close to our chests," Beryl said.

"You think there's a possibility that the case connects to another we discussed?" he asked. "You really think that is likely?"

"I believe we would be foolish not to consider it. But if you would like us to resolve this as swiftly as possible, it would be expedient for us to consult a local expert on that other matter. We would need to do so in an official capacity, however," Beryl said.

"The other party is not likely to be forthcoming without some pressure to do so?" he asked.

"That's exactly what I mean. Without revealing reasons for our interest, I think it unlikely we will receive cooperation," Beryl said.

"Very well. You have my permission to share what you know

with that solitary party. But no one else, mind," Mr. Melton said.

"We will get on it at once," Beryl said.

"See that you do. The longer this takes, the higher the stakes become," he said.

Beryl heard the line disconnect, and she replaced the receiver on the wall. Just as she was contemplating whether or not she ought to head out to the outskirts of the village to collect Edwina, Crumpet raced along the passageway and sat in front of the door, his tail wagging enthusiastically. A moment later Edwina pressed open the front door and stepped inside. Beryl wondered how the dog always knew his mistress was near at hand.

"I have rather a lot to tell you about my trip to the farm," Edwina said, placing her hat on the hall tree.

"I have rather a lot to tell you about our dissatisfied client," Beryl said. "I was just about to come to collect you." Beryl gestured towards the telephone.

"I hurried back as soon as I could. There was a lot to investigate, and the distance is not an inconsiderable one," Edwina said.

The day had turned warm, and Beryl could well imagine that it had taken some physical effort for Edwina to cycle home. Her hair appeared to be wavier than usual, and little beads of perspiration shimmered on Edwina's forehead. As much as Beryl understood Edwina's passion for hats, she thought it likely they made her friend unnecessarily uncomfortable whilst exercising.

"Since you're here now, you can fill me in on what you've learned while we drive down into the village."

"We need to go into the village straightaway?" Edwina asked.

"As a matter of fact, we do. At least we do if we don't wish to lose our client," Beryl said.

"Is it as bad as all that?" Edwina asked, her eyes widening with worry.

"Let's just say Mr. Melton just gave us permission to discuss the case with Constable Gibbs."

Edwina reached for her hat and popped it back onto her head. She admonished Crumpet to stay in the house with Beddoes and hurried out the door, with Beryl following in her wake.

Chapter 12

It could not be said that Constable Gibbs appeared cheered to see them enter the police station. Her customary scowl was stamped firmly on her face, and she drummed her stubby fingers on the countertop separating the public from the inner sanctum of the police station. The countertop was a high one and came in just below the constable's formidable bustline. Beryl noticed Constable Gibbs reaching for a stack of papers and a pen as soon as they stepped through the doorway. She could only surmise that the constable wished to appear busy in order to find an excuse not to have time to speak with them.

"If you're here to ask about your employee, I assure you your efforts have been wasted," Constable Gibbs said. "I will release him only if I decide he's not guilty, and at the moment things are not looking all that good for him."

"We are actually here to speak to you on another matter of importance," Edwina said.

"We believe it may be connected to your burglary case," Beryl said.

"I told you to stay out of that case, along with what happened to the magistrate," Constable Gibbs said.

"Yes, I do seem to remember that," Beryl said. "However, I'm afraid we are not going to be able to honor your request."

"It was not a request. It was an order," Constable Gibbs said.

"I'm afraid that we answer to a higher authority than your own," Edwina said. "Isn't that right, Beryl?"

Beryl nodded her head. "Yes, we do. You see, our investigation is no mere local matter. It is, in fact, a matter of national security. Isn't that what the man said, Edwina?"

"Yes. That's exactly how he phrased it. A matter of utmost national security," Edwina said. "And now we have been authorized to bring you in on the investigation."

"You aren't suggesting that you will allow me to participate in *your* investigation rather than *you* participating in mine?" Constable Gibbs said.

"Actually, it was not our suggestion in the least," Beryl said. "It came from the outside."

"And who exactly is this outside authority, pray tell?" Constable Gibbs said.

"The registrar-general," Edwina said.

"The registrar-general? You expect me to believe that the registrar-general has hired you two to meddle in my burglary investigation?" Constable Gibbs said. "This is simply too much to be believed."

"We were afraid that you would say that. Do you have that telephone number?" Edwina said, turning to Beryl.

Beryl nodded. "I wrote it down on this paper. Please feel free to telephone in and make enquiries yourself as to our credentials. I told the district registrar that you would be likely to need proof, and although he did not advise you to waste his superior's time with your impertinent and unnecessary questions, I convinced him that it was likely such precautions would be necessary in order to convince you."

She slid the piece of paper with the telephone number written on it across the counter to Constable Gibbs. The constable looked down at it with an even deeper scowl.

"You expect me to believe that this is the telephone number for the registrar-general and that I am expected to cooperate with two civilians on the subject of an ongoing investigation? What sort of fool do you take me for?" Constable Gibbs asked. "I would have expected something like this from you, Miss Helliwell, but frankly, I am rather shocked at you, Edwina."

The telephone on the side wall of the police station erupted into a furious spate of ringing. Constable Gibbs looked pleased to have a reason to interrupt her conversation with the two of them. She turned her back on them and lifted the receiver from the wall. Beryl could hear the sound of a man's voice rumbling through the earpiece. Constable Gibbs stood up straighter and turned her head to glance over her shoulder at the two other women. Her complexion had paled slightly, and she seemed at a loss for words.

"Yes, sir. I completely understand and will give them every possible assistance," she said just prior to replacing the receiver in its cradle. She stood with her back to Beryl and Edwina for a moment longer, exhaled deeply, then turned around. Her scowl had been replaced with a look of complete bafflement.

"Was that the registrar-general's office?" Beryl asked.

The constable nodded.

"Did he order you to cooperate with us?" Edwina said.

"He said it was a matter of national security that he could not discuss over the telephone line," Constable Gibbs said. "I suppose this means I ought to invite you into the back room." With that, she unlatched the small door designed to keep the hoi polloi on the correct side of the barrier and allowed them to pass through to her inner sanctum.

Constable Gibbs gestured at a table tucked away in a corner

of the room and ringed by four chairs. Beryl and Edwina took seats, and Constable Gibbs joined them.

"I guess you had better tell me what this is all about," Constable Gibbs said.

Beryl leaned forward and lowered her voice. "Is there anyone else here in the building?" she asked.

"Only Declan O'Shea, who is locked up in the cell at the end of the corridor," the constable said.

"Your helper isn't here today, is he?" Beryl asked.

Constable Gibbs shook her head. Beryl was relieved to hear it. Mr. Wilkes had formerly served as the village constable, and nowadays he helped out from time to time when Constable Gibbs needed an extra pair of hands or set of eyes. Beryl had not found his lecherous attentions welcome in any way. She had turned them to her advantage on occasion, but she did not enjoy the necessity of doing so. She also doubted very much he would be as discreet as Constable Gibbs.

One thing Beryl had noticed about women in unorthodox professions was their innate understanding that they must hold themselves to a higher standard than men doing the same jobs. She was certain there was no possibility that Constable Gibbs would spread gossip about what they would reveal to her. Beryl had no such confidence in former constable Wilkes.

"If anyone comes in, we shall have to pretend we're here on another matter," Edwina said.

"It really is serious, then?" Constable Gibbs said.

"I'm very sorry to say that the district registrar arrived at the Beeches this morning to report that the census schedules for all of Walmsley Parva have been stolen," Edwina said.

"Stolen?" Constable Gibbs said.

"Right off the back of Mr. Crossley's bicycle," Beryl said.

"Or out of his cottage," Edwina said. "He doesn't seem to remember exactly when he last had them."

"But this is outrageous. What will happen if the Triple Alliance hears that the government can't be trusted with such sensitive information as their census schedules?" Constable Gibbs said.

"That is exactly why it's a matter of national security," Edwina said. "Will you help us?"

"Of course I will," Constable Gibbs said. "Do you think this is related to the ongoing burglary investigation?"

"It might be. And it might not be," Beryl said.

"How can I help?" the constable asked.

"We were hoping you could give us a list of the homes that have been burgled," Edwina said.

"We would also like to know if you have a list of the items stolen at each of those households," Beryl said.

"I have both such lists," Constable Gibbs said. "But how do you think they will help you?"

"We are not entirely sure that it will. But at least it would give us someplace to start," Beryl said.

"Has Declan said anything else that leads you to believe he is, in fact, the one responsible?" Edwina asked.

"To be entirely honest with you, I'm no further ahead than I was when I took him in for questioning. But I have to say this connection with such an outrageous theft makes him look all the more guilty," Constable Gibbs said.

"How do you figure that?" Beryl asked.

"All the trouble being stirred up lately in Ireland makes me feel predisposed to suspect him of being some sort of an agitator. Maybe the thefts aren't connected at all and this was a deliberate attempt to provide one more reason for the Triple Alliance to criticize the government," Constable Gibbs said.

"You can't suspect him simply for being from a country that wants independence," Beryl said.

"I can suspect him of just about anything at all. It is part of my job to be suspicious," Constable Gibbs said. "There's no denying the fact that his arrival and the timing of the burglaries are one and the same."

"I can't see that flinging about accusations on account of personal prejudices is part of your job," Beryl said.

"I think it would be for the best if we were able to come to some understanding about working on the case together," Edwina said.

Constable Gibbs gave her a long look. Then she nodded her head.

"This is far too important for any sort of petty squabbling. You two clearly have the trust of the registrar-general, and that has to mean something. Besides, with just one of me to cover all the incidents that crop up here in the village, I could do with some help that is actually helpful," Constable Gibbs said.

"You mean you don't think you should rely simply on the assistance of former constable Wilkes?" Beryl asked.

"Constable Wilkes is more willing than able. But don't go repeating that," Constable Gibbs said. "He means well, after all."

"I found him to be willing *and* able," Beryl said. "And I don't think he meant well at all when he laid his hands upon my person. But I am glad that we will have a chance to be on the same side of the case for once."

"What shall we give out as a reason that you have involved us in the investigation?" Edwina asked. "It's not as though such a thing is a common occurrence. After all, you have successfully policed the village for years without any assistance from us, or anyone else for that matter," Edwina said.

Beryl thought Edwina was laying it on a bit thick now that they had already gotten a buy-in from the constable concerning their part in the investigation. But she was happy to defer to Edwina's better sense of how to keep on the good side of any of her fellow villagers. One thing that Beryl had realized over her

time in Walmsley Parva was that it was one thing to charm people for the short run when one was a visitor requiring assistance
with aeroplane repairs or directions to the next village. It was
quite another matter entirely to maintain an even course when
one continued to see the same faces again and again, day after
day. She unreservedly admired Edwina's capacity for simultaneously taking little guff from those around her and giving
even less offense. It was a fine balance and one that Beryl was
not entirely sure she would ever master.

"What if we give out the story that because the magistrate is
a prominent person with connections to someone from Miss
Helliwell's former life, I have asked you to assist in that part of
the investigation? We could say that all three of us are following those leads that we think are connected to the case," Constable Gibbs said.

"Are you quite certain, Doris?" Edwina said. "We know
how hard you've worked to remain in your position, and we
would not wish to do anything to cause you any difficulties in
that regard, would we, Beryl?"

"I am all for women taking on whatever roles in the world
they wish to assume," Beryl said. "I have never been in the
habit of making difficulties for other spirited females. We shall
do everything possible to indicate that we are the ones assisting
the constable, not the other way around."

"Then it's all settled," Constable Gibbs said. She pushed
back her chair and stood. Beryl and Edwina followed her lead,
and she escorted them to the public side of the police station
once again. "Should I have anything to share with you, you can
rely on me to do so. I expect that you will do the same."

"Certainly we will," Edwina said. "Before we go, however,
would you be willing to share with us that list of burglary victims, as well as any statements they made regarding the actual
losses themselves?"

"Let me just pull out the files, and I will be happy to let you copy everything down," Constable Gibbs said.

Edwina could not help but feel a bit topsy-turvy. She had never expected to experience a cease of hostilities between the pair of them and the constable. She felt almost heady with power. If anyone had told her when she awakened that morning that Doris Gibbs would invite her to participate in the investigation, she would have told them they should book an appointment with the local physician.

"Well, that certainly makes things easier, now doesn't it?" Beryl said as she and Edwina stepped out into the sunshine.

"The constable's attitude or the information she provided for the investigation?" Edwina asked.

"Both, I should think," Beryl said. "Hold up a minute. Isn't that Terrence Crossley?"

Beryl raised a gloved hand and pointed at a figure lurking about at a corner of the police station. Edwina barely managed to catch sight of him before he disappeared down the alley between the station and the cloth merchant. Casting the idea of propriety to the wind, she broke into a trot and headed after him. She felt Beryl close on her heels as the two whizzed along the high street and rounded the corner of the building. There stood Terrence Crossley, pressed against the brick wall at the end of the alley, shrouded in shadow. He made a valiant effort to appear simply to be inspecting a bit of litter on the cobblestones with the toe of his shoe.

"Terrence Crossley, what were you doing lurking about the police station?" Edwina said, stepping up to the census taker. Her finger itched to jab him in the chest, as she had often seen Beryl do with male suspects. But she refrained. There was something not quite nice about touching gentlemen, especially those embroiled in calamitous affairs.

"I was planning to go in and speak with Constable Gibbs, but I wanted to wait until the two of you came out," Terrence Crossley said.

"That seems like a fishy story," Beryl said. "If you wanted to speak with her, why did you rush off when we followed you?"

"It was more of an impulse," Mr. Crossley said. "I had come into the village with the hope of spotting the bag of census schedules. When I saw you entering the police station, I decided to wait around until you came out to speak with her."

"What did you wish to speak with her about? You know you're not supposed to discuss the census-schedule loss with anyone other than your employer and with us," Edwina said.

Even though both Beryl and Edwina knew that they had revealed the secret to the constable, there was no reason that Terrence Crossley needed to be informed. As far as Beryl was concerned, the fewer people who felt free to speak on the subject, the better.

"It wasn't really about the census schedules. At least not in any way I can understand. I actually wanted to give her some information about what happened to Mr. Faraday," Mr. Crossley said.

Beryl stepped closer and towered over the nervous man. "I think it would be best if you shared with us what you were going to say to the constable before you head inside."

"I thought you were supposed to be working on the census-schedule case. I don't know that Mr. Melton will be pleased to hear that you're spending time poking your nose into what happened to the local magistrate instead," Mr. Crossley said, straightening his shoulders and looking more assertive.

"We have every reason to suspect that the cases are connected. Which is why we were in speaking with the constable ourselves," Beryl said.

"What did you want to tell her about Mr. Faraday's death?"

Edwina said. "I assume that that's the part of his troubles you wish to mention."

Mr. Crossley nodded his head. "I remembered something that happened when I was dropping off the census schedules at Groveton Hall last week. I thought it might help the constable in her investigation."

"And what was that?" Beryl said.

"You must understand that I don't intend to listen at doors and windows before knocking when I drop the schedules off, but there was no way I could avoid doing so at Groveton Hall that day," Mr. Crossley said.

"What was it that you did not intend to hear?" Beryl asked.

"A heated argument," Mr. Crossley said.

"Who was it that you heard arguing?" Edwina asked.

"I recognized the voice of Mr. Faraday. His was rather distinctive. He was arguing with a woman, but I don't know who she was," he said.

"Did she sound like she had an accent or anything else that would help to identify her?" Beryl asked.

"I can't say that there was anything particularly unique about her voice, but I can tell you that just as I was about to knock on the door, the shouting stopped. An older woman with a high color to her face opened the door as soon as I was about to grasp the door knocker. She could have been the second person involved in the argument," Mr. Crossley said.

"About how old would you say that she was?" Edwina asked.

"Probably in her early sixties," Mr. Crossley said. "She had rather a superior air about her."

It sounded as though he might be speaking of either Mrs. Breen, the domestic servant, or Miss Meechum, Timothy Faraday's nanny.

"What was the argument about? Do you know?" Beryl asked.

Mr. Crossley looked sheepish and uncomfortable. "I really don't want you to take the impression that I listen at doorways," he said.

"In the summer it's impossible not to overhear raised voices that float out through open windows. We shall hold no such thing against you, and we will not consider that you were carrying tales or behaving as a gossip. Mr. Faraday is dead, and I am sure that you would be doing your civic duty to share what you know with those trying to get to the bottom of what happened to him," Edwina said.

Mr. Crossley nodded his head ever so gently. Edwina couldn't help but wonder if he was still feeling the ill effects of a night of excessive drinking. In the low light of the alley, it was difficult to see if his skin still retained the greyish-green tinge it had had when they visited him at his cottage earlier. Still, he seemed coherent, and his story might help to get to the bottom of everything.

"I couldn't hear things word for word, mind you," he said.

"Whatever you have to tell us, we would be grateful to hear," Beryl said.

"They seemed to be arguing back and forth about someone named Alan. The woman who was speaking sounded very concerned about his presence at Groveton Hall," Mr. Crossley said.

"Did she say exactly what her concern was?" Edwina asked.

"She just said she felt that he was not a very good influence and that the sooner he left, the better it would be for all concerned," Mr. Crossley said.

"Were you able to hear Mr. Faraday's response?" Beryl asked.

"I did hear him say something about how it wasn't her place to comment on such things, and that it would not be her concern for much longer, in any case," Mr. Crossley said.

"Did you hear her response?" Edwina asked.

"There wasn't one," Mr. Crossley said. "At least not one that

I heard. It was just after this that the argument stopped and I decided to go ahead and knock on the door. As much as I don't like to barge in on family conversations, I don't have time to waste dithering about on each and every doorstep I visit."

"Of course you don't," Edwina said soothingly. "And the woman you saw seemed to still be quite agitated?"

"She had two flaming red cheeks and a wild look in her eyes," Mr. Crossley said.

"And you heard nothing else at all?" Edwina asked.

"Not as regarded the argument," Mr. Crossley said.

"Is he the one you spoke with about the census schedule?" Beryl asked.

"Yes. The woman let me in, and then I asked to speak with the head of the household," Mr. Crossley said. "Just as I always do."

"Did he seem angry, too?" Beryl asked.

"No, he seemed brusque and blustery, as I often have come to expect when calling upon householders. I spent a few minutes with him explaining the ins and outs of filling out the census schedule and asked if he had any questions," Mr. Crossley said.

"Did he have any questions?" Edwina asked.

"I'm not sure that I should reveal that. After all, I have a duty of confidentiality to uphold," Mr. Crossley said.

"You weren't all that concerned with that when you left the census schedules unattended in the center of the village," Beryl said.

Mr. Crossley winced.

"Any little bit of knowledge you provide may help us to track down what you so carelessly lost," Edwina said.

"I suppose you make a good point," Mr. Crossley said. "As a matter of fact, he asked me about the time frame for the census and also about how the information tends to be used."

"How it tends to be used?" Edwina asked.

"Yes. He was very interested in posterity. He seemed to be

concerned about filling it out with accuracy and about how any inaccuracies might impact the future," he said.

"Do you tend to get that kind of question from most of the households you visit?" Beryl asked.

"It is a fairly common question. Especially from superior sorts of people. Those who have trouble reading and writing don't seem to pay quite as much attention to such things as those who are well educated. But it's something I do end up answering at least a couple of times each day when I'm dropping off the schedules," Mr. Crossley said.

"Did he seem upset in any way as a result of his argument?" Edwina asked.

"I think it's safe to say that he was not entirely tranquil. He had an intensity about the questioning, which I attributed to his agitated state. But if you are asking if he turned ill humor upon me, I would say that he was very courteous," Mr. Crossley said.

"Would you say that the argument sounded heated enough that the woman might have wished Mr. Faraday ill?" Edwina asked.

"I'm sure I couldn't say that for sure. As I said, I could not hear every word that passed between them, at least not clearly. I had the impression that the woman who was speaking did not have as much power in the conversation as Mr. Faraday did. I think it took quite a bit of boldness on her part to bring herself to mention what she did," Mr. Crossley said.

"I think it would be a good idea for you to go ahead and share this information with Constable Gibbs, as you had intended to do. It may help her with her investigation," Beryl said.

"If you really think it will help, I suppose I will," Mr. Crossley said.

"It may help her to continue to examine all options," Edwina said.

"I thought she had a suspect in custody?" Mr. Crossley said.

"Yes, she has a suspect, but that does not mean she definitely has gotten to the bottom of all that transpired at Groveton Hall the day the magistrate died," Edwina said.

Mr. Crossley nodded his head, and the two women stepped back to make way for him to pass along the alley and head back towards the police station. They followed him and watched as he let himself inside.

"It sounds to me as though we need to make a point to speak with Nanny Meechum and Mrs. Breen," Beryl said.

"What reason do you think either of them could have for objecting to Alan Faraday's presence at Groveton Hall?" Edwina asked.

"I haven't the foggiest notion," Beryl said. "He doesn't seem to be the sort of young man that anyone would object to. I would not consider him to be some sort of a bad influence, from my brief encounter with him at the pub. At least if you don't count his prejudices towards Declan."

"I wonder if the woman's objection had anything to do with the reasons the magistrate and Alan fell out in the first place?" Edwina said.

"I suppose we shall have to ask both women about it as soon as possible," Beryl said. "I say we head on out to Groveton Hall straightaway."

"I don't think that shall be necessary if we want to start by speaking with young Alan Faraday himself," Edwina said, indicating with her head towards the village green. Alan Faraday stood with his back to them, staring across the duck pond. "I think it would be best if just one of us went ahead and spoke with him. If there are two of us, he may feel quite ganged up on."

"I think I will leave young Mr. Faraday to you. He and I did not leave things in the best possible light when we met at the pub on Saturday night," Beryl said.

"What do you plan to do whilst I am speaking with him?" Edwina asked.

"I'm sure I will be able to find some way to pass the time. At the very least, I can pop into the pub and ask Bill Nevins if he remembers what time Mr. Crossley staggered out of the Dove and Duck on the night of the theft," Beryl said.

With that, the two parted ways, and Edwina struck off for the village green.

Chapter 13

Edwina walked slowly towards the duck pond. She wanted a moment to appraise Alan Faraday's comportment before he realized he was being observed. He did not look downhearted and bowed low with grief. He simply stood with his back to the high street, his hands in his trouser pockets. A slight breeze ruffled the edges of his hair.

"Alan, I thought that was you," Edwina said, coming up beside him.

"Hello, Miss Davenport," Alan said. "How lovely to see you."

"That's very kind of you to say, I'm sure. Especially considering what you've been through lately," Edwina said. She scrutinized his face for signs of grief as he turned towards her.

"I understand from Deirdre that you and your business partner were the ones to find my brother's body," Alan said. "Whilst I am sorry that you were in for such a terrible shock, I am very grateful that neither Monica nor Timothy was the one to find him instead."

"Mrs. Faraday said much the same thing. It never is pleasant to encounter someone who has passed away, especially in such surprising circumstances. But it is vastly preferable that a loved one is not the person who makes the discovery," Edwina said. "We were happy to have been able to spare the family such a thing."

"We do appreciate it," Alan said.

"Will you be staying in Walmsley Parva for some time?" Edwina asked. "At least through the funeral services?"

"I shall be here for at least that long," Alan said. "I may be here for a good while longer."

"Had you decided to return home permanently before your brother met with his accident?" Edwina asked.

"I had not entirely made up my mind on that front," Alan said. "I suppose it's common knowledge that my brother and I had a falling-out some time ago."

Edwina nodded her head. "I'm afraid that everyone had a great deal to say about it to anyone within range of hearing," she said. "Frankly, I was a bit surprised to hear you had come back to the village. I hope this means that the two of you had reached a reconciliation before he passed on."

"As a matter of fact, we did. Gordon invited me to come to Groveton Hall for Father's Day as a sort of an olive branch. I thought it was the least I could do to accept," Alan said.

"I'm glad you were able to put aside your differences before it was too late," Edwina said. "Oftentimes what seems like a large problem in the moment appears to be much smaller upon reflection. Perhaps that was the way for the two of you?" she asked.

Edwina did not wish to appear to be prying, but it would be best to know Alan's version of the cause of the estrangement. She also wondered if he was telling the truth entirely about their reconciliation. She would not have said that he was lying entirely about making peace with his brother. But she felt as though he was still holding something back, as if the situation was slightly more complicated than he was letting on.

It could simply be that he felt such information was none of her business. And indeed, truly, it was not. She had not become entirely accustomed to the sorts of impertinent questions a private enquiry agent was required to ask in order to be successful at her business. If her mother could see her now, Edwina would surely be sent to bed without dinner.

"That's just it exactly. I'm afraid that I took offense where none was meant and foolishly said some things that I wished I could take back. Gordon was inclined to be easily offended and did not appreciate my attitude," Alan said.

"It can be very difficult for the young to endure the well-intentioned counsel given out by their elders. It can be easy to bridle and chafe under such admonishments," Edwina said.

"It was particularly difficult in our case. My brother had always served as a sort of a father figure to me more than that of a brother. I felt the estrangement acutely," he said. "I was very glad to receive his letter inviting me to come down in time for the census."

"I can't seem to remember what Mr. Faraday said the two of you quarreled about. In fact, maybe he never mentioned it at all but had simply said you had left the village rather abruptly," Edwina said.

"Gordon did not particularly like to air family business to all and sundry, so I expect he said very little and instead simply allowed others to draw their own conclusions about my whereabouts and the argument."

In fact, Mr. Faraday had said nothing whatsoever about his younger brother. It was as though he had no longer existed. One moment Alan Faraday had been part of the thriving life in Walmsley Parva, and the next he had simply ceased to exist. Edwina had often wondered what had happened to the younger man. With so many families suffering the loss of their loved ones, it had seemed to her particularly ungrateful of Gordon Faraday to not attempt a reconciliation, considering he was fortunate enough to have his younger brother still drawing breath and apparently unscarred.

"Very sensible of him, I'm sure," Edwina said. "It seems to me there are far too many people who are inclined to unburden their minds of late. We never did such a thing when I was a child. My parents would be absolutely aghast to know the sorts of things that are spoken about in mixed company these days."

"It shouldn't have been any sort of a secret. Gordon wished for me to enter the law and follow in his footsteps. I was far more interested in a career as an architect. When I told him I no longer wished to become a solicitor, he lost his temper and refused to continue to support me until I came to my senses," Alan said.

"I should not have thought he would have an objection to a field of study as well respected as that of architecture," Edwina said.

"I don't really think it had a whole lot to do with law versus architecture. I think it had more to do with the fact that my brother preferred to direct everyone's lives than it did my new degree. He really was not the easiest of men to live with," Alan said with a shrug of his bony shoulders.

Edwina noticed that he appeared to be almost gaunt. There were hollows under his eyes, and as she looked more closely, she saw that his shirt appeared to be slightly more worn than was particularly suited to gentlemen of his stature. When he said that his brother had cut him off without a penny, perhaps that was exactly what he meant and it was not an exaggeration. She could well imagine that Alan Faraday was very grateful to have received an invitation from his brother to return to his home. She wondered what he had been doing with himself to keep body and soul together in the intervening time. It did not look as though any career he had decided to undertake had been a thriving one.

"He had much the same reputation in the village. Still, I am sure that no one wished him to come to the sort of end that he did," Edwina said.

"That's very kind of you to say, Miss Davenport, but I expect that there were at least a few members of the public who will not be sorry never to encounter him sitting on the magistrate's bench again," Alan said. "In fact, doesn't the constable have someone in custody who was given a very large fine for his part in a minor incident?"

"Constable Gibbs does have a burglary suspect in custody at present, but I don't think that she has determined for sure whether he is responsible for what happened to your brother. You don't have any reason besides the harshness of his sentencing to think that anyone would wish to harm him deliberately, do you?" Edwina asked.

Edwina kept her eyes trained on the younger man. He squinted, but perhaps that was more on account of the brightness of the sun rather than any dishonesty or hesitation in his answer.

"He never received any direct threats, as far as I know. But then, I might not have been aware of such things. Gordon was appointed magistrate after I left the village, and as I have said, our contact has been almost nonexistent in the meantime," Alan said. "In fact, the only way I knew anything about what was going on was that Monica sent me letters."

That was an interesting bit of news. Edwina would not have expected such a young woman to have taken on that sort of responsibility in a family. Or the risk. Life with her stepfather sounded as though it had not been easy under the best of circumstances, and Edwina could not imagine Mr. Faraday would have made light of the mutiny he would have seen communication with his estranged brother to be. Monica was a brave young woman. Or a foolhardy one. Sometimes it was difficult to tell the two apart.

"Have you and Monica always been close?" Edwina asked.

"I am not sure you could say that she kept me informed out of any particular attachment. I think it was more a case of the enemy of my enemy is my friend," Alan said.

"She and your brother did not have a warm relationship?" Edwina asked.

"It was warm if you mean that they both made each other hot under the collar," Alan said.

"She did not seem particularly grief stricken when I encountered her at Brightwell Farm earlier today," Edwina said.

"She isn't. And I can't say as I blame her. It has been lovely chatting to you, Miss Davenport, but I promised my sister-in-law that I would pick up a few things at the bakery for tea this evening, and I don't want all the best things to be sold out. Timothy is particular to a treacle tart, if there are any to be had."

With that, he gave Edwina a pleasant smile and strode off in the direction of the high street. As Edwina watched him go, she was more convinced than ever that he was not any more grief stricken than was Monica Billington.

Beryl shielded her eyes with her broad hand and watched as Edwina progressed towards her from the village green. Clearly something was on Edwina's mind, judging from the way she appeared almost oblivious to her surroundings. It was a wonder Edwina had never been struck down by a passing motorist, considering the lack of care she displayed in crossing the street. Beryl thought it was a good job her friend had never taken to city life. With her total disregard for vehicular hazards, she would not have lasted long in a place more crowded than little Walmsley Parva.

"Did you have a fruitful interview with young Mr. Faraday?" Beryl asked once Edwina had joined her beside the motorcar.

"Indeed, I did," Edwina said. "But I don't know that I am any more sure of who might have been involved than I was before I spoke with him. It seems the more information we turn up, the more people we find who do not seem to feel grieved at the magistrate's passing."

"I'm afraid I wasn't able to narrow down the time frame very much at the Dove and Duck, either," Beryl said. "Bill Nevins said he remembered Mr. Crossley staggering out at some point during the evening, but he was not entirely sure when."

"So that does not help determine the timing of the theft of the census schedules," Edwina said as she yanked open the door of the automobile and slid inside.

"No, it does not. It only confirms what we already knew from Simpkins. Bill said that Mr. Crossley was well and truly lubricated by the time he staggered out the door that evening. That in itself seems to have been a noteworthy event," Beryl said.

Beryl settled herself behind the wheel and gave Edwina a significant look.

"Mr. Crossley said he was not inclined to imbibe with regularity. At least not such a large quantity. I wonder what made him decide to do so that particular evening," Edwina said.

"I wondered the exact same thing. Perhaps there is a little bit more to Mr. Crossley than he has admitted," Beryl said.

"Or perhaps he just found himself caught up in the atmosphere at the pub and overindulged accidentally," Edwina said. "I have heard that is the way it often happens."

Beryl was quite certain that Edwina was obliquely referring to herself. Any blame attaching itself to Edwina concerning such things could be laid squarely at Beryl's feet. On the rare occasion that Edwina became the least bit squiffy, it was as a direct result of Beryl deliberately plying her with strong drink. She had only done so for Edwina's own good, but she could see how Edwina might prefer to assume such a thing had been an accident. Perhaps in Edwina's mind it was.

As far as Beryl was concerned, on occasion Edwina benefited greatly from not only the loosening up associated with partaking in cocktails but also the way that it caused her to become quite emboldened. She wondered if Terrence Crossley had some reason to desire being emboldened himself.

"Or perhaps he was steeling himself for some sort of difficult task," Beryl suggested. "I wonder what could have been on his mind that would require such drastic measures."

"But what could have been troubling him? He's new to the area, and the trouble with the census schedules had not come up as of yet. At least they had not if he is telling us the truth about when he thinks he lost them," Edwina said.

"That is perhaps an additional line of enquiry we should pursue. Until now we have given Mr. Crossley's story a great deal of credence. Perhaps we should reconsider doing so," Beryl said.

"I agree that we should look into it further, but I am inclined to believe that he was simply bored cooped up here in the village and was looking for something to occupy his time after a long week at work. I think a better use of our time would be to speak with one of the burglary victims from the list Constable Gibbs provided," Edwina said.

"Where do you propose we start?" Beryl asked.

Edwina pulled her trusty notebook from her pocket and flipped open the cover. She ran a slim finger down the list of names and stopped at one halfway down the page.

"Sally Cartwright, Larkspur Cottage. I believe we should start with her," Edwina said. "I know her slightly from the Women's Institute and have always found her to be a sensible young woman. If she has anything useful to contribute to the investigation, I'm sure she would be happy to share it with us."

Beryl readily agreed and started the automobile. In a flash they were tooling along the high street of Walmsley Parva, the wind ruffling their hair and Edwina taking up her customary stance of clinging to the door handle, as if evaluating the safety of leaping from the vehicle whilst it was rolling along. Beryl had thought it possible that Edwina's attitude towards high rates of speed might take a turn for the better after she learned how to drive herself, but alas, it was not the case. If anything, her friend had become even more critical of everyone else's driving, particularly Beryl's. She seemed to be using her newfound knowledge against Beryl in ways that Beryl did not find particularly pleasant. Even when Edwina managed not to vocalize her concerns and recriminations, her body language spoke volumes.

Beryl felt rather miffed when Edwina exhaled a sigh of relief as they slid to a stop in front of Larkspur Cottage. As she stepped out of the automobile, Beryl evaluated the scene around her. The cottage lay slightly outside the main village and on a plot of land large enough to leave it well away from the prying eyes of neighbors. Adding to its solitary feel were the dense evergreen shrubberies and trees flanking it on both sides. As far as Beryl could see, there was nothing to indicate it should have been named Larkspur Cottage. Left to her, she might have called it Hemlock Lodge or Pine Grove Place.

Edwina stood in the middle of the street, giving the cottage a once-over of her own. She turned towards Beryl. "This seems rather an isolated sort of place, doesn't it?" she asked.

"I was just thinking the same thing. I wonder how many of the properties on the constable's list will prove to be much the same," Beryl said.

"The woman I delivered the yarn to, who claimed to have been the victim of an attempted burglary, was also a bit off the beaten path," Edwina said. "It seems that our burglar is careful when it comes to choosing locations."

"Groveton Hall is also well out of the way," Beryl said. "Do you think that this burglar seems like the same sort of person who would take a bag of census schedules off a bicycle right in the middle of the village?"

"I think it's too soon to say for sure, but it's something to keep in mind," Edwina said. With that, she stepped onto the brick path leading to the glossy black front door and lifted the door knocker. The pair of detectives waited patiently for someone to answer.

From within they heard the sounds of a baby crying and then footsteps approaching. A young woman with warm brown eyes, a smattering of freckles across her nose, and hair making a valiant effort to escape its pins stood in front of them.

"Miss Davenport, what brings you all the way out here?" she asked.

"We hoped we might have a few moments of your time to ask about the burglary that occurred at your home recently," Edwina said. "Have you met my business partner, Beryl Helliwell?"

"I have not had the pleasure of making your acquaintance, ma'am, but I have heard a great deal about you," Sally Cartwright said, stepping back and holding the door wide open to allow them to pass into the small, dimly lit hallway.

Beryl noticed a small blue hat and jacket hanging on a peg on the wall, next to a woman's cardigan and a man's straw boater. The smell of bread baking floated towards her from somewhere in the back of the building, and Beryl was suddenly reminded by a rumbling in her stomach that they had not made time for a proper meal since breakfast. She did hope Sally would not feel obligated to offer to feed them. With the economy being what it was, it never did to accept hospitality if it meant taking food from the householder's own family.

"I've heard of you, too," Beryl said, hoping the sound of her voice drowned out any noise from her digestive system. "Edwina tells me you are involved with the Women's Institute."

Sally nodded her head. "When I heard about the institute's plans for food production, and for making the best of what we had during the war years, I knew it was something I wanted to get involved with. What I learned there, I have continued to use ever since, even though things aren't quite as stringent as they used to be."

Beryl thought she remembered Edwina nattering on at one point concerning the value of the Women's Institute. Beryl had nodded and feigned interest but, truth be told, had been rather dismissive of such an organization. Beryl had never warmed to domesticity or to groups populated entirely by women. She found she did far better interacting with men when it came right down to it, and she often found herself chafing at the notion of fulfilling those roles assigned exclusively to women. Making jam or organizing fund-raisers built around white elephant sales and church fetes was not her cup of tea. Not that anything was her cup of tea. She simply couldn't abide the stuff.

"Very industrious of you, I'm sure," Beryl said as Sally led them into a small sitting room off the hallway. Their hostess gestured towards a large sofa, beside which slept a snoring elderly dog. Tiny garments and a scattering of children's toys lay about the room. Sally bent over to gather them quickly, as if embarrassed by evidence of family life in front of unexpected visitors.

"Please don't trouble yourself, Sally. We should have asked if you were available to meet with us this afternoon before simply springing ourselves upon you," Edwina said, taking the seat closest to the decrepit canine. It stirred slightly as she lowered herself into her seat but did not creak open an eye. Beryl placed herself gingerly at the other end of the sofa and nodded her agreement.

"I shouldn't like you to think me an untidy housekeeper," Sally said as she plucked a small shoe from the seat in front of her.

"I should think nothing of the sort. You are a busy woman with a family to care for, and we are inconveniencing you. But we do have an important investigation under way, and we need some information from you in order for it to continue. Do you have a few moments to spare?" Edwina asked.

"Anything I can do to assist you would be my pleasure," Sally said, taking the seat and placing the shoe in her lap.

"We wanted to ask you about the burglary and the items that were taken," Beryl said.

"It was really very astonishing. I never would've expected such a thing to occur in Walmsley Parva. Although, I don't know that it was much of a break-in, considering the doors were, of course, left unlocked. Although, I've broken that habit since it happened," Sally said.

"Did you come home and discover things were missing, or were you here when it happened?" Edwina asked.

"I had just taken little Luther out for a walk. He's gotten so he can toddle along quite well now, and I wanted to be sure to check for wild strawberries in a particularly nice patch I know about," Sally said. "I'm still making jam, just like you taught us."

"I'm glad to see the skills have continued to be useful to you. Was the field quite a distance away?" Edwina asked.

"It was far enough that I needed to carry Luther part of the way," Sally said.

"Were you gone for a long time?" Beryl asked.

"Probably about three hours in total," Sally said. "It took us about half an hour each way to walk, and then we spent a couple of hours picking fruit. It isn't particularly efficient to do so with a small child in tow. At least not one as inclined to try to dash off as Luther is."

"According to the statement you gave to Constable Gibbs, you returned home and found that your house had been burgled. Is that correct?" Edwina asked.

Sally nodded. "I telephoned down to the police station as soon as I realized something had happened. It was shocking."

"Did you lose things of much value?" Beryl asked.

"Only a few bits of silver from the china closet . . . and one other strange thing," Sally said, looking at Edwina.

"What was that?" Edwina asked, reaching for her notebook.

"My aunt Cynthia's apricot brandy," Sally said, arching an eyebrow.

"You can't be serious," Edwina said, holding her pencil poised above her notepad in disbelief.

"I was absolutely astonished. I came into the house and found the door open. At first, I thought it might have been done by the breeze. As soon as I stepped inside, I knew something was wrong. So, I checked the place over immediately. It's quite a small house, so it didn't take long to notice the silver missing from the china cabinet. After all, we haven't much in there, so I was sure to miss anything that had gone missing. It wasn't until later that I realized that the brandy was missing also."

"But who on earth would take your aunt Cynthia's apricot brandy?" Edwina asked.

"It's the most baffling thing of it all," Sally said.

"What's so strange about someone raiding someone's liquor cabinet?" Beryl asked. Not that she wished to sound as though she might be the sort of person who would do the same thing. Still, it seemed rather an ordinary item to take advantage of.

"It's not that it was someone's liquor cabinet that was the focus of the theft. It was that it was the particular liquor taken," Edwina said.

Beryl sensed something passing between Edwina and Sally that she did not have access to. As so often happened in the village, Beryl had noticed that there were undercurrents and unspoken histories flowing between people. It was something she had never experienced herself, and whenever it occurred, it left her feeling a little hollow inside, as if there was a part of life that she had missed out on by being so eager to ramble from place to place.

"What Miss Davenport is being too polite to say is that my

Aunt Cynthia's apricot brandy was legendary in Walmsley Parva," Sally said.

"It did have a well-deserved reputation," Edwina said.

"Anyone who has ever been a victim of my aunt Cynthia's home brewing will tell you, without reservation, that it was the ghastliest thing they have ever tasted," Sally said. "Absolutely sinister stuff."

"Since you put it that way, Sally, I would have to agree it really was quite dreadful," Edwina said. She turned towards Beryl. "It was the sort of thing you never wanted to see show up at one of the jumble sales or any other event being held in the village. Unfortunately, Cynthia was an extraordinarily generous woman, and it was a social discomfort one was forced to navigate with frequency."

"No one ever made the mistake of bidding on it more than once. In fact, I think that not too long after she had taken up her new hobby, I was the only one who did so," Sally said.

"You bid on your aunt's brandy, even though you knew it was terrible?" Beryl asked.

"No one else was going to do so. I couldn't let the poor old dear feel ashamed of what she contributed, so I would bid on it anytime it appeared at an event. Unfortunately, that led her to believe that I actually liked it. In fact, the only thing she gave me for Christmas in the past ten years was a bottle of her brandy," Sally said.

"So, you had a lot of it, then?" Beryl asked.

"I did. Whilst she was alive, I would pour out a little at a time what I had bought at any of the auctions, so that when she visited, she thought I had been drinking it. She always was eager to get her bottles back, so I would return them to her. Unfortunately, like a bad penny, they kept turning up."

"But you ended up with some in the end?" Edwina asked.

"When my aunt died and I cleared out her estate, there were about a half dozen bottles in her cupboards. Somehow, they made me feel quite sentimental, and I couldn't bring myself to get rid of them. I had tucked them into a cupboard here in the sitting room for safekeeping. I certainly would not have wanted Luther to get into them," Sally said. She got to her feet and walked towards a small door tucked beneath a sloping wall and gave the doorknob a tug.

"They were right here, in among some badminton rackets and out-of-season clothing. When I made a careful search after the burglary, I realized that they had disappeared."

"How bizarre. So, just the silver and the apricot brandy were taken?" Edwina asked.

"Yes, that is it," Sally said. "I suppose I was lucky that the thief didn't take anything more."

"I would have to agree," Edwina said, closing her notebook. "Was there anything you noticed in the house to indicate who had been here?"

"What sort of thing?" Sally asked.

"A footprint, a smudge, maybe even a smell lingering in the air?" Beryl asked.

"No, nothing of that sort," Sally said as she closed the small door and pushed it firmly in place. "I wish there had been something to indicate who had done it. Frankly, I've been a bit jumpy ever since it happened. My husband is frequently late getting home in the evening, and I don't feel as comfortable out here as I once did. Especially not with a small child to worry about as well as myself."

Beryl looked down at the dog. He was clearly no help whatsoever, but she thought she had better ask.

"And your dog didn't seem to have dissuaded the intruder in any way?" Beryl asked.

"As you can see, he's not much of a guard dog."

"He didn't even seem to notice when I sat down next to him," Edwina said. "He looks to be quite elderly."

"He's deaf and blind, as far as I'm able to tell," Sally said. "I don't think he would've been able to cause too much fuss even if someone had stepped on his tail."

"Still, he should have been able to smell something, shouldn't he have?" Beryl said. Not that she was an expert on dogs, but she had noticed that Crumpet was inclined to prioritize his sense of smell over all his other senses. Whenever she volunteered to take him out on a walk, he was forever following a trail with his nose that was completely invisible to her.

"Perhaps I should have given him more credit for preventing further losses," Sally said.

"Maybe the burglar was surprised by him. Perhaps he had managed to wake the dog partway through his or her traipse through your house, and that's what prevented the thief from taking more of your possessions," Edwina said.

"I shall have to tell my husband what you said. He keeps mentioning that we should put the poor boy out of his misery. Perhaps he is earning his keep, after all," Sally said.

"Will you be available if we have any further questions?" Beryl asked.

"I will make a point to be. As I said, I've been uncomfortable since the burglary occurred, and anything I can do to help get to the bottom of it would be my pleasure," Sally said.

She showed them to the cottage door and closed it only when the sound of a child's cries could be heard from the second floor of the small house.

Chapter 14

"What do you think of her story?" Beryl asked. "Do you really think it's so very odd that someone would take the apricot brandy?"

"I think that what we heard at Larkspur Cottage is going to convince Constable Gibbs even more that Declan was involved with the burglaries," Edwina said.

"Why is that?" Beryl asked.

"Because anyone who had spent time here in the village for long would have recognized Cynthia's apricot brandy for the criminal waste of fruit that it was. He or she would never have considered making off with it. It was not the sort of thing you could pay someone to take," Edwina said.

"Was it really as bad as all that?" Beryl asked.

"Let me put it this way. Charles Jarvis ended up with a bottle of it as a thank-you for preparing Cynthia's will. He confided to me that a single sip of it dislodged one of his fillings. After that, he decided to harness its effects for good rather than evil," Edwina said.

"And how did he manage to do that?" Beryl said.

"He began using it as a cleaning solvent for his oil-paint brushes," Edwina said.

"I have to admit I've never heard of anything quite as bad as that before," Beryl said.

"You see what I mean? Things are looking very grim for young Declan," Edwina said.

Although she hated to admit it, Beryl had to agree. Although, a thought did occur to her as she fired up the motorcar and eased out onto the lane.

"It seems to me that whoever took it would be inclined to at least look at the labels. Did this Cynthia woman name it in some way?" Beryl asked.

"Yes, she took quite a lot of time over that part of the process. She hand-lettered the name *apricot brandy* on each bottle and added the date, if I remember correctly," Edwina said. "Why do you ask that?"

"Well, in my experience, no Irishman worthy of the name would consider ruining his palate with something as ghastly as apricot brandy. He certainly wouldn't load up on this stuff without sampling it first. And he absolutely would have realized that it wasn't worth drinking if he had done so," Beryl said.

"You have had quite a lot to say about prejudice from the moment Declan came into our lives," Edwina said.

"What does that have to do with anything we learned here today?" Beryl asked.

"It seems to me that assuming that Declan would be a connoisseur of spirits based on his nationality is just as prejudiced as assuming anything else about someone based on their ethnicity. Admit it, you are just as likely to label people with attributes and characteristics as the rest of us," Edwina said, sitting back in her seat and folding her gloved hands primly in her lap.

When they had arrived at Larkspur Cottage, Beryl had promised herself she would drive more sedately on the way back into the village. Seeing the rather smug look on Edwina's face now, she changed her mind. With a feeling of satisfaction, she applied herself to the accelerator and enjoyed seeing Edwina reach up and hang on to her hat.

As much as Beryl was disinclined to approve of gossip, there was something to be said about the expediency of asking Prudence Rathbone for her insider knowledge on just about any topic. Prudence, the owner of the post office–cum-sweetshop–cum-stationer, was the foremost purveyor of gossip in all the village. Her closest friend, Minnie Mumford, came in a close second, but when time was of the essence, Beryl had found it expedient to drop in on Prudence for a chat.

It was always easy enough to come up with an excuse for entering her shop. After all, one could always claim to be in need of postage stamps. Beryl had often distracted Prudence from impertinent questions by making enquiries into the cost of postage to far-flung destinations. That seemed to be one of the most reliable ways to use a sleight-of-hand technique to get more information than one gave.

Prudence looked up from a display of new fountain pens she was straightening in a case on the far side of the shop. Perhaps the pens would be a better way to engage Prudence than even enquiries as to the parcel postage rates to Kenya would be. Edwina sensibly headed for a rack displaying picture postcards and made quite a fuss about inspecting them one at a time. Beryl could feel Prudence itching to keep her eye on both women at the same time. A distracted Prudence was a vulnerable Prudence, and Beryl was quite certain that if there was anything to be gained by their visit, they would come out on top.

"Good afternoon, Miss Helliwell," Prudence said. "What brings you into my shop this afternoon? I thought you would be far too busy tracking down criminals to have any time for shopping."

"It seems that you are rather well informed about our business," Beryl said. "We do find ourselves run right off our feet of late, but it does not do to allow one's basic needs to go unmet even during the course of performing one's duties."

"I know just what you mean. Many's the time I find I simply must flip the OPEN sign to CLOSED and pop out to run some errands up and down the street," Prudence said.

Beryl took that to mean that Prudence, because of her shop's enviable position and large plate-glass window, often found herself overcome by curiosity concerning the affairs of others and made the difficult decision to close up shop in order to investigate.

"As it happens, I am in dire need of a new pen. With so much to keep track of with the new business, I seem to have rather worn out my old one," Beryl said. "I see you have a rather nice display here."

Beryl tapped on the glass in front of her with a gloved finger. Even though she was not above annoying Prudence when it served her needs, there was no call to do so until provoked. Prudence was a fiend when it came to buffing and polishing her glass display cases. There was no need to get on her bad side before the questions even got under way by leaving finger marks all over her establishment.

Prudence was a savvy businesswoman and was always eager to make a sale, especially considering she so often closed shop. It behooved her to make the best of the moments when both she and eager customers were available at the same time. She gave Beryl one of her long toothy smiles and indicated the assortment of pens before her.

"You are in luck," Prudence said. "I have just received a particularly nice new line of pens. Do you see one that you think might suit?"

"I should very much like to try that one," Beryl said, indicating a cigar-shaped black pen with a flat top. Beryl liked its clean lines and sturdy-looking silver clip. Prudence lifted it from the velvet-lined tray in which it sat and laid it on the counter in front of Beryl.

"Would you like a piece of paper to try it out?" Prudence asked.

"Yes, I would," Beryl said. "You never can tell with a pen, can you, until you've tried it out for yourself?"

Prudence nodded and reached for a box secreted away in the cabinet below. She extracted a piece of newsprint and placed it on the case in front of Beryl. Beryl knew from experience that newsprint never did give a particularly good practice run for pens. It feathered and bled far too easily. However, newsprint was the cheapest sort of paper available, and she could see how Prudence's lack of generosity with her customers was showing itself in her choice of test paper on offer.

Beryl posted the pen by placing the cap on the end. She hefted it slightly and liked the weight of it in her hand. With a flourish, she signed her name in a bold scrawl across the sheet of paper. The nib gave no feedback whatsoever. It was an extremely wet writer, and Beryl enjoyed the way the ink laid down in a wide, bold line.

"You know, I think this is exactly what I am looking for," Beryl said. "I should like to take it, please."

"Will you be requiring any ink to go with it?" Prudence asked as she removed a pen box from the cabinet and returned the scrap paper to its resting place.

"Edwina, do we need any fountain-pen ink for the office?" Beryl asked, turning to her friend.

"I should think it would depend on the color you are considering," Edwina said. "We have almost a full bottle of blue, but we are nearly out of black." Edwina approached the counter and stood next to Beryl. She looked at the pen and nodded with approval.

"We should like a bottle of black, then, too, please," Beryl said.

"Prudence, you don't happen to have any black-banded stationery in stock, do you?" Edwina asked.

Beryl could almost hear Prudence's thoughts whirling in her head. Of course, Edwina would think of just the right angle to introduce the topic at hand without appearing to do so.

"That would entirely depend. What sort of stationery are you considering? Something for condolences perhaps?" Prudence asked, leaning over the case ever so slightly.

"As a matter of fact, that's exactly what it is for. We have, of course, already paid a call to Mrs. Faraday, but I always think it best to follow up such a visit with a note, don't you?" Edwina said innocently.

"It's the least one could do as a neighbor after such a nasty business," Prudence said. "Whoever thought such a tragedy would befall such a lovely lady as Mrs. Faraday."

Beryl was intrigued. It was not like Prudence to have positive things to say about her neighbors. Perhaps Prudence had decided to take a new tack. The stationery shop down the street had been the recipient of Beryl's Derby winnings earlier in the month, when she had decided to place an order for a Remington portable typewriter. She could have purchased the same machine through Prudence's shop but had decided not to do so. She found the woman to be so toxic, it was with trepidation that she dared to consume chocolates purchased in her store.

She did not want to give Prudence the satisfaction of making a far more expensive purchase there. Perhaps Prudence had taken note of the sort of conversations Beryl and Edwina did not prefer to engage in and was adjusting her behavior accordingly. After all, it was common knowledge that Simpkins had come into a great deal of money, and perhaps Prudence thought she and Edwina had some sway over how he spent it.

The truth of the matter was they had no such influence. Edwina had made a great show of directing him to her friend local solicitor Charles Jarvis when he had come into his fortune, and Charles had assisted him in acquiring financial advice. The only say in the matter Beryl had was to accept his offer of purchasing rounds of drinks down at the Dove and Duck from time to time. But Prudence need not know any of that. In fact, it was far better that she did not.

"That's just what we thought," Beryl said, looking over at Edwina, who nodded vigorously. "Such a tragedy for all the family."

Beryl waited to see if Prudence would take the bait. Out of the corner of her eye, she watched as Prudence busied herself sorting through her stock of stationery. Her cheek moved strangely, as though she was chewing it furiously from the inside. How difficult it must be for Prudence, Beryl thought, to keep from saying those things she ought not to. Beryl was counting on it being an impossible task. But still, it would not do any harm to speed things along. After all, time was of the essence in this case.

She glanced over at Edwina and gave her a slight nod. Edwina cleared her throat slightly.

"Although, it has been said by some people that perhaps his passing is not an entirely negative occurrence for absolutely everyone concerned," Edwina said.

Prudence dropped the box of note cards like it had singed her, and turned her body back towards Beryl and Edwina. Everything about her body language had changed from someone holding herself in check to someone bursting at the seams with something to share.

"I have heard it said that the Faraday family was not an entirely happy one," Prudence said.

"How sad," Edwina said.

"There are those in the village who say that the magistrate and his stepdaughter did not get along anywhere near so well as one would hope," Prudence said. "And I daresay I, for one, saw a bit of coldness between the magistrate and his wife from time to time, when they were in the shop."

"I thought they were a very devoted couple, by all accounts,"

Edwina said. "Wasn't that the impression you had when we
stopped by to pay our condolence call?" Edwina asked, turning
towards Beryl.

"Indeed, it was. She seemed deeply saddened by her husband's death. I suppose that she must feel rather daunted at the
notion of being a widow rather than a married woman. After
all, there are hardly enough gentlemen to go around these days,
and I'm sure she felt herself rather fortunate that her husband
made it out of the war unscathed," Beryl said.

She had always found it best to provide Prudence with
something to contradict. The postmistress seemed to like nothing better than to know more than those around her, and with
her contrary nature, she delighted in arguing with her customers. Especially if she could disguise such behavior as being
for their own good.

"I have noticed she's the sort of woman to attract admirers
wherever she goes," Prudence said. "I would be very much surprised if she remained a widow for long. Men of all stations of
society seem to take quite an interest in her."

"Are you suggesting she has a fleet of admirers trailing in
her wake already?" Beryl said. "That was a bit of quick work,
wasn't it?"

"The poor magistrate isn't even cold in his grave, and she has
men in here asking after her," Prudence said with a decided
smack of her lips.

"How ghastly," Edwina said. "How unseemly. She must not
know that such a thing is occurring, or she would have done
something to quash it immediately."

"I suppose it's possible she doesn't really know. The admirer
in question is not the sort of person I would expect to be in her
immediate social orbit," Prudence said, her face breaking into a
wide smile of satisfaction.

Beryl could tell that extracting the tasty tidbit from where
Prudence clutched it to her scrawny chest, like a dragon guard-
ing its hoard, would prove futile if she displayed the least bit of

interest in knowing the name of the party involved. It would be best to make less of Prudence's news.

"Well, if they're not, I'm sure no aspersions can be cast on social intimates of the recent widow. After all, one would never expect a lady of quality like Mrs. Faraday to not attract admirers from the lower classes," Beryl said. "Will we be all set for postage, Edwina, or should we buy some to go with the condolence card?"

Beryl could feel Prudence scrambling to reclaim the floor.

"I suppose it's possible that Mrs. Faraday was not always such a very great lady. After all, the admirer in question seems to have known her for many years previously," Prudence said as a triumphant look flashed across her face.

"I really know very little about her past. I never made her acquaintance until she arrived in Walmsley Parva," Edwina said. "But I can't imagine that the magistrate would have married a woman of a station far below his own, can you?" Edwina asked Beryl, pointedly turning slightly away from Prudence.

"I should not have thought he would have been the sort of man not to value the social station of his wife," Beryl said. She turned back towards Prudence. "I'm sure you must be mistaken about any level of intimacy between Mrs. Faraday and some unnamed workingman who just popped into the shop and began nattering away at you."

Two spots of color appeared on Prudence's sallow cheeks. Beryl could tell she was working herself up into a fit of pique.

"There was no mistake about it. Mr. Crossley, the census taker, made a point of asking me about Mrs. Faraday as soon as he came to town," Prudence said triumphantly. She turned her back on Beryl and Edwina and extracted the box of black-banded stationery from the shelf behind her and smacked it down on the case in front of her with a vehemence that suggested she was not going to take lying down any questions about the quality of the tale she carried.

"Mr. Crossley, the census taker, asked about the magistrate's wife?" Edwina said. "When did this happen?"

"Like I said, as soon as he came to town. Most people make a point of stopping in at the post office when they first move into the village to inform me of their address," Prudence said.

"He seemed to know her personally?" Beryl asked.

"He knew enough to ask if she was still beautiful," Prudence said. "If that doesn't mean he had made her acquaintance previously, I don't know what does."

There were hidden depths to Mr. Crossley, that was for sure, Beryl thought. She wondered if Mr. Crossley had a reason for moving to the little backwater of Walmsley Parva that went above and beyond his job with the census service. Beryl wondered how he knew Mrs. Faraday and whether or not she had been glad to see him.

Whilst Mr. Crossley was certainly not the sort of man one crossed the street to avoid, she would not have expected him to be invited to dine with the magistrate and his family. His economic situation, at least from the look of his cottage, did not make it seem likely he would be the Faradays' sort of person. Even if he had fallen on hard times, he would likely possess a finer wardrobe, even if it had become rather shabby. No, he was decidedly of a lower class than were Mrs. Faraday and her husband.

"That does seem to indicate a connection between the two of them, doesn't it?" Edwina said.

"I thought as much myself. As I said, I doubt very much Mrs. Faraday will be on the marriage market for very long," Prudence said. "Now, did you need those stamps?"

"What do you think of that?" Edwina asked.

"I think that the case has taken a turn I did not expect in the least," Beryl said.

They had completed their transaction with Prudence and

had hurried out of the shop as soon as was seemly. Of course, it did not do to look as though one were eager to rush away and chew over a tasty bit of gossip, but that was exactly what they needed to do.

"I'm asking myself if it is strange that Mr. Crossley did not mention a connection with the Faradays before now," Edwina said. "Does this make him look guilty in some way, or am I just becoming increasingly suspicious with each passing investigation?"

"I can't say as though the opportunity would have presented itself for him to mention it casually in conversation with us," Beryl said. "And if he had wanted to keep such a thing a secret, would he have been so foolish as to make an offhand public comment such as he did in the village post office?"

Edwina thought about that for a moment. She had to admit that if Mr. Crossley was intelligent enough to be hired as the census taker, he was most likely the sort of person who had his wits about him sufficiently not to share business he considered secret with a virtual stranger, and certainly not one who ran the local post office.

"Still, I think we should ask him about his connection with Mrs. Faraday, don't you?" Edwina said.

"We should be sure to ask him, but I think we should also make a point of asking Mrs. Faraday about their manner of meeting," Beryl said. "Don't you have an appointment this afternoon?" Beryl reached out a finger and ran it along the bottom edge of Edwina's hair.

Edwina had impetuously bobbed her hair earlier in the month and had enjoyed the results so much, she had decided to book a standing appointment to keep it in trim. Alma Poole, of Alma's House of Beauty, had recommended a maintenance trim every three weeks if she wished to keep a clean and severe outline to her new style. Edwina had readily agreed as she was entirely delighted by this change in her appearance. When she had booked the appointment, she had had no notion that she would be on a case burdened with a serious time crunch.

"I am booked in to see Alma for a trim, but I don't know that I can spare the time now that we are on a case," Edwina said.

"Nonsense. You won't be in dereliction of your duties in any way whatsoever. Alma's House of Beauty is almost as good a place to glean information as the post office. You can have your hair done while working on the case," Beryl said, taking Edwina by the elbow and steering her in the direction of the beauty parlor.

"What will you do whilst I'm at Alma's?" Edwina said.

"I shall endeavor to speak once again with Mrs. Faraday and ask her about her connection with Mr. Crossley. That is, I will if you don't mind me going out there on my own," Beryl said.

"That suits me just fine. You take your motorcar and drive on out to Groveton Hall. I'll have my hair done, and then I'll walk back to the Beeches. We can compare notes when we both arrive back home," Edwina said.

With that, the two friends parted company. Edwina made her way along the high street until she came to the turnoff for Alma's House of Beauty. She pushed open the door and heard the small bell jingling above her head. Alma's shampoo girl stood sweeping the floor with a decided lack of enthusiasm. The young woman brightened up as she saw Edwina approach.

"Here for your trim, are you, Miss Davenport?" the girl said.

"I am indeed," Edwina said.

The girl gestured towards the shampoo sink, and after removing her hat and placing it, along with her handbag, on a rack near the door, Edwina settled into the seat in front of the sink and relaxed under the girl's capable ministrations. The last time she had sat with her head in the sink, Edwina had had far more hair to be washed and rinsed. In less time than she could have thought possible, she found herself swathed in a towel and seated in the chair Alma had reserved for cutting.

There was a faint hint in the air of the chemicals used for permanent waves. For years Edwina had spent time every few weeks having her hair contorted into unnatural curls. It had been her mother's idea to begin that process when she was in her early twenties. Edwina had never enjoyed either sitting long enough for the intense-smelling concoctions dabbed onto her head to do their work or the results it gave. It was with intense relief that she considered the change she had made to her appearance and how much easier her new bob had made her life.

Alma appeared at her side with a pair of shears and a comb in her hands.

"I wasn't sure if I would see you here today, Edwina," Alma said, running the comb through her hair.

"Why is that?" Edwina asked.

"I thought maybe you would be involved with this latest bunch of goings-on here in Walmsley Parva. You have seemed to be up to your pretty little neck in it every time there's been something going on recently. Why should this time be any different?" said Alma.

"It is rather terrible business about the magistrate and all the burglaries, isn't it?" the shampoo girl said.

"You had best get back to your sweeping, young lady," Alma said, pointing the shears at her shampoo girl. "I have to stay on top of her every minute of the day, or she'll get distracted and we'll be up to our knees in the hair." Alma had lowered her voice to a whisper, and despite her grumbling, Edwina wondered if Alma was as concerned about losing her help in the shop as everyone else was about losing domestic staff in their homes.

"She has a point, however. It really has been quite a ghastly business," Edwina said. "You haven't had any problems here at the shop, have you?"

"You mean have we been burglarized?" Alma asked, snipping little bits of hair from along the back of Edwina's neck.

"Yes, either here at the shop or even at your home. It seems that things have gotten out of hand," Edwina said.

"We've had a bit of trouble lately, but not from a burglary," Alma said.

Edwina had heard nothing of the sort. "I'm sorry to hear that. Whatever has gone on?"

"It did involve the Faradays, but not in the way you might be thinking," Alma said. "Alan Faraday was in here earlier this week." Alma's thin lips pressed together in a grimace.

Edwina wondered if it was simply because Alma did not prefer men to make an appearance in the shop, which she and her customers considered to be a respite from the gruff sex. No woman in the village wished to be seen by any man in the sort of state she would be in during her visit to Alma's House of Beauty. The whole point to visiting a beauty parlor was to appear more attractive, not less. Men were entirely discouraged from putting in any sort of appearance, and that even included Alma's husband, Sidney Poole, purveyor of fine meats. It certainly would have extended to someone as recently returned as Alan Faraday.

"He didn't want you to cut his hair, did he?" Edwina said. Even though Alma was well known for her skills in the art of hairdressing, just down the street there was a perfectly good barbershop, where all the men in town were known to have equal access to quality haircuts. There was no call for them to enter Alma's place of business. At least not for any good reason.

"He certainly did not want me to cut his hair. But he did want something from me." Alma was distressed enough that she lowered her shears. Edwina was glad that she did so. Edwina had seen some unfortunate results of Alma feeling agitated as she proceeded to ply her trade. Occasionally, a woman in the village could be found with a decidedly uneven set of bangs or with marcel waves that were not evenly distributed across her head. Alma was skilled at her job, but she did need to focus on the task at hand whilst doing it.

"What did he want, then?" Edwina said, turning slightly in her seat to look up at Alma. The other woman came round and sat herself in the seat next door to Edwina.

"You know how young Alan left the village under strained circumstances several years ago?" Alma said.

"I do remember when that happened. It seems such a sad thing for a family to grow distant almost willingly when so many other families were suffering losses they could do nothing about," Edwina said. "What does that have to do with Alan paying a call to your establishment?"

"Someone told Alan about the betting pool we ladies have. He came to ask if he could take part in it," Alma said.

"He did what?" Edwina said. "But that is entirely outside the norms for the pool."

"My thoughts exactly. He wanted to be allowed to place a wager on whatever was the highest stakes we had going," Alma said.

"Did you allow him to join in?" Edwina asked. The thought was preposterous. Alma's betting pool was exclusively for the ladies.

"Of course I didn't allow him to place a bet. The whole point of the ladies' wagering pool is that it's for ladies. But he didn't like my answer," Alma said.

"What did he do when you refused him?" Edwina said.

"That's when it all became ever so nasty," Alma said. "He told me that if I did not allow him to participate, he would tell the husbands what we were up to."

"What did you say to that?" Edwina asked.

"I told him that if he ever thought to threaten me that way

again, I would lay a charge against him before the magistrate. I told him I knew very well that his gambling problem was what had forced the estrangement between him and his brother, and that if he did not want for me to tell Mr. Faraday the elder that his younger brother was up to no good once more, he would leave my shop and not return to it," Alma said.

"When did this happen exactly?" Edwina said.

"He was in here Monday evening, just before closing time. It made me so upset I had no appetite when I went home for my tea," Alma said. She patted her ample stomach with the flat side of her comb, as if to emphasize the unusual nature of the event.

Edwina considered the fact that she and Beryl had found the magistrate's body on Tuesday, around midmorning. Could the confrontation Alan had provoked with Alma have anything to do with Mr. Faraday's death? After all, it had occurred not all that many hours later. Had a situation involving his brother caused Alan Faraday to make a clumsy and desperate attempt to join Alma's wagering pool?

"Did Alan happen to say why he was so desperate to place a wager with you?" Edwina asked.

"He didn't say why he wanted to join the betting pool, but he did say something that sent a shiver right down my spine," Alma said, taking what felt like a dramatic slice from the back of Edwina's hair. "He gave me the coldest stare I've ever received, and then said that by not letting him have a chance to win some money, I had already done the most damage to him I could do."

"How odd," Edwina said. "It sounds as though he was quite desperate."

"I felt just dreadful about the whole affair. As soon as I threatened to expose him to his brother, he dashed out the door and down the street. He slammed the door so hard, it knocked the bell from its hook and dashed it to the ground," Alma said.

Edwina could scarcely wait for Alma to finish trimming her

hair. She felt quite desperate herself. Although she was not happy to think young Alan Faraday could have been involved in his own brother's death, she could not deny she was enjoying the exhilaration she had come to associate with making headway on an investigation.

As soon as was possible, she hopped out of the chair and asked Alma to put the cost of the appointment on her account. Not so very long ago she would have done so with a deep sense of shame, having no idea where the money to settle the account would come from. But now she realized with a rush that she could pay for a weekly appointment at the salon out of her own earnings. Fueled by high spirits and a sense of urgency concerning the case, she hurried out of the shop at a rate of speed her mother would surely have considered unsuitable for a lady.

Chapter 15

Beryl pulled up the drive to Groveton Hall once more and turned off the automobile's engine. She sat there, giving the place a careful look. As country manor houses went, the building before her was unremarkable. The mellow stone walls and the gravel driveway were exactly what one would expect from such a place. Some sort of evergreen shrubbery ran around the perimeter of the building, hugging it closely. Two large stone griffins flanked the front door. Dotted here and there about the roofline, the requisite early Victorian—era gargoyles squatted and peered down menacingly as Beryl exited her automobile.

No, she thought to herself, she would not wish to be the mistress of Groveton Hall if someone offered it to her for free. It would require a great deal of cash to keep such a monstrosity afloat. Although, like most Americans, Beryl was inclined to feel unrepentantly romantic about the past, especially when it came to historic buildings, she could muster up no fond feelings for something as blandly predictable as Groveton Hall.

A swell of indignation grew up in her chest as she considered how little Mr. Faraday had likely understood the impact of the fine he had levied on Declan. The magistrate had probably spent more on having the gravel in his driveway kept neat and tidy in the average week than the total wages the poor Irishman could hope to earn in that same amount of time.

Beryl mounted the steps and rapped sharply on the tiresomely predictable lion's head brass door knocker. A harried-looking woman, slightly older than her, opened the door. She wore an apron, but it was not the sort parlormaids wore as part of their usual uniform. Rather it looked like one of Edwina's aprons used in the kitchen. Beryl thought she detected a spot of brown sauce sullying its sprigged floral print. This must be the Mrs. Breen that Mrs. Faraday was so eager to keep in her employ. Mrs. Breen made the formidable Beddoes appear friendly and obliging by comparison. The woman positively scowled at her as she wiped her raw red hands on her apron.

"What is it you want?" the woman asked.

"I would like to speak with the lady of the house, if she's in," Beryl said.

"Aren't you that woman who found the magistrate's body?" she asked.

How times had changed, Beryl thought with a start. Not so many months ago, the question she would have been asked was whether or not she was the famous Beryl Helliwell. Now it seemed she had become so common a sight about the village that those who had not met her before associated her with village goings-on. Beryl was not entirely sure how she felt about such a change of circumstance.

On the one hand, it might make matters easier when trying to proceed with an investigation unobtrusively not to be recognized everywhere she went. It also meant that her desire to change her life completely by settling in an out-of-the-way little village had succeeded. On the other hand, many doors had opened to them because of her celebrity. And Beryl was not all that keen to blend in with the woodwork. She was at an age when she had a niggling fear just such a thing would occur no matter what she did to try to stop it sooner or later. There was no need to allow it to happen any sooner than was completely necessary.

If only their latest case were not one to which they were sworn to secrecy. It would be very satisfying to have their faces appear in the newspaper as the triumphant, celebrated detectives with one more solved case to add to their files. Perhaps she should write to her friend Archie Harrison and ask if he wanted to do a follow-up interview with her and Edwina. She would not be able to mention the current case, of course, but she was sure that between the pair of them, they would be able to come up with enough fodder for a worthwhile article in one of London's smaller newspapers. But for now, the case beckoned.

"That's right, I am. Which is exactly why I'm here. I have a question I need to ask on behalf of the local constable," Beryl said.

She was gratified to see the unpleasant servant take a step backwards. It was as though she did not wish to be in the orbit of the word *police*. Beryl hoped she had not given Mrs. Faraday's domestic staff the excuse they had been looking for to quit her employ. Beryl had been surprised at how often English servants felt any diminishment in their employers' status.

They seemed remarkably unwilling to associate with anything disreputable. A death in the house was never welcomed, and one under mysterious and potentially criminal circumstances was unlikely to have favorably disposed the Breens to remain at Groveton Hall. Prolonged scrutiny by the police or their associates certainly would not help matters.

"You'd best see the mistress, then," the woman said, motioning for Beryl to follow her inside.

Beryl closed the door behind her and found herself being led into the very same room where Mrs. Faraday had received her and Edwina previously. Mrs. Faraday sat at the secretary desk, bent over a letter. She turned when the servant announced Beryl's arrival.

"Someone to see you, madame," the woman said.

She turned her back without waiting for a response from her mistress and rushed out of the room. Beryl thought she smelled the faintest whiff of smoke in the air. Perhaps something burning on the stove explained her rudeness.

"Do come in, Miss Helliwell. I hope you will excuse Mrs. Breen's abruptness. She and her husband are quite distressed over our current upheaval. The servants do not like anything unusual to befall their own household. They seem to love nothing better than to gossip about things happening in other people's homes, but they have no tolerance for it whatsoever when it occurs in their own sphere," Mrs. Faraday said.

She gave Beryl a half-hearted smile and gestured for her to take a seat. "What brings you by again so soon?"

Beryl did not think she detected a note of reproach in the other woman's voice. But it was a fair question. The bereaved should not be expected to entertain visitors more than the bare minimum number of times polite society demanded.

"I'm very sorry to trouble you once again, especially as I'm sure you are inundated with correspondence," Beryl said, gesturing towards the tall walnut secretary, whose drop-down front was littered with piles of envelopes and sheets of notepaper. "But I needed to speak to you about Mr. Terrence Crossley."

"Mr. Crossley?" Mrs. Faraday said, tilting her head to one side. "Should I know that name?"

"He is the man in charge of distributing and collecting the census schedules for the village of Walmsley Parva and the outlying homes in the district." Beryl kept her eyes fixed on Mrs. Faraday's face, hoping to detect any change in her expression that would indicate she did indeed know to whom Beryl referred.

"Oh, that Mr. Crossley. I don't know if he introduced himself when he came to the door to drop off the census schedules," Mrs. Faraday said. "Why would you possibly want to speak with me about him?"

"I'm going to confide in you something we are not mentioning any more often than necessary," Beryl said. "Miss Davenport and I are working closely with Constable Gibbs on the burglaries that have occurred in Walmsley Parva. Constable Gibbs has asked us to pay particular attention to anything connected with your household as regards the crime. She is a more than competent investigator, but with so many burglaries occurring in the area, she felt it would be advisable for her to delegate some of the footwork to other experienced investigators."

"The investigation into what happened to my husband and the burglary at our home has been foisted off on private enquiry agents rather than the actual police?" Mrs. Faraday said, crossing her arms over her chest.

"I believe the constable meant it as a way to ensure that your portion of this larger case received the individual attention that it deserved. She wanted you to feel as though someone as important as the magistrate and yourself were not being treated with the same sort of attention as the more common victims in the crime spree," Beryl said.

She had noticed how willing the upper classes all across the United Kingdom were to assume they were deserving of special attention from all quarters of officialdom. In Beryl's experience, the mentioning of such exclusivity, even if it was in no way true, often softened otherwise intractable individuals. It seemed to be working once again. Mrs. Faraday unfolded her arms and placed her hands in her lap.

"I see. Well, I suppose it makes sense for me to speak with you in her stead. Besides, there's something not quite nice about being interviewed by the police. And the servants are quite agitated by it all. But that still doesn't explain what Mr. Crossley has to do with anything," Mrs. Faraday said.

"We've taken a statement from a witness who says that Mr.

Crossley claims to have made your acquaintance in the past. I wanted to ask you about such a connection," Beryl said. "And whether or not he also knew your husband." Beryl suddenly wished she had Edwina's notebook and pencil tucked away in her pocket. She thought it always gave Edwina such an air of authority when she pulled them out and began recording the responses of those they interviewed.

"Yes, I suppose Mr. Crossley did mention that in passing when he delivered the census schedules. I would not say I knew him particularly, but we did meet on occasion in the past," Mrs. Faraday said.

Beryl noticed a slight tightening in Mrs. Faraday's facial features. Clearly, Mrs. Faraday was not enthusiastic about admitting the connection she had to Mr. Crossley. Beryl could not blame her. She would not necessarily wish to renew a connection with him, either, if she were not required to do so. He seemed the sort of person who could become a bit of a nuisance, and she had not found him to be an interesting conversationalist. Nor was he particularly easy on the eyes. Still, she wondered if Mrs. Faraday's reluctance went deeper than those superficial things. If Mrs. Faraday's life had been anything like her own, there were any number of men she would be delighted never to need to fend off again.

"And how did you meet him on occasion in the past?" Beryl said.

"I was an ambulance driver during the war, and Mr. Crossley was a soldier I met at one of the field hospitals during my time overseas," Mrs. Faraday said.

"Did you recognize him when he arrived at your door?" Beryl asked.

"No, I did not. As I said, our acquaintance was slight and fleeting, and I had not seen him in many years. He seemed to remember me, but I suppose that's not unusual, considering the circumstances," Mrs. Faraday said.

"Which circumstances would those be?" Beryl asked.

"There were far more men than women where we met. I expect I stood out to him rather more than he stood out to me," Mrs. Faraday said.

Beryl thought it likely Mrs. Faraday made a good point. Even though women did serve as nurses and ambulance drivers at the edge of the conflict, women still appeared in far fewer numbers than did men. A woman as attractive as Mrs. Faraday would certainly have made a memorable impression.

"Did he know your husband, as well?" Beryl asked.

"Yes, I'm sure he did. My husband was in a leadership role, and all the officers serving would have known who he was."

"Did he ask to see your husband when he dropped off the census schedules?" Beryl asked.

"As a matter of fact, he did. I opened the door to answer it, and he mentioned our previous acquaintance. Then he asked to speak with the head of household, and I took him down to Gordon's study."

"Did you stay for the conversation between the two of them?" Beryl asked.

"No. I had better things to do with my time than to sit there listening to two old soldiers reminisce about how valiantly they fought for king and country. I've heard rather enough of that over the years to know to avoid it whenever possible," Mrs. Faraday said with a fleeting smile. "My husband was rather inclined to be tedious on the subject of his war years. But I have found that so many men are, haven't you?"

Beryl wasn't sure she agreed with Mrs. Faraday's assessment of the situation. Although she often had interesting conversations with women who had also spent time so close to or even at the front, she doubted an exchange with Mrs. Faraday would turn out to be one of them. Although Beryl generally did not discuss the war, and spent as little time thinking about it as possible, it was her opinion that if talking about it made anyone who had endured that horror feel the least bit better, it was fine by her.

"I happen to have rather a soft spot for soldiers myself," Beryl said. "Thank you for your time, Mrs. Faraday. I don't think I shall need to trouble you again today." She stood and left Mrs. Faraday to get on with her correspondence.

Beryl pulled the door closed behind her on her way out. As she did so, she caught a glimpse of rustling black fabric out of the corner of her eye. Unless she missed her guess, the woman exiting a room near the end of the hallway was Nanny Meechum. Beryl could not believe her good luck. She would be able to interview two suspects before returning to the Beeches to report on her part of the investigation to Edwina. She raised her hand in greeting to the elderly woman, who did not seem particularly glad to see her. Beryl thought if she had been able to get away with it, she would have turned her back and hurried off in the other direction as quickly as her aging legs would take her.

"Would you by any chance be Nanny Meechum?" Beryl asked.

"That is correct, madame. Did you wish to speak with me?" Nanny Meechum said.

"As a matter of fact, I do have a question for you. Do you have a moment?" Beryl said.

"I must attend to young Master Timothy, so you will have to be quick, but I can spare you a moment of my time," the nanny said. "What is it you wanted to ask?"

"My business partner, Miss Davenport, and I have been asked by Constable Gibbs to assist with the portion of the burglary investigation as pertains to Groveton Hall. She felt it fitted the status of the household for investigators to be assigned to concentrate their efforts on what happened here. Especially in light of the tragedy that befell Mr. Faraday," Beryl said.

"I'm happy to help in any way that I can to unravel whatever befell him, but I can't see that I have any information to contribute to your investigation," the nanny said.

"It's really just a small matter that I was hoping you would be able to clear up for me," Beryl said. "We have a witness who says you were heard arguing with the magistrate quite heatedly in the days before his death. We are making enquiries into anyone who had reason to harbor ill will towards Mr. Faraday. I would like to know the nature of your argument with him."

Nanny Meechum took a startled step backwards and threw a knobby-knuckled hand to the base of her throat. Beryl had had her share of governesses during her youth and, truth be told, had not been fond of the sort of strict oversight they had, as a rule, employed. Even with all her energetic high jinks and spirited and outrageous exploits, she had not managed to leave any of them looking particularly shaken. It was as though governesses and nannies were cut out of the sort of cloth that was incapable of showing signs of wear. She found it quite surprising that Nanny Meechum betrayed any sign of inner discomfort.

"I don't know the sort of person who would be carrying tales like that, but it seems to me, he or she deserves to go to bed without any supper," the nanny said. "May I ask the name of the eavesdropper?"

"I'm afraid that's not the sort of information I am prepared to disclose during an ongoing investigation. I have to assume from your reaction that the person carrying the tales was rude but truthful," Beryl said.

Nanny Meechum pursed her lips and exhaled noisily through her slightly flared nostrils. "I suppose it would do no good to deny it now. Yes, Mr. Faraday and I had some rather heated words not long before his death. They concerned his brother's visit."

"You don't approve of the younger Mr. Faraday?" Beryl asked.

"It's not so much that I don't approve of him as a person. It's more that I feel he is having a deleterious influence upon young Monica," Nanny Meechum said.

"What makes you say that?" Beryl said. "Miss Davenport says that Miss Billington is quite a lovely young woman. You feel that she has changed in some way?"

"She has become quite unmanageable of late. I don't like to make such accusations lightly, but I suspect she has developed an attachment to a man," Nanny Meechum said.

"And you suspect that man is Alan Faraday?" Beryl said.

"As a matter of fact, I do. In my experience, proximity is a dangerous thing. Having Mr. Alan Faraday in the same household with an impressionable young woman like Monica is a recipe for disaster. I said as much to the magistrate, not that he took my concern seriously, mind you," the nanny said.

"What did he say exactly?" Beryl asked.

"He said whilst he thought that Monica was no more sensible than any other girl, he expected she would be able to see through his brother at the very least and would not involve herself with someone like him. He said that any problems with her or with his brother were well in hand, and that I should restrict my attention to my duties, which exclusively involved the care of young Timothy," the nanny said.

"What do you think he meant by having problems in hand?" Beryl asked.

"I have no idea whatsoever. I just felt it was my duty to make him aware of the goings-on under his own roof. He paid very little attention to his stepdaughter, other than to criticize her for insignificant infractions that were unlikely to lead to larger troubles. Now, if there isn't anything else, I must get back to Timothy. Even without the magistrate to remind me of my duties, I do know what they are," Nanny Meechum said.

With that, she hurried off into the conservatory at the end of the hall, and Beryl watched as she hesitated ever so slightly before she grasped the banister of the wide staircase at the foot of which Beryl and Edwina had so recently found her employer dead.

Even though Beryl could not say she felt particularly more enlightened as to who might have wanted the magistrate to come to harm or who might have taken the census schedules, she did have an even stronger sense that the magistrate had created enemies wherever he went. Even within his own household. He seemed like exactly the sort of man who would not realize how he had imperiled himself until it was too late.

Chapter 16

Edwina did not know if it was her new haircut or her sense of adventure that propelled her down the street and towards a destination she found herself surprised to be undertaking. Before she could talk herself out of it, Edwina pushed on the brass hand plate on the door of the pub and crossed the threshold. She could always blame her unladylike behavior on the investigation.

Surely unorthodox activities undertaken in the service of the king would be forgiven even by the ghost of her mother. Not that Edwina believed particularly in ghosts. She simply could not afford to. Walmsley Parva would be blanketed with them, should anyone bother to acknowledge their presence.

Edwina stood hesitantly for a moment just inside the doorway of the Dove and Duck before taking herself firmly in hand and attempting to stride confidently towards the bar. A peculiar mixture of smells filled her nostrils as she made her way towards the long wooden expanse, where Bill Nevins stood wiping down the bar's surface with a polishing cloth. He looked up as she approached, and did not make an attempt to hide his astonishment.

"Miss Davenport, what brings you into my humble establishment?" he said, draping the cloth over his shoulder.

"Miss Helliwell and I are working on a case, and I hoped I might find Chester White here," Edwina said.

"He's in the gents', but I'm sure he'll be back in just a moment," Bill said. "I don't suppose you'd like a pint or something, would you, whilst you're waiting for him to return to his table?"

Edwina looked beyond him at the wall of bottles. To Bill's left, there stood a row of gleaming taps. She wondered if she would ever be the sort of woman that Beryl was. Would there ever come a day when she would enter a country pub and breezily ask for a double whiskey or a pint of the house's best? Even with her vivid imagination, Edwina thought it unlikely she could imagine something like that occurring. The day might come when she found herself accompanying Beryl into a public house much like this one, but she could not imagine herself ordering anything stronger than a lemon squash. Even that seemed a stretch.

"Whilst I appreciate the offer, I prefer to keep my professional dealings separate from my private life," Edwina said.

"As you prefer, miss. That's Chester's table right over there, with the ledger spread out on it. If you'd like to wait for him over there, I'm sure he'll be right back," Bill said.

"Thank you so much," Edwina said.

No one else seemed to be in the pub, and she wondered if that was often the case. Edwina had made it a practice of long standing to keep her eyes firmly fixed in front of her as she passed the Dove and Duck whenever she was in the village. She did not particularly wish to know exactly what her neighbors got up to inside the pub. She found it difficult enough to hear of their exploits when Simpkins and Beryl returned home from a night of cavorting. Seeing it with her own two eyes was more than she wished to do.

After all, she would be encountering those same people out on the streets, in the shops, and even occasionally at church. She did not wish to alter her opinion of any of her fellow villagers based on what might be occurring within the pub. She crossed the room, noticing the sound of her hard-heeled shoes against the wide pine floorboards. She scraped back a chair at the table containing a ledger and a half-empty glass of an amber-colored liquid and took a seat. Just as she was pulling off her gloves, Chester White appeared beside her.

"Miss Davenport, are you here to place a bet? I didn't think of you as the wagering kind," Chester White said as he settled into his seat and patted his large leather ledger.

"Actually, I'm here on business that concerns another matter entirely," Edwina said.

"Well, should you change your mind, I'm always happy to explain how wagering works to a novice. Come back and see me anytime and I'll set you up an account," Chester said. "Although, I suppose if you wanted to learn the ropes, you could simply ask either of your housemates."

Edwina did not quite like the gleam in Chester's eye as he mentioned both Beryl's and Simpkins's residence in her home. She doubted she would ever get entirely used to the notion that her jobbing gardener now slept beneath her roof. She certainly did not need any reminding that both he and Beryl had an unfortunate tendency towards wagering.

"That's very kind of you, I'm sure," Edwina said. If she wanted information from Chester, especially as pertained to gambling, there was no need to be insulting. No matter how tempting it might be to remind him of how little chance there was that she would be inclined to indulge in as sordid a form of entertainment as gambling. If she were ever inclined to try her hand at that sort of thing, she would most assuredly entrust her inaugural attempt to the likes of Alma Poole and the ladies' wagering group rather than the sort of grubby affair that backing horses and other sporting events at the pub would prove to be.

"So, what is it that I can help you with?" Chester asked.

"I wanted to ask you about troubles with Mr. Faraday," Edwina said.

"Which one?" Chester said.

"Either one, I suppose," Edwina said. "Although I had heard that the younger Mr. Faraday was the one who was likely to have had business here with you."

Chester took a sip of the contents of his glass and carefully regarded Edwina over its rim as he did so.

"I assume that you will keep whatever I say to you to yourself. I would think that our businesses are not entirely dissimilar, are they?" he said.

Edwina felt the urge to contradict him burbling up in her throat, then thought better of it. She smiled conspiratorially instead.

"I should think we both flourish by having a reputation for being discreet and for understanding the value of a good tip," Edwina said.

"I see we understand each other completely," Chester said. "Mr. Alan Faraday was in here last Monday afternoon, trying to place a bet."

"You said, 'Trying to place a bet.' Does that mean he did not do so?" Edwina said.

"It does indeed. I told him I couldn't take his money. Not that it was his money," Chester said.

"Not his money?" Edwina asked.

"That's right. He tried to pay me with a cheque rather than cash, which is contrary to my long-standing policy. Cash is the only way to do things in this business," Chester said, giving Edwina a broad wink.

"Was it not his cheque?" Edwina asked.

"That's right. It was not. It was a blank one belonging to his brother. Well, I say it was blank, but the signature had been filled in," Chester said significantly.

"And you thought there was something not quite right about that?" Edwina said.

"I was sure of it. Not only do I not take cheques in lieu of cash, but I also don't take them from a third party. I most assuredly don't take them from someone who says he got a cheque from a person who expressly forbade me to accept any more bets from his brother just before the young scalawag arrived in the village," Chester said.

"Gordon Faraday forbade you from accepting bets from his brother Alan?" Edwina said.

"In fact, he did. He threatened to haul me up before his bench if I ever took another bet from his brother. He said he would come up with some sort of charge and make it stick, and stick for a good long time. There was no way on God's green earth that Gordon Faraday would have signed a blank cheque for his brother to give to me. I told him to take that cheque and walk right back out of the pub. I said I never wanted to see him at my table again," Chester said.

Edwina leaned back in her chair. Things did not look good for young Alan Faraday. "What did Alan say to that?"

"He didn't say a thing. He just got a thunderous look on his face and stomped out the door without a word. To tell the truth, I kept looking over my shoulder all the way home that night. I didn't want to encounter him alone in the dark."

Edwina pushed back her chair and stood. "You've been a great deal of help, Mr. White," she said. "Please do feel free to call upon Beryl and me in the future if you need a favor returned."

"I'll keep that in mind, but I don't suppose I shall need to do so. Your father and I were friends, and it's a pleasure to be able to help you out."

Edwina was astonished. She had no idea that her father was well acquainted with Chester White.

"You considered my father to be a friend?" Edwina asked.

"I certainly did. Many's the time he put a wager on a horse with me over the years," he said.

"I never heard any such thing," Edwina said. In a village like Walmsley Parva, one could usually count on hearing every manner of gossip. She was simply astonished not to have realized her father was a frequent gambler or a gambler of any sort.

"Like you said yourself, Miss Davenport, your business and mine both rely on discretion. It was important to your father that your mother not hear of his tendency to enjoy a flutter now and again. We all like to have our secrets, don't we?" he said, giving Edwina another broad wink.

She left the pub with even more to think about than she could have imagined.

Beryl looked around the parlor with satisfaction. Although she could not describe her relationship with Beddoes as a warm one, she had to admit there was a great deal of benefit to be had in having a servant at the Beeches. The glassware on the drinks tray gleamed in the low candlelight. Beryl lifted the lid of the ice bucket and noted with pleasure that the bucket was filled to the brim with already chipped ice. The soda siphon stood filled with water and at the ready. Beddoes had even laid out a dish of olives threaded onto wooden picks.

Simpkins had assisted the maid in opening out the card table and ringing chairs around it. It was rather an ingenious contraption. By day it simply appeared to be an ordinary square wooden table. If one paid close attention, it might be noticed that the tabletop was perhaps a bit thicker than ordinary. But should the occasion arise, the top could be folded back to reveal a felt-lined inner table that was perfect for playing any manner of games involving cards or dice.

Beryl wondered how Edwina's family had come to own such a specialized item. To hear Edwina speak of her parents did not encourage one to believe them to be card fiends. Perhaps the table had been purchased by one of Edwina's more sociable ancestors. So many of the items at the Beeches were possessions passed down from one generation to the next. Beryl could think of only a very few things scattered about the large house that Edwina had added to its furnishings.

In fact, the most prominent of the additions had been provided by Beryl herself. The typewriting machine in the morning room and the wireless in the parlor were easily the most modern conveniences in the household. Beryl supposed she ought to feel grateful that someone had had the presence of mind, and the cash, to take action upon the notion to add indoor plumbing to the house at some point in the past.

Even though Beryl was not above making do with whichever sorts of facilities presented themselves when she was out on an expedition or traipsing off to exotic locales across the globe, she did have rather a soft spot for remaining indoors should the call of nature occur in the middle of the night. She did prefer that the call of nature did not involve quite so much nature if it was at all possible. She also found the charms of an oversized porcelain tub to be entirely irresistible.

Edwina bustled into the room, carrying a tray of sandwiches and what she would most assuredly refer to as biscuits. Edwina placed the tray down on a sideboard near the card table and glanced around the room approvingly.

"Charles should be here very soon. Simpkins still plans to join us, doesn't he?" Edwina asked.

"He was more than happy to agree to join us when I told him that we would be playing poker rather than bridge," Beryl said.

Beryl had promised to give Simpkins an opportunity to brush up on his poker game, but she had done so knowing full well that Edwina was at least as eager as Simpkins to improve her game. Edwina had a rather endearing passion for the romance of the Old West, and Beryl was tickled by the notion of her friend imagining herself in a dusty saloon, besting a table full of hardened cowboys.

Crumpet went racing down the hallway, barking furiously. Edwina followed him and returned with Charles in tow. Simpkins joined them a moment later, and the four gathered around the card table. Even though the purpose of the evening was entertainment, Beryl and Edwina had agreed prior to offering an invitation that Charles was someone they wished to interview concerning the magistrate's background. Beryl always preferred to kill two birds with one stone whenever possible. Doing so at the card table was one of her favorite ways to accomplish such things.

She allowed the first hand to pass by without interjecting any discussion of the investigation, but as Edwina dealt the cards for a second go-round, Beryl broached the subject of the magistrate's death.

"Charles, you must be affected by the magistrate's death. Did you know him well?" Beryl asked.

Charles looked up from the card Edwina had just dealt him with a grimace on his face. Beryl wondered if the look on his face was caused by what he held in his hand or by the question she had posed.

"To be entirely honest, Gordon Faraday's death has opened up some time in my schedule this week. I know that sounds rather crass, but until a new magistrate can be appointed, all the pending cases are on hold, and so I have had some extra time on my hands," he said.

"They say every cloud has a silver lining. What have you done with your time?" Beryl asked.

"I've taken the opportunity to get in a few extra sessions with my paintbrushes," Charles said.

Beryl noticed him sneaking a glance in Edwina's direction. On her first visit to Charles's house, Beryl had spotted a large number of watercolors he had painted himself hanging in the main hallway. A surprising number of them featured a figure of a woman who bore a marked resemblance to Edwina. Ever since, she had been doing her best to encourage her friend to take a romantic interest in Charles. So far Edwina had seemed to be resistant to the notion, but Beryl was hopeful that eventually she would convince her.

"Did you know him well?" Beryl said.

"I wouldn't say I knew him well, but I would say I knew him as well as I would like to," Charles said, with a surprising level of candor.

He was a remarkably tight-lipped man unless pressed to reveal what he knew. Beryl supposed that was a good thing in a solicitor, but it could be quite tedious during the course of an investigation. She wondered at his frankness and whether or not it indicated the strength of his antipathy for the other man.

"That seems to be the sort of feeling shared by most of the people we've spoken to about him," Edwina said. "No one seems to have warmed to him particularly."

"I suppose that's what you get for fining people and tossing them in the local pokey," Simpkins said, reaching for his hand of cards. "It seems to me it's a surprise that he lasted as long as he did, rather than that he met with his death so soon."

"Charles, Mr. Faraday's younger brother Alan says that he and his brother fell out over his choice of profession. Do you remember Mr. Faraday mentioning that he was interested in his brother pursuing a career in the law?" Edwina asked.

"I would have remembered something like that if Mr. Faraday had brought it to my attention. Any conversations we had concerning Alan were of a far less pleasant sort," Charles said.

"Did the magistrate confide concerns about his brother to you?" Beryl asked.

"I am not sure I should say anything," Charles said, indicating he would like a card. "It was exceedingly awkward at the time, and I cannot see that it would do anyone any good now to rehash the whole tawdry affair."

"If it has any bearing on the magistrate's death and the possibility he may not have met with an accident, it would be worth revisiting a bit of discomfort, wouldn't it?" Beryl asked.

"I suppose when you put it like that, it would be my duty to assist you in your enquiries," Charles said. "I heard that the two of you are helping Constable Gibbs lately."

"You know something about the estrangement between the two brothers that goes beyond a mere disagreement about Alan's profession, don't you?" Edwina said.

"I'm afraid something far less benign caused the rift," Charles said. "Do I have your word that you will not repeat anything that I share with you here?"

The rest of the party nodded encouragingly.

"Of course our intentions are never to spread malicious gossip about fellow residents of the village, Charles. You know that," Edwina said.

"Edwina, surely you remember that Gordon Faraday was a career military man," Charles said.

"He was inclined to mention it whenever he could wedge it into conversation," Edwina said.

"Alan and Gordon quarreled over Alan's reluctance to volunteer when war broke out," Charles said.

"Alan attempted to avoid serving?" Beryl asked.

"I suppose that that is what it all boiled down to in the end," Charles said.

"I heard that boy was a shirker," Simpkins said. "Bit of a gambler, too."

Charles looked at Simpkins appraisingly. "It seems as though you know something about what happened with young Alan," he said.

Simpkins cleared his throat loudly, and for a fleeting moment, Beryl wondered if he might forget himself and spit on Edwina's oriental rug. She felt a wave of relief when he did not. Edwina might be persuaded to overlook many of Simpkins's less refined habits, especially now that he paid Beddoes's wages, but Beryl doubted she would forgive treating her parlor like a barn.

"There were rumors about young Alan at the time. It is hard to keep something like that a secret," Simpkins said. "Not that I blame the lad for trying to keep out of the whole mess."

"What exactly happened, Charles?" Edwina asked.

Charles fortified himself with a sip of his cocktail before speaking. "It all started when Alan refused to attest under the Derby Scheme. Gordon was disappointed when his brother did not immediately volunteer and had hoped that he would do so when pressured to do so by a recruiting canvasser."

Beryl remembered thinking the Derby Scheme had seemed repugnant to her at the time. Although Beryl had readily consented to assist wherever she was needed during the war, she did not feel justified in judging the willingness of others to do the same. The Derby Scheme had employed respectable older men in communities to go door to door and cajole those eligible to serve to attest in front of them that they were willing to do so. The canvassers were often highly skilled political agents or fathers of men already serving. Those who consented agreed to report to a recruiting office within forty-eight hours. The pressure to acquiesce was enormous and was not an experience Beryl would have relished facing.

"I cannot imagine Mr. Faraday looking kindly on any reluctance on Alan's part," Edwina said.

"That is putting it mildly. He told Alan that he had to join up as a volunteer before conscription went into effect, or he would cut him off from any financial support. Alan left Groveton Hall that very same day. He took what money was in the house and helped himself to a few blank cheques from Gordon's cheque-book," Charles said.

"How do you know all this?" Beryl asked.

"Gordon told me what had happened when he discovered that money had been fraudulently withdrawn from his account. He wanted me to act as an intermediary between them," Charles said.

"What did he want you to do?" Edwina said.

"Essentially, he wanted me to draft a letter to his brother threatening to report him to the police for the forgeries and the theft if he did not report for service."

"Did you assist him?" Beryl asked.

"I told him that it would be very difficult to track Alan down and that it would cause a lamentable scandal for him to do so. He decided it was not worth the effort, especially as he was headed to the front himself," Charles said.

"I heard he didn't report for duty even after he was required to," Simpkins said.

"I believe that is correct. Gordon wrote to me later to say Alan had been rounded up outside a known gambling den in London in the autumn of nineteen sixteen. It was all very unpleasant," Charles said.

Beryl stood and crossed the room to the drinks table. She mulled over the new insight into the relationship between the Faraday brothers as she mixed up a fresh batch of martinis. Edwina's thoughts seemed to run along the same lines as her own, because before Beryl finished rattling the cocktail shaker, her friend spoke.

"So, Alan is a known thief with a previous history of problems with his brother. And I have it on good authority that Alan helped himself to another of his brother's blank cheques the day before he died," Edwina said.

"He was eager to point a finger at Declan, too," Simpkins said, turning to Beryl. "Do you remember how he practically accused him of the thefts that night we saw him at the pub?"

"I remember it very clearly. He makes a very strong suspect indeed. But there is a wide gap between filching money and killing a family member," Beryl said.

"You never know what a person will do if he is desperate enough," Charles said.

"There is nothing you two can do about it tonight, no matter what," Simpkins said, holding out his empty glass to Beryl. "If he is guilty, he will still be tomorrow."

"Right you are, Simpkins. Who's up for another hand of poker?" Beryl asked.

Chapter 17

Beryl pulled to a stop in front of Terrence Crossley's cottage. The district registrar had been quite insistent upon meeting with them in person to hear an account of their progress in the case. Although Beryl made it a point never to permit herself to feel nervous, she had to admit she felt less than enthusiastic about the interview with their client. She did not like to consider the possibility that the two of them had gotten in over their heads, but if she were to be entirely honest with herself, she would have to acknowledge that very little progress on any front seemed to have been made.

Even though Beryl was firmly of the opinion that the best way to learn was through experience, she did feel somewhat unprepared for the responsibility of accounting for her actions to a paying client. In her previous pursuits, Beryl had simply gone about being herself and, by dint of that, had never failed to appear a resounding success. It was rather clearer cut when one set out to break speed records either on the ground or in the air. Either one set a new record or one did not. There were no particularly grey areas.

But in the realm of investigation, the same could not be said. She felt they had been asking the right sort of questions of the correct people, but she could not honestly say that their efforts had yielded fruit likely to impress someone as eager to get to the bottom of the matter as Mr. Melton appeared to be.

Edwina did not look quite up to the task of facing an angry client, either. She had armed herself with her very best hat and a pair of net gloves. Beryl had overheard her enquiring if Beddoes had found the time to polish her shoes that morning. Clearly, she wished to present herself in the best possible light in order to endure the trial that lay ahead of them.

Although it could never be said Edwina enjoyed riding along in the automobile with Beryl at the wheel, she had been even less inclined to pass the time in pleasant conversation than usual. She had clung silently to the door handle and stared out the window without even bothering to voice her concerns about their safety. Perhaps, Beryl had thought, Edwina hoped that they would in fact become involved in some sort of road incident that would delay their arrival at the meeting. But in Beryl's capable hands, they had arrived right on time.

Terrence Crossley opened the door of his cottage with the same sort of look on his face that Beryl had seen on Edwina's. It appeared he was no more eager to endure the grilling his superior was likely demanding than were they. He ushered them into the small, stuffy sitting room and gestured towards a pair of mismatched chairs near the fireplace. Mr. Melton got to his feet as they entered but did not smile.

"May I offer you ladies something to drink?" Mr. Crossley asked, gesturing towards a small sideboard covered in a variety of bottles. Beryl saw Edwina leaning forward slightly in her chair. A strange look flickered across her face, but before Beryl could intimate that she wished to know the cause, it was gone. Beryl was surprised to hear Edwina answering yes before Beryl could get a word in herself.

"I would like to have whatever's in that green bottle," Edwina said. "It looks rather intriguing."

Mr. Melton shook his head. "I'm a teetotaler and would prefer to simply get down to business."

"I'll take whatever you are having," Beryl said, gesturing towards a glass next to the only empty chair in the room.

Mr. Crossley poured them each a drink, and after delaying things by fussing about with glasses and ice for as long as he could, he handed them each their beverage and seated himself next to his employer.

Out of the corner of her eye, Beryl watched as Edwina took a tentative sniff of the contents of her glass. She wondered if her friend was concerned about being poisoned or if there was something wrong with the sanitation. As she had a legendary capacity to down any manner of unwholesome foodstuffs, Beryl plunged in and took a sip of a decidedly uninspiring whiskey.

"What I want to know is, have you made any progress whatsoever on this case?" Mr. Melton asked.

Beryl was about to reply when Edwina spoke up.

"We have been working on the assumption that the theft of the census schedules and that of the items at homes all throughout Walmsley Parva have to be connected. I would like to assure both of you that we are hopeful a breakthrough in the burglaries is imminent," Edwina said.

"Do you think that that will lead you to the recovery of the census schedules?" Mr. Melton asked.

"I think that it would be premature to make any promises on that score," Beryl said, giving Edwina a questioning glance.

"These things take time, Mr. Melton," Edwina said, placing her glass on the small table beside her chair. "I assure you we are as eager to recover the census schedules as you are. After all, our personal data is involved in the theft. And whilst you are responsible for the appearance of the government, I don't believe that you are amongst those affected by the theft in a personal way."

"I hadn't given that any particular thought," Mr. Melton said. "Of course, you two ladies have been directly affected by what happened. Do you have any idea how much longer it will take to get to the bottom of this? My superiors are applying a great deal of pressure. There will be questions before long from those not in the know about the delay in turning in the schedules. I shan't be able to hold them off much longer," Mr. Melton said.

"I suppose you could create a village worth of falsified census schedules, couldn't you?" Beryl asked. "After all, wouldn't you be able to get ahold of a whole bunch of blank ones?" Beryl could hear the gasps from the others seated in the room.

"The census is an official document. One does not falsify such things under any circumstances," Mr. Melton said. "After all, what would happen if we did not have reliable information in the event of something as important as another armed conflict?"

"But I thought the Great War was supposed to be the war to end all wars," Edwina said. "Mr. Melton, you aren't suggesting that you've heard rumblings of new difficulties, are you?"

Beryl could hear the sound of distress in Edwina's voice. Beryl had no such hopes that any given war would be sufficient to dissuade those in power from reaching out to take what it was they wanted through force, through the blood and sweat of those over whom they held sway. Sometimes she thought it surprising that most acquaintances who knew them would guess that Edwina was the practical one of the two of them.

Beryl was often accused of being capricious and even a bit naïve when it came down to what was or was not possible. Beryl thought the reality was quite different. Although she was unwilling to accept the restrictions placed upon women or machinery or even possibilities, she believed she was sadly more realistic when it came to the behaviors of others than was her seemingly earthbound friend.

The reality remained that whilst Americans had also given to the cause, they had not endured threats on their own soil. Edwina's inability to brook a suggestion that another such conflict could be in the future likely stemmed from how close to home the first one had felt. She reached out a hand and placed it on her friend's trembling arm.

"I'm sure that Mr. Melton is only speaking hypothetically," Beryl said. "No nation worth its salt would find itself lacking information on the number of men it could call up in aid of their country, should the need arise. Besides, the censuses are also for matters concerning public health and even planning for the growth of cities and expansion out into the countryside for roadways and so on." Beryl was gratified to see Edwina nod her head, as if relieved.

"Regardless of the reasons for requiring information, the necessity for their veracity remains," Mr. Melton said. "It is our civic duty to complete the information honestly and completely. Unless I am instructed to authorize such a suggestion by my superiors, I would utterly discount the possibility of falsifying census schedules from the residents of Walmsley Parva. I am utterly relying on the two of you to locate the schedules and return them shortly."

"As soon as we have anything else to impart, we will be sure to do so," Edwina said.

"As there is nothing else to be accomplished by prolonging my visit to Walmsley Parva, I will return to my office and update the registrar-general. Good day to you all," Mr. Melton said as he got to his feet, grabbed his hat from a rack on the wall, and took his leave.

As Mr. Crossley accompanied his superior to the door, Edwina made some furious hand gestures towards the contents of her glass. Beryl could only surmise that Edwina wished for her to take a sip. Edwina handed her the glass and made some furious gestures with her free hand. Beryl took a surreptitious sip and handed the glass back to Edwina before Mr. Crossley could return.

Her eyes began to water and smart. Her nostrils stung, and her taste buds went into a full-scale rebellion. The flavor was as if someone had steeped a pair of well-worn socks in a vat of honey. She thought she tasted a dash of bitterness, as if the pith from a grapefruit had been tossed in for good measure. Edwina silently slid from her chair and made her way to a window on the far side of the room. It was a long one and nearly reached the floor.

Quick as a wink, Edwina reached up and unlatched the brass catch on the lower window sash. Before Terrence Crossley shut the front door to his cottage, she had returned to her seat, looking as if she had never left it. Edwina whispered hurriedly in Beryl's ear, and in a flash the two devised a plan.

"Mr. Crossley, you look as though you could use a bit of cheering up. This meeting can't have been easy for you, and while I appreciate your hospitality, you must permit me to repay it," Beryl said. "Why don't you join me at the Dove and Duck? The drinks are on me." She stood and stepped towards the door.

"Since Mr. Melton made it clear he was on his way out of the village directly, I suppose it would be safe enough to head into town. And never let it be said I would turn down such an appealing offer from a lady like yourself," Mr. Crossley said.

"Are you coming, Edwina?" Beryl asked.

"You know I never go to the pub," Edwina said right on cue. "You go ahead with Mr. Crossley, and I shall find my way home on foot. After the tongue-lashing we just endured, I feel a great need for a walk in the open air to clear my head."

"Well, Mr. Crossley, it looks like it will be just the two of us. Climb on into the old bus and I'll show you what it can do," Beryl said, yanking open the driver's side door and patting the leather seat beside her. "I'll see you back at the Beeches in a couple of hours, Edwina."

As she pulled out of the driveway, she could see Edwina slowly making her way away from the cottage in the rearview mirror.

Edwina made a show of continuing along the path leading away from Mr. Crossley's cottage until Beryl had pulled out of sight. As soon as she could no longer see the back end of the motorcar, she scanned the area to be sure she was well and truly alone before heading back to the cottage. She made her way around to the side where she had unlatched the window. She tucked her fingers underneath the sash and pressed upward. She was relieved to feel it slide with more ease than she might have expected in such a poorly maintained structure.

She regretted wearing her newest and smartest summer-weight suit for their interview with Mr. Melton. Even though the latest fashions for women involving the slimmer cuts suited her slender frame, they were not particularly conducive to climbing furtively through windows. After looking around once more to be sure she was unobserved, Edwina hitched her skirt up above her knees and hooked one leg over the window ledge. In a flash she reentered the small cottage and closed the window behind her.

She made straight for the sideboard containing the drinks bottles. Just as she suspected, the tall green bottle from which Mr. Crossley had served her displayed a familiar beige label marked APRICOT BRANDY. She felt a nervous excitement working its way through her stomach as she bent down and opened the doors to the sideboard. There she discovered five more bottles of the stuff. She straightened and closed the doors. Edwina searched the sitting room for any further signs of contraband. Finding none, she moved on to the kitchen. There, too, she found nothing except the normal items associated with the running of a bachelor's household.

Despite her misgivings, Edwina took herself firmly in hand and entered the only other room in the cottage. Edwina had very little experience of finding herself in a man's bedchamber. She found herself once again wishing that she were the one who felt blithely unconcerned at the idea of heading to the pub. Beryl would certainly be better equipped to evaluate if anything was out of place in such a chamber. Still, she told herself, if she was correct in her suspicions, she would not need to be an expert in the male of the species in order to confirm them.

Sure enough, as she slid open the bottom drawer in the chest of drawers, she found no fewer than five cigar boxes filled to the scuppers with an assortment of jewelry, cuff links, pocket watches, and silver flatware. When she inspected the wardrobe, a variety of other household items of value threatened to tumble out onto the floor. Edwina had never seen such a collection of silver serving trays and ivory-handled carving knives in her life.

Without a doubt, Edwina had discovered the identity of the local burglar. She decided to head back into Walmsley Parva rather than back to the Beeches. Under ordinary circumstances, she would never consider helping herself to someone else's property. However, time was of the essence, and Edwina did not think Terrence Crossley deserved the same consideration as the average individual. She relatched the window sash, then exited the front door and pulled it shut firmly behind her.

She rounded the side of the cottage and helped herself to Mr. Crossley's bicycle, regretting once more her unfortunate choice of ensemble. After hitching her skirt above her knees once more, she mounted the cycle, placed her very best hat in the basket clamped to the bicycle handlebars, and pedaled off in the direction of the village. She could hardly wait to tell Beryl what she had discovered.

Chapter 18

Sooner than she would have thought likely, Beryl looked up to spot Edwina standing on the pavement outside the front window of the pub. She gestured for Beryl to join her outside. Beryl made her apologies to Terrence Crossley and settled her bill at the bar with Bill Nevins. When she emerged from the Dove and Duck, Edwina had positioned herself partway up the street, looking unnaturally absorbed in a display window at the men's haberdashery. When she saw Beryl moving towards her up the pavement, she appeared to be almost trembling with excitement.

"So, what did you find?" Beryl asked.

"It's him. It's Terrence Crossley," Edwina said. "I found most of the items from the list we got from Constable Gibbs hidden away in his cottage."

"That apricot brandy really was trouble," Beryl said. "I've never tasted anything so ghastly in my life."

"We shall have to tell Constable Gibbs, of course," Edwina said.

"Yes, but I can see that causing more complications for the government, can't you?" Beryl said.

"I'm sure that we will be able to appeal to her better nature. Let's see if she's in at the police station," Edwina said.

Constable Gibbs stood behind the counter in her usual spot at the police station. She glowered at Beryl and Edwina as they entered, but Beryl had to wonder if it was more from habit than from any actual animosity. In fact, as they stepped towards the counter, she opened the door and ushered them into the private side of the station without a word of criticism.

"From the look on Edwina's face, the two of you must have something important to tell me," Constable Gibbs said, gesturing towards the staff table and taking a seat herself.

"I am delighted to say we've solved the burglaries," Edwina said.

Constable Gibbs's eyes widened slightly, and she reached for a piece of paper and a pencil and placed them in the middle of the table. Beryl reached out a hand and placed it on top of the writing implement.

"I think it would be best if we kept this as unofficial as possible," Beryl said.

"What do you mean?" Constable Gibbs said. "Are you unable to prove who did it?"

"No, we know who did it, and can prove it, too. I found most of the stolen items in his possession," Edwina said.

"Why don't you tell me who it is that's been causing all this trouble?" Constable Gibbs said.

"The census taker, Terrence Crossley," Edwina said.

"Are you sure?" Constable Gibbs said. "That's quite a responsible job, and I would be surprised for someone of poor character to be given it."

"If he's never been caught stealing before, no one would know that he has less than a blameless record," Beryl said.

"I'm afraid that his job as a census taker gave him a perfect excuse to be lurking around people's homes. And he would have a legitimate excuse for knocking on the door and waiting for a response," Edwina said.

"So, if he didn't get one, he went ahead and let himself in?" Constable Gibbs asked.

"I think that's exactly what he did," Edwina said. "When I was speaking to Mrs. Corby, she said she thought she heard someone trying to enter the house when she hadn't responded. At first, I thought she was just imagining things in order to be part of what was going on. You know how it is with lonely old ladies."

Constable Gibbs nodded, indicating that she indeed did know how it could be. "How did you discover it was him?" she asked.

"It was the apricot brandy," Edwina said.

"Ghastly stuff," Constable Gibbs said.

"The worst I've ever tasted, and I think of myself as quite the connoisseur," Beryl said.

"He offered us some when we called upon him to give a report on the theft of the census schedules to his superior, Mr. Melton, this very afternoon. As soon as I saw the bottle on his drinks table, I recognized it," Edwina said.

"Well, of course you did. Anyone who's lived in Walmsley Parva for a year or more knows what those bottles look like. And they know better than to drink from them," Constable Gibbs said.

"He had no idea what he had taken. I sampled some just to be sure, and then, after the meeting, Beryl invited him to the pub to get him out of the cottage so that I could take a look around," Edwina said.

"I'll pretend you didn't tell me that," Constable Gibbs said. "Cooperating with the police does not give you permission to simply poke about in people's homes uninvited."

"I should think that the same could be said of Mr. Crossley," Beryl said. "You aren't considering pressing charges against Edwina for breaking and entering, are you?"

"Perhaps not," Constable Gibbs said. A wistful expression passed across her face, as though she were saddened by a golden opportunity slipping through her fingers. "But I am going to need to arrest Terrence Crossley."

"See, that's where things get a bit troublesome," Beryl said. "If you arrest him, it will cause a great deal of damage to the reputation of the government. After all, if it would bother people to know that their census data had been stolen, how much would it also trouble them to know that the person they had entrusted it to in the first place was a common criminal?"

"I see the problem, but I'm not sure what you're suggesting for a solution," Constable Gibbs said. "It's clear to me that we cannot simply allow this man to continue operating in the village."

"No, of course not. I suggest that we do not publicly name him as the thief. We could turn over the responsibility for prosecuting him to someone far above our pay grade by letting the registrar-general note that he's the one responsible for the burglaries," Edwina said.

"I suppose that would take care of keeping his identity secret, but what would it do for returning the items to the people who lost them or for clearing the names of those who have been suspected of being the burglar?" Constable Gibbs said.

"We could return the items to the victims and still not reveal the name of the burglar. They might be just happy enough to get them back that they would accept that they would never know for sure," Beryl said.

"It does bring up an important question, however," Edwina said. "The question of who might have done it would continue to cling to the rest of the people suspected."

"I suppose I could give them a false perpetrator. I could tell people that it was a serviceman who had lost his wits and was wandering about the countryside. I could tell them that I have bundled him off to a rest home where he can get some help. I expect that most people would not wish to ask any more questions about it than that," Constable Gibbs said.

Beryl looked at the constable with new respect. It was just

the sort of magnificent story she would have concocted to explain such a thing. She had not expected Constable Doris Gibbs to be the sort of person who would be so willing to be flexible with the rules and regulations that she would even accept this as an option if someone else had come up with it, let alone that she would come up with it herself. Perhaps a new era of cooperation was ahead of them.

"I think that's a marvelous way to resolve the problem," Edwina said, smiling at Constable Gibbs. "Rather ingenious, too."

Beryl was surprised to see that Constable Gibbs appeared to be blushing. Being the sole police officer in a small village must be quite a difficult task, she thought for the first time. Doris Gibbs was likely almost as much of an outsider in her own village, where she had lived all her life, as Beryl had been in the places she had visited only temporarily. She felt slightly ashamed of herself for treating the policewoman as an opponent to be bested rather than as a colleague to be respected.

"Do you think that he is also responsible for what happened to the magistrate?" Constable Gibbs asked.

"I really don't know that for sure. What I can say is that I did not find any of the items taken from the magistrate's house in amongst the items he had tucked away in his cottage," Edwina said.

"That's interesting. I don't seem to remember that the items taken from Groveton Hall would be so different than those taken from other houses to explain why they weren't amongst the rest of the hoard," Constable Gibbs said.

"As we've been looking into the theft of the census schedules and the other burglaries, it has become clearer and clearer that Gordon Faraday was not a popular man," Beryl said. "I think it would be unwise to consider that his death was definitely accidental."

"Even though I'm not going to publicly name Terrence Crossley as the burglar, or even arrest him officially, I am going to ask him some very pointed questions about his time at Groveton Hall," Constable Gibbs said. "It seems strange to consider that two burglars would be operating in the same small village."

"According to Mr. Crossley, Mrs. Faraday, and the nanny at Groveton Hall, Terrence Crossley arrived at the hall to deliver the schedules when someone was home, and stopped in and picked them up when someone was there, too. He would not have had an excuse to come back to Groveton Hall and commit the burglary if he had taken care of his business already," Edwina said.

"He needs to be apprehended sooner rather than later. Do you know where he is now?" Constable Gibbs asked.

"When we last left him, he was at the Dove and Duck. Even if he left, I don't think he would have gotten very far yet," Beryl said. "I drove him into town, so he did not have his bicycle."

"Well, he will have it if he spots it where I left it," Edwina said.

"Leave Mr. Crossley to me. If you really don't think he is responsible for the theft of the census schedules, I suggest the two of you get on with your investigation into what happened to them," Constable Gibbs said, pushing past them as she headed out the door.

They followed the constable out of the police station. Constable Gibbs assured them she would be discreet when confronting Terrence Crossley about his crimes. She gave them her word that she would not tax him with what he had done in front of any witnesses or behave in any way that would raise people's suspicions. She also said she would stop in at Prudence's shop and ask her if she had seen a disheveled-looking man with a limp skulking about the village.

With Prudence's inclination to gossip, it would not take long before the whole village was convinced that a stranger was roaming the highways and byways of Walmsley Parva. It would be a very short leap from that rumor to the story that a drifter had been breaking into the houses.

Beryl and Edwina promised to assist by sowing their own seeds of the story whenever the occasion arose. As so often was the case, it did so almost immediately. Before they were two doors away from the police station, Minnie Mumford put down the watering can that she was using to hydrate her window boxes and as an excuse to keep a close eye on the street. She waved them over, with an eager look on her face.

"I saw that you were just leaving the police station," Minnie said. "Does this mean there's been some sort of a break in the burglary case?"

"Why do you ask?" Beryl asked.

"I've been having a terrible time sleeping. I just can't seem to drift off when I'm lying in my bed worrying that the same thing that happened to poor Gordon Faraday could happen to me," Minnie said.

"I'm sure that Constable Gibbs has the situation well in hand and that there is nothing for you to worry about. In fact, she just asked us if we would keep our eyes out for a disheveled-looking ex-serviceman wandering about the village," Edwina said.

Minnie glanced hurriedly up and down the street. Edwina noticed her eyes lingered on the post office, where Prudence Rathbone stood in the doorway, looking as though she wished she could overhear what they were discussing. Although Minnie and Prudence were the best of friends, they did enjoy healthy competition as to who would be the first with any juicy tidbits of gossip to spread about the village. Most often Prudence took the lead, making any advantage Minnie might have all the more satisfying.

"I'll be sure to keep an eye out for someone like that. One doesn't know what to think anymore," Minnie said, bending over and plucking her watering can from the ground. She splashed water over the display of marigolds and forget-me-nots tucked into the window box. "We never used to have ruffians wandering about, getting up to heaven knows what. And I thought it was bad enough seeing a well-bred young lady like Monica Billington screeching like a fishwife. To think that now there are strangers terrorizing our streets, as well. What is the world coming to?"

"That doesn't sound like Monica in the least," Edwina said.

"I shouldn't have believed it of a nice young lady like her, but I saw it with my own eyes. If I didn't think that Gordon Faraday was the victim of an accident, I would say that she should top the list of suspects in his death," Minnie said, leaning towards Edwina and lowering her voice. She shot another look across at Prudence's shop, as if to be sure her voice could not be overheard.

"When did this happen? What was the argument about?" Beryl asked.

"I'm sorry to say I was witness to a very distressing and embarrassing scene at the bank. Monday, I think it was," Minnie said.

"Monica Billington was raising her voice at the bank?" Edwina said.

"If by 'raising' it, you mean she was peeling the paint off the ceiling, then I say that she sure was. It seems that her stepfather had closed her account and she was unable to retrieve any funds," Minnie said.

"Are you sure?" Beryl asked.

"Everyone in the bank would have been sure. Not that there were many people in the bank at that time of day, for which I'm sure the clerk was very grateful. I hardly knew where to look," Minnie said. "The words she used made my face sting with shame just to have heard them."

"And this happened on Monday?" Beryl asked.

"Monday afternoon, just before closing time. I remember

going in particularly to collect some change to keep in the till for the next day," Minnie said. "I'd say it's a good thing for Monica Billington that Constable Gibbs has a burglar she suspects is responsible for her stepfather's death, wouldn't you?"

"I'm sure she's very grateful," Beryl said.

"You remember to keep a lookout for a scruffy wanderer," Edwina said.

Minnie nodded, clutched her watering can to her chest like a shield, and darted back inside her tea shop.

Chapter 19

"I should think being cut off from one's money would cause anyone to be enraged," Edwina said.

"I think we need to speak with Monica again," Beryl said. "I wonder where she'll be."

"We can always telephone Groveton Hall and ask if she's at home," Edwina said.

By stopping in at the Woolery and using the telephone, they ascertained that Monica was at the stables, accompanying Timothy to a riding lesson.

"I think we should hop in the old bus and head over to Brightwell Farm immediately."

"That is just what I was thinking," Edwina said.

They strode down the street as quickly as was seemly and within moments were out on the open road, headed for the horse farm. Edwina had cast a guilty glance at Mr. Crossley's bicycle, still propped up against the wall of the pub, as they had walked past. She was still mulling over what would become of such a lovely machine should he be sent to prison when Beryl pulled to a stop in front of the barn at Brightwell Farm.

Monica stood in much the same place Edwina had seen her on her previous visit. She leaned against the fence enclosing the paddock, holding out a handful of juicy grass to a sleek chestnut-colored horse. Edwina thought she noticed Monica's posture stiffening as they approached.

"Are you two ladies thinking about signing up for riding lessons?" Monica asked.

"I am not in need of any lessons," Beryl said. "I am actually quite a good rider but find that I am far less inclined to spend my time on horseback now that I've had a chance to drive a motorcar. Besides, in my opinion, horses have nothing on camels for the pleasure of riding."

Edwina was gratified to see Monica's eyes widen. If there was one thing Beryl was good at, it was knocking people off-balance with her outrageous claims. Although knowing Beryl as well as she did, she knew it was unlikely that the claim was untrue. Beryl had certainly spent enough time in the sorts of places where camels were easily found to have had plenty of opportunities to ride one. It would be just like her to prefer the experience to a more pedestrian one.

"We actually came to speak with you, Monica," Edwina said. "We have a question about an incident that occurred earlier in the week."

If anything, Monica's face became even more guarded than before.

"What sort of an incident?"

"We have it on good authority that you discovered, much to your dismay, that your stepfather had cut off your access to your bank account. Is that true?" Edwina asked.

Edwina could not believe she had actually managed to squeeze out a question on the subject of money. If there was one thing her mother had indelibly impressed upon her over the years, it was that nice ladies did not speak about such things. They certainly did not go prying into the financial affairs of others. Edwina reached up and felt the back of her hair, touching it almost as though it were a talisman. The fact that she had cut it off reminded her that she was taking her life in an unprecedented direction and was throwing off many of the restrictions of the past.

"Gordon was always so unfair," Monica said. "It was just like him to do something so high handed and leave me to be discovering it in an embarrassing way in public."

"Had you any reason to suspect that he would do such a thing?" Edwina asked.

"We had not been getting along at all well of late. I should have realized he would retaliate in some especially odious way," Monica said.

"What was the source of your discord?" Edwina asked.

"What wasn't? Gordon and I had never gotten along particularly well, even from the time I was a small girl," Monica said. "You must remember that things were not harmonious between us ever, Miss Davenport."

Edwina was sorry to acknowledge that what Monica said was true. She had been the sort of child one often saw wandering around the village on her own, looking as though she hadn't a friend in the world. The women of the village had taken quite an interest in Monica when her mother died. The girl had been only seven or eight years old, and they all had felt concerned for her. Gordon Faraday had packed her off to a third-rate boarding school not long after her mother had passed, and Edwina had seen little of her except for during school holidays. The truth be told, Monica seemed to have been happiest during the war years, when her stepfather was stationed at the front and they had no contact whatsoever.

"But there must've been something particular that had occurred recently for him to make a change in your financial status," Beryl said.

"He didn't like my politics. To be entirely honest, he didn't like that I had an opinion about politics whatsoever," Monica said.

"And that was enough for him to cut off your bank account?" Beryl asked.

"Actually, I believe it was when I voiced support for Irish independence that he finally snapped. I should have gone ahead and cleared out this month's allowance before being so foolish as to tell him what I really thought," Monica said.

"He did seem to have rather a bee in his bonnet about the Irish, didn't he?" Beryl said.

"He absolutely hated them," Monica said. "When I wouldn't back down from my position about Irish independence, he told me that university was what was filling my head with all sorts of leftist nonsense. He didn't just cut off my allowance. He also announced he would not pay for my schooling anymore."

"That must have made you exceedingly angry," Edwina said.

"Indeed, it did. But it's all sorted now," Monica said. "Or it soon will be."

"You should be careful what you say, Monica, or people will start to get the idea that you had something to do with your stepfather's death," Beryl said.

"Well, that's just ridiculous. How could I have?" Monica asked. "He either tripped or had a run-in with that burglar."

"I think that you will find that he did not have a run-in with the burglar," Beryl said. "Someone could just as easily have made it look as though he had, though, couldn't they? It is common knowledge throughout Walmsley Parva that someone was breaking into homes."

Monica's eyes widened once more, and she looked at Edwina. "But I couldn't have done anything to Gordon. I was here at Brightwell Farm when he died."

"Can anyone confirm that? Mr. and Mrs. Johnson were not on the property at the time, and Declan has already said that he was here entirely alone," Beryl said.

"Declan's just trying to protect my reputation. We were here together all morning," Monica said.

"You and Declan spent time together here, unchaperoned, all morning long?" Edwina asked.

"That's right. We have been spending time together for weeks. You can ask him yourself if you like. He's working in the stables right now. I was actually waiting for him to finish up in order to get to speak to him. He doesn't like for me to be in there with him, because he says I distract him and slow him down," Monica said.

"We're going to go and ask him for his side of the story, but I would like you to stay out here. It will look better for you if you aren't there giving him any coaching as to what to say," Beryl said.

"Suit yourself. It's the truth, and it won't matter if I'm here or there. Declan will confirm my story," Monica said. She turned her back on the two other women and reached out to scratch the velvety nose of the chestnut horse.

Beryl shrugged at Edwina and strode off in the direction of the stables.

Declan stood at the back of the stable, stripped to the waist, a pitchfork in his hands. Beryl once again thought what a fine specimen he was and felt a pang of envy as she considered the fact he was already spoken for. At least he was if Monica was telling the truth. When he caught sight of her, he plunged the fork into a nearby pile of hay and brushed his hands on his dirty trousers.

"I've been meaning to stop in at the Beeches to thank you for helping me to get out from under the eye of the constable. I understand I have you to thank for my release," he said.

"It was our pleasure to help exonerate the innocent. Besides, I was sure you were not involved," Beryl said.

"If you are here to ask when I'll return to work, I'll be back to the Beeches to work off your fee as soon as I get caught up here. Mr. Johnson has been very understanding, but things are really starting to pile up in my absence."

"I am delighted to hear it, but there is no rush. I am actually here to ask you a question about Monica Billington," Beryl said.

"What about her?" he asked, crossing his well-muscled arms across his chest.

"I wanted to ask if the two of you are rather well acquainted."

"What makes you think a thing like that?"

Although she did not have Edwina's keen ability to sense untruths of every stripe, Beryl did know a great deal about affairs of the heart and whether or not someone's heart was available or if it had already been given. She was entirely convinced there was someone Declan loved. Now the trick would be to discover if it was actually Monica or if she had made the whole thing up.

"Monica said to ask you about the relationship. She said it would be fine for you to talk to us. It would be best for both of you if you were honest with me."

"Does this have something to do with the burglaries? Does Constable Gibbs think Monica is involved now that I am off the hook?" he asked.

Beryl decided there was no reason to share any more information with him than was strictly necessary. Even though she was certain he was not involved with the burglaries, there was still the matter of the magistrate's death to clear up. And the missing census schedules.

"Monica has asked me to verify your relationship with her. You can rest assured that if it has no bearing on the investigation, I will not breathe a word of what you've been up to to anyone besides Miss Davenport," Beryl said. She heard a noise behind her and turned to see Monica approaching.

"Go ahead and tell her the truth, Declan," Monica said.

"Monica and I were here together at the time her stepfather met with his accident," Declan said. "I knew that Mr. and Mrs. Johnson would both be away, and we wanted to be alone."

"He's very concerned about my reputation. It's rather sweet of him," Monica said.

"So, the two of you were here at the farm?" Beryl asked.

"Yes, up in my room," Declan said. "Is that the information you needed?"

It was not the sort of claim most young people would be willing to make if it were not true, even if it was to save their skins. Surely, they could have said that they were anywhere else, doing anything else, in order to provide each other with an alibi. She was inclined to believe them both.

"And no one else saw you as far as you know?" Beryl said.

"No. There were no visitors to the farm, and Monica didn't arrive until after Mr. and Mrs. Johnson had left," Declan said.

"Well, for once, getting up to no good may just have provided you with an alibi," Beryl said.

"Does that mean that we are not under suspicion?" Monica asked.

"It means that it seems unlikely that either of you were involved with what happened to your stepfather. As the burglar has been discovered, as well, I think the two of you can breathe easy for now," Beryl said.

At least, Beryl thought, if it was not proved that either of them was responsible for stealing the census schedules.

Edwina did not want to be involved in the conversation Beryl was having with Declan, and when Monica entered the stable to join them, she kept her distance. Whilst Edwina did understand that oftentimes young people were inclined to get themselves into romantic entanglements, she did not wish to discuss what the two of them might have been doing unsupervised at the farm. She should have guessed from the neatness of

Declan's bedroom above the stable that he liked to have it company ready whenever the occasion should arise. Most young men were not inclined to be quite so neat and tidy without a good reason. She saw no reason why Declan should have been any different.

As she looked about at the far end of the stable, keeping as much distance as she could and hoping that Beryl would be done with her conversation soon, she stopped in front of one of the stalls and looked inside. There was nothing to see besides straw and horse droppings. She moved along and saw no horses in any of the stalls. As it was such a fine day, she expected they were all out cavorting in the sunshine. She would not have preferred to be cooped up inside if she were them.

She came to a stall whose door was propped open by a large tan sack. As she looked into the stall, she noticed it was not used for housing horses. Instead, it seemed to be serving as a sort of storage room for a whole pile of sacks. As she casually glanced over them, she noticed that the corner of one sack seemed to be a slightly different color than all the others. Curious, she stepped into the stall and loosened the drawstring on the top of one of the closest sacks. The sack was filled with some sort of grain. Even though the sacks were quite heavy, she found that she was able to move them without a great deal of effort.

She lifted three of them away from the pile and placed them along the far wall of the stall, revealing the sack whose color did not match the rest. As she pulled it towards her, she could see that it was an entirely different sort of sack altogether. Whereas the grain sacks were made of burlap and were very coarse, this darker-colored sack was made of canvas. She lifted it from the pile and loosened the drawstring on the top. Her voice caught in her throat as she peered inside. There in front of her was an entire sack full of census schedules.

She peeked back out of the stall and noticed Beryl was still completely absorbed in her conversation with the young couple. With any luck, they would be far too engrossed in their conversation to pay any attention to her. She hoisted the sack and wrapped her arms tightly round it. With a final backward glance at the others, she made a beeline for the motorcar.

Her heart hammered in her chest as she hurried along. She kept expecting to hear someone calling out for her to stop as she raced towards the vehicle. When she reached the boot, she opened it with trembling hands and lowered the sack inside it. She had just slammed the lid of the boot shut when Beryl appeared in the stable doorway. Edwina gestured for her friend to join her, then jumped into the passenger-side seat.

Chapter 20

"I'm still not sure we ought to do this," Edwina said.

"If we are going to get to the bottom of what's going on, I can't see that we can do any differently," Beryl said.

"It just feels like such an invasion of privacy," Edwina said. "I'm not convinced that we are right to do this."

"We owe it to the entire government to discover what we can about who actually took the census schedules," Beryl said. "It's not just enough to have found the schedules themselves. If we don't, the same person who stole them before may well do it again."

"But not for another ten years," Edwina said.

"You don't think that all the schedules for the surrounding community have been collected, do you? Or those throughout the entire country? For all we know, it's an organized gang determined to bring down the entire government. You wouldn't want that, now would you?" Beryl asked.

"Are you sure we shouldn't telephone to the district registrar first? I'm sure I would feel much better if we had his permission before going through the sack," Edwina said.

"I have always found it better to ask for forgiveness than for permission. It's far more expedient. Besides, we need not tell him that we looked them over if it does not aid our case. And neither of us is going to reveal anything we find here that is not connected to the crime," Beryl said.

"I suppose you're right," Edwina said. She took a deep breath and loosened the drawstring on the top of the sack. "How shall we go about doing this, then?"

"I suggest that we each take half of the census schedules and that we check off the names on the list Mr. Melton gave us as we encounter them," Beryl said.

Edwina upended the sack, and they divided the pile of census schedules in half.

"So, we're agreed that we are only going to look at just enough information written upon them to check the names off, correct?" Edwina said.

"Of course. Now let's get on with it. I don't think either of us wants to have another unpleasant meeting with Mr. Melton," Beryl said.

Carefully, they set about opening each schedule and glancing at the name and address listed inside. One by one, they checked off the addresses listed on Terrence Crossley's register. Beryl found the work tedious, and although she was tempted to spend a little more time perusing each schedule than what they had agreed, she kept her eyes mostly where they ought to be.

The pile was nearing the end when Beryl opened the schedule that Edwina had filled out for the household ensconced at the Beeches. Edwina seemed to be engrossed in what she was doing, and Beryl thought there would be no harm in looking a little more carefully at the information Edwina had chosen to provide.

She let her gaze wander over the entire document. Edwina had carefully and conscientiously marked down their names, ages, and marital status. Beryl noted with amusement that Edwina had written *divorced* multiple times after Beryl's name. Edwina had listed herself as a spinster. The schedule did include two pieces of information that Beryl found interesting. One was that Edwina had made the decision to provide multiple occupations for herself, Beryl, and Simpkins.

After Simpkins's name she had written *international businessman, gardener, private enquiry agency stakeholder*. Beryl was both surprised and pleased to see Edwina had owned up to Simpkins's involvement in the private enquiry agency. Although he insisted on remaining a silent and even secret partner, Beryl had felt somewhat saddened to consider he would not get credit for his generous investment in their fledgling company. Edwina was inclined to be unwaveringly truthful, but Beryl had wondered if her friend would be able to bring herself to report accurately on Simpkins's habitation at the Beeches, let alone his involvement in their business.

But the most remarkable thing contained in the census schedule was confirmation of Beryl's own suspicions. She felt her heart swell with pride at the notion that Edwina had become the sort of person who would say what she wanted before she had any outside validation for her dreams. Edwina had listed herself as a private enquiry agent, which in itself was an enormous change from what would have been recorded in the previous census. But the piece of information that stood out the most for Beryl was the fact that her friend had recorded the word *novelist* on her occupational line, as well.

So that was the bee that had been buzzing round inside Edwina's bonnet just as soon as the theft of the census schedules was reported. Edwina had not even admitted to the household that she was working on a book. She certainly would not have wanted it to become common knowledge around the village before she was ready to disclose it.

Edwina was the sort of person who liked to keep those things she valued most quite private until she was ready to reveal them. Beryl suspected that Edwina had spent some time debating whether or not to record *novelist* on the census schedule. She was just trying to decide whether or not to say anything to Edwina on the matter when she realized that her friend was calling her attention.

"Beryl, did you have the schedule for Groveton Hall in your pile and forget to mark it off?" Edwina said.

"I don't remember seeing the one for Groveton Hall. Is it checked off on the list?"

"It's checked off by Terrence Crossley but not by one of us. And I've finished going through the schedules in my pile, and I don't have it. I see that you have a few remaining," Edwina said.

Edwina reached for three of the half dozen remaining schedules and quickly looked through them. She carefully marked each of the addresses as she verified them. Beryl did the same with the last three schedules in her pile.

"It wasn't in these three I just checked," Edwina said.

"Nor was it in mine," Beryl said. "What do you think that means?"

"I think it means we need to go and speak with the members of the household at Groveton Hall," Edwina said, getting to her feet.

They hurriedly replaced the schedules in the sack, and Beryl tugged the drawstring firmly shut. They tucked the sack out of sight in a cupboard in the morning room and headed straight for the motorcar.

Chapter 21

Edwina held on to her hat with one hand and the door handle with the other. Whilst from a personal standpoint, she could not approve of the way in which Beryl was driving, as a private enquiry agent, she had to admit her friend was providing value to their team. Beryl slowed down enough before the driveway to Groveton Hall that she did not squeal the brakes when she stopped in front of the stately home. Edwina took a moment to compose herself and to allow her heart to still before she pressed open the door and stepped out onto the gravel drive. She thought she could still hear her heart hammering over the sound of the scrunching gravel beneath her feet as they walked to the front door.

Beryl stepped up the front steps and rapped sharply on the door with the knocker. A moment later the door opened, and in front of them stood young Timothy Faraday, holding a balsa-wood toy aeroplane in his hand.

"Hello, Timothy. Do you remember me?" Edwina asked.

The little boy nodded solemnly. He held the toy over his head and made a sort of a buzzing noise. "I saw you at the stables with Monica the other day," he said.

"That's right. This is my friend Miss Helliwell. We're here to speak with your mother. Is she home?" Edwina asked.

He nodded again.

"I like your plane," Beryl said. "I flew one just like it a couple of years back."

"It's my very favorite toy. I thought I lost it forever, but Mummy gave it back to me today," Timothy said.

Edwina looked closely at the plane. She thought about the list of items from the burglary at Groveton Hall. "Is that the plane that was stolen during the burglary at your house?" she asked.

"Yes. It was gone, but now it's back," he said.

"Timothy, are you absolutely certain that's the aeroplane you lost when the burglar broke into your house?" Edwina asked.

"It's my very favorite toy. I wouldn't be likely to forget it," he said.

"Are you sure that your mother didn't just buy you a replacement for it since you missed it so much?" Edwina asked.

"No, this is the same one. One of the strings on it broke a little while ago, and Nanny fixed it for me using some red string since she couldn't find the same color that was on it before," Timothy said, holding the little plane out for Edwina to inspect.

Beryl and Edwina both peered at the outstretched chubby hand holding the toy. It was clear upon closer inspection that the plane was well used. There were dirty smudges and scuff marks all along its wooden frame. There was a chip in one end of one of the propellers. One section of the string holding the plane's wings together was indeed colored red, unlike the other ones, which were white. If this was a replacement aeroplane, someone had gone to a great deal of effort to replicate the original.

"Timothy, this looks as though it was handmade rather than purchased in a shop. Is that not the case?" Beryl asked.

"That's right. My father made it for me," Timothy said.

"Mummy said it was a good thing I got it back, since he can't make me another one."

"You said your mother was here. May we speak with her, please?" Edwina asked.

"Come with me and I'll take you to her," Timothy said, turning from the door.

Edwina looked at Beryl before following in the small boy's wake. Her friend was not known to enjoy the company of children. In fact, it was one of the few things Edwina had noticed Beryl found to be rather frightening. She, on the other hand, liked children. Besides, she had no intention of allowing Timothy to leave her sight before she was able to ask his mother about the miraculous reappearance of the stolen aeroplane. Unless she was very much mistaken, there was more to the story of what had happened at Groveton Hall then Deirdre Faraday had been letting on.

Timothy led them to a small sitting room near the back of the house. He pushed open the door and ran inside. His mother looked up with a smile, which faded when she saw the two sleuths approaching.

"Timothy was just showing us his lovely aeroplane. He says it's his favorite and that he is delighted to have it back after it was lost in the burglary," Edwina said.

"Timothy just forgot where it was, and we assumed it had been stolen during the burglary," Mrs. Faraday said. "Isn't that right, darling?"

"That's really strange. Constable Gibbs provided us with a list of items taken at all the burglary scenes, but when the items were recovered, nothing you had listed was found amongst them. Can you imagine why that would be?" Edwina asked.

"I should think that the burglar already sold them on. Some of it was quite valuable," Deirdre said.

"Timothy, where did you tell me that you had put your

plane when it was stolen?" Edwina asked. "Do you remember telling me about it when I met you at the stables?"

Timothy nodded. "I said that it was in the silver box Father always kept on his desk," he said.

"Did you try to find the box after your father had his accident?" Beryl asked.

"Mummy said the box was stolen with all the other things the burglar had taken," he said.

"Timothy's just confused," Mrs. Faraday said, shifting in her chair. "I'm sure you didn't come here to ask me about my son's toy plane."

"No, as a matter of fact, we're here to ask you about your census schedule," Beryl said.

"My census schedule?" Deirdre asked. Edwina noticed her fingers begin to fidget in her lap.

"Yes, the census schedule that Terrence Crossley picked up here the day your husband died but that is not amongst the schedules he collected," Edwina said.

"Timothy, why don't you go and find out what Monica is doing? Please stay with her until I call you again," Mrs. Faraday said with a trembling voice.

Edwina waited for the door to close behind Timothy before she continued. "Mrs. Faraday, is there something you would feel better if you told us?" She sat down in the chair next to the window and gave Mrs. Faraday the sort of frosty glare she generally reserved for errant parlormaids. Beryl took the other available seat and gave Mrs. Faraday her full attention.

"I don't know what you're implying," Mrs. Faraday said, shrinking back into the depths of her seat.

"We know who the burglar is, and we know that he did not take items from your home. We also know that someone has deliberately removed the census schedule for your house from amongst the rest of them. The fact that you miraculously dis-

covered a toy that everyone assumed was in a burglar's possession points a lot of fingers in your direction," Beryl said.

"It was an accident," Mrs. Faraday said with a catch in her
voice. "I didn't mean for any of this to happen."

Edwina could feel the misery rolling off Mrs. Faraday. She
reached out and took the younger woman by the hand and
gave it a squeeze. "You will feel better if you tell us what happened."

Mrs. Faraday drew a deep breath and then let it out slowly
before nodding.

"If it weren't for the census, none of this would have happened," she said. "Gordon simply could not bring himself to
record any falsehoods on the census schedule. I didn't even
know that he knew."

"That he knew what?" Beryl asked.

Mrs. Faraday struggled to her feet and headed for a small
walnut secretary desk placed against the far wall. She lowered
the front and reached into one of the many cubbyholes contained within. Edwina felt herself tensing as the notion flitted
through her mind that Mrs. Faraday might have the same pro-
clivity for pistols as Beryl. When Mrs. Faraday drew her hand
from within the desk, it simply contained what appeared to be
a census schedule. She returned to her chair and handed the
schedule to Edwina. "See for yourself."

Edwina opened it carefully and looked over what was written. On the line asking the names of the occupants of the household, she was surprised to see the words *Timothy McDonald,
age six*, carefully printed in block letters. She passed the schedule to Beryl, who quickly read it through.

"Timothy is not your husband's son?" Edwina asked.

"No, he is not. But I allowed Gordon to believe that he was
in order to preserve my marriage and to give my child a comfortable home," Mrs. Faraday said.

"How does any of that explain what happened to your husband?" Beryl asked.

"Mr. Crossley served in the same unit as my husband during the war. In fact, Gordon was instrumental in vouching for him in order for Mr. Crossley to obtain the job as census taker. Unfortunately, seeing Mr. Crossley again just stirred up all sorts of old memories for Gordon, I suppose," Mrs. Faraday said. "Gordon was quite cruel about it, actually. After I handed the census schedule to Terrence Crossley, Gordon waited until he was out of sight, and then he told me that he had not claimed Timothy as his own son on the census schedule. Up until that moment, I had had no idea that he knew that he was not Timothy's father."

"So, you killed him?" Beryl asked.

"No, that's not how it happened at all," Mrs. Faraday said. "Well, not exactly."

"What exactly did happen?" Edwina asked. "Did you shove him down the stairs because he recorded someone else as Timothy's father?"

"No. Gordon wasn't content to leave it at that. He told me the truth about something that I had suffered in silence about for years." Mrs. Faraday took another deep breath, and a flood of tears slipped down her cheeks.

"Take your time," Edwina said, handing the distressed woman a handkerchief from her handbag.

"Gordon and I were married in a hurry on a weekend leave from the front not long after the war broke out. He seemed so commanding and stable in a world that had turned upside down that I believed myself to be in love with him. I knew it was a mistake quite soon after we wed, but since no one knew what the next moments would have in store, let alone the future after the war was over, I didn't see any reason to try to get out of it." She looked at Beryl, as if asking for agreement. Beryl nodded.

"I understand perfectly. Everything had a quality of unreality to it at the time," Beryl said. "Nothing brings out impetuous behavior like fearing for one's life."

"That was it exactly. And I suppose it explains why I let myself be swept into an illicit romance with a handsome Irishman named Patrick McDonald," Mrs. Faraday said.

"That still doesn't explain how your husband came to harm right here in his own home so many years after the war was over," Edwina said.

"I was getting to that. Terrence Crossley knew Patrick because they both served in Gordon's unit. Gordon was in charge, and Terrence had a habit of trying to stay on his good side in order to make things a little easier for himself in a terrible situation. I didn't know it had happened at the time, but somehow Terrence Crossley found out about the affair. Gordon told me that Terrence had brought it to his attention whilst we were still stationed at the front."

"Why didn't your husband confront you at the time?" Beryl asked.

"He said that he had more important things on his mind at the time than an indiscretion by his wife. Besides, I think that he found it convenient to have me around once we returned to Walmsley Parva. After all, he was saddled with a stepdaughter with whom he did not get along and had a large household to run with an insufficient number of domestic staff. Trifling over such a small matter would likely not have been worth it to him. Especially considering he had already avenged himself sufficiently, at least in his own mind," Mrs. Faraday said. Another river of tears flooded from her eyes, and she dashed it away with the back of her hand.

"What do you mean, avenged himself?" Edwina said.

"When he told me that he had always known the truth about Timothy's parentage and that he had decided to record that truth for posterity on the census schedule, I asked him why he had not accused me of it at the time. He said he had taken care of the matter to his satisfaction, and then he asked me if I could not guess how he had done so," Mrs. Faraday said before letting out a deep sob.

"Were you able to guess what he had done?" Beryl asked.

Mrs. Faraday nodded slowly. "Gordon was the commanding officer of his unit and as such was in charge of any court-martialing that took place on the field. He accused Patrick of cowardice and an attempt at desertion. He had him executed by firing squad the day after Terrence Crossley told him about our relationship."

Edwina looked over at Beryl, who was nodding slowly, as if she was well aware such things could occur. Edwina felt deeply shocked. She felt tears sliding down her own cheeks, and hurried to wipe them away before anyone else might notice it. Somehow it did not seem professional to be so moved by Mrs. Faraday's story. She might still be considered a criminal. At the very least, she was guilty of adultery and making a false statement to the police.

"It would have been easy enough to get away with it, too, considering he was Irish, wouldn't it?" Beryl said.

"Unfortunately, yes, it was all too easy to convict Patrick of the crime with almost no evidence. It was commonly believed that the Irish were more likely to abandon their duty than were English soldiers. Gordon looked so proud of himself as he told me what had happened that I couldn't stand to be in his presence anymore," Mrs. Faraday said.

"I wouldn't blame you if you meant to harm him," Beryl said.

"But I didn't. The argument took place near the top of the stairs, and as I pushed past him to try to flee his presence, he reached out to grab for me and lost his balance. If I had not pulled away in time, he would have knocked me over with him, and we would've both been found at the bottom of the stairs," Mrs. Faraday said.

She looked from Beryl to Edwina, as if willing them to believe her story. Edwina did not feel that it was their place to pass judgment upon her but rather simply to collect the evidence.

"Did you fake a burglary to try to explain what had happened to him?" Edwina asked.

"It was the only thing I could think to do. Everyone else was out of the house at the time, and I gathered up a few items from around the house that I thought would be easy enough for a burglar to spirit away. I spent a little time overturning items in the rooms on the first and second floor to make it appear as though the house had been ransacked. Then I hid the items I said were stolen in a cupboard in the attic," Mrs. Faraday said.

"How did Timothy's plane come to be amongst them?" Beryl asked.

"It's just as Timothy said. He had been playing a game with Monica and had hidden it in that silver box. They played it all the time. But then they both had things they needed to go off and do, and they decided to leave the game until they returned. I made the mistake of taking the box he had placed his plane in when I gathered all the other items I pretended had been stolen," Mrs. Faraday said.

"You must have felt terrible when you realized what had happened," Edwina said.

"I was horrified when I asked him to think of the last place he remembered having it and I realized what had happened. I couldn't bear to get rid of the toy. It was his favorite, and it had belonged to Patrick. He gave it to me shortly before he died. He said if it were within his power to do so, he would take me away in a real aeroplane somewhere where Gordon would never find us," Mrs. Faraday said.

"Did you steal the census schedules, too?" Beryl said.

"I did. But I only wanted to get my schedule back. I didn't know who was going to read them, and I thought that if anyone noticed that Timothy's surname did not match his father's, and then recalled the accidental death, it might cause trouble for me. Plus, I didn't see any reason for the secret not to die with my husband."

"Did you steal them from Terrence Crossley when he went to the pub?" Edwina asked.

"No. I snuck out after everyone in the house was asleep and drove to his cottage in Gordon's motorcar. There was a perverse satisfaction in finally being able to drive it. I am a very good driver, after all. Unlike Gordon, who could never manage not to grind the gears. I stopped well short of Mr. Crossley's cottage so he would not overhear me and crept round the back. I couldn't believe my luck when I noticed he had left the bag of census schedules on the back of his bicycle."

"So, you grabbed them and decided to hide them?" Beryl asked.

"Well, first, I looked through them to find the one for my household. Then I put the rest of them back in the bag and drove out to the stables. I remembered seeing a bunch of feed bags in one of the stalls when I was there one day, watching Monica ride. I remembered that they looked remarkably like Mr. Crossley's bag, so I decided I would hide the bag in the pile, since it didn't seem likely it could be easily traced to me if I left it there."

"And with so much attention focused on Declan as the most likely burglar, it didn't hurt to hide Mr. Crossley's bag where he was working and lodging, did it?" Beryl asked.

"I suppose that it didn't slip my mind that he would make a viable suspect," Mrs. Faraday said.

Edwina suddenly felt her sympathy for the other woman ebbing away.

"We are, of course, going to have to report all of this to Constable Gibbs," Edwina said.

"What will happen to me now?" Mrs. Faraday asked.

"That will be for a magistrate to decide. I guess it's too bad that the one you had the most sway with won't be able to help you now," Beryl said.

Chapter 22

Edwina sat in her favorite chair in the library, struggling to keep her attention focused on a book of poems she had pulled off the shelf. Beryl lay stretched out on the window seat, making no effort whatsoever to pretend she was doing any else but lolling and daydreaming. Edwina heard a rap upon the door, and Beddoes popped her head around it.

"Mr. Charles Jarvis to see you, miss," Beddoes said, pushing the door open wide.

Charles stepped through, looking immaculate in a summer-weight suit of grey wool. A shell-pink rosebud sat tucked in his jacket buttonhole. Edwina could tell he looked both excited and nervous about something. Her stomach did a slight flip-flop as she considered the possibilities for his visit. Beryl had made a number of pointed remarks over the past few months concerning Charles and his likely romantic interest in Edwina. Why he should arrive at her home unexpectedly and so formally turned out, she did not wish to imagine.

Beryl creaked one eye open and gave Charles a welcoming smile. She swung her large feet off the end of the window seat and placed them on the floor.

"I'm so sorry to have disturbed you ladies. I seem to have caught you at a moment of well-earned repose," Charles said.

Beddoes gave a bob of her head and stepped back out into the hallway, pulling the door shut behind her.

"Don't be silly, Charles," Beryl said, crossing the room to meet him. "You know we are always delighted to see you. Any news about Mrs. Faraday and her family?"

Charles had been retained to represent Mrs. Faraday in the matter of her husband's death, and the whole village had been on pins and needles awaiting news of whether or not she was to be tried as a murderess.

"Indeed there is," Charles said. "I am delighted to tell you that the crown prosecutor has decided not to bring charges against Mrs. Faraday, or anyone else for that matter."

"So the matter is to be considered an unfortunate accident?" Edwina asked.

"That is my understanding. The case has been officially closed," Charles said.

"Tongues are sure to continue to wag in a village as small as this one, even if the magistrate was a heartily disliked man," Beryl said. "I wonder if the family might be better off making a clean start somewhere else."

"Mrs. Faraday said much the same thing when we parted company after our last meeting. She has decided to take Timothy and Nanny Meechum on an extended holiday. After all, Groveton Hall will go to Alan Faraday, and she has no other real ties to Walmsley Parva," Charles said.

"What will become of Monica?" Edwina asked.

"I heard a bit of gossip on that score from Nanny Meechum. It appears that Monica and Declan have hurried off to Gretna Green. I expect they have married by now."

"I do hope they will be happy together," Edwina said. There was something terribly romantic, if ill advised, about the relationship between the pair of them. Edwina could well imagine that after her unhappy childhood, Monica would be eager to make a home of her own.

"Carrying tales about the neighbors is not the only reason for my visit. I'm also here to make an important proposal to Edwina," Charles said.

The flip-flops in Edwina's stomach magnified, and she felt as though she had suddenly found herself in a plane piloted by Beryl that was doing somersaults over the open sea. The room around her went a bit swimmy, and she felt a trickle of sweat run down the back of her neck in a markedly unladylike fashion.

"Propose away, Charles. Do you need me to quit the room and give you a bit of privacy?" Beryl asked, elbowing Charles in the ribs.

Charles winced and swallowed extravagantly. Edwina could not tear her eyes from the large Adam's apple bobbing in his throat. She willed him to be suddenly struck mute. As much as she liked Charles and respected him, too, she liked her life as it had come to be even more. Ten years ago, when her mother had filled out the census schedule and had printed the word *spinster* after Edwina's name, she had felt lonely and grieved. Now the word felt like a symbol of freedom.

With her business success, her bobbed hair, and her novel well under way, she felt her life was satisfyingly full and in no need of any complications. Certainly, she would not want to hurt Charles's feelings in any way, but she simply could not imagine wanting to give up anything about her new life in order to make room for a husband. After all, Simpkins was more than enough male presence at the Beeches.

"Certainly not, Beryl," Charles said with a slight smile. "As a matter of fact, I may need you to help convince Edwina to accept my suggestion."

Beryl nodded and dropped into the chair next to Edwina. "I'm happy to do whatever I can," she said.

Charles sat in the only remaining seat. "Edwina, I have been asked to put forward a name as a replacement for Mr. Faraday as the magistrate for Walmsley Parva."

Edwina felt a rush of relief wash over her. Of course, Charles was there only to solicit her opinion on the subject of who would be suitable as a new magistrate. Why she ever let Beryl's foolish teasing make her uncomfortable in the presence of her dear friend Charles she could not imagine.

"And you've come to me to ask my opinion on who it should be?" Edwina asked. "You are not going to suggest the doctor, are you? I don't think that would be best for the village. With him needing to be on call in case anyone is ill, it could really slow things down in court. I think the same could be said for Vicar Lowethorpe. Also, a man of the cloth should probably rise above such things, don't you think?" Edwina could feel herself beginning to babble with relief.

Charles reached out and touched her hand. Edwina gulped. Perhaps she had been too hasty in her assessment of his reason for visiting. "No, Edwina, I am not here to ask your opinion about whose name I should put forward. I am here to ask if you would be willing to serve as the magistrate."

Edwina gulped again. It sounded as if Charles was asking her something impossible to be believed. She looked over at Beryl, who was smiling broadly and nodding her head vigorously.

"I think that's a marvelous suggestion. I can't think of anyone who would be better at such a role than Edwina. What you say, Ed?" Beryl asked.

"Are there any women magistrates?" Edwina asked.

"There are a few, but not many. You would be one of the first, but I can't imagine why that would bother you," Charles said. "After all, if you can take on the role of a lady private enquiry agent, why should you not be able to be a magistrate, as well?"

"Do you really think I'm the best person for the job?" Edwina asked.

"You are intelligent, fair minded, and one of the kindest people that I know," Charles said.

"But don't I need some sort of legal experience?" Edwina asked.

"You already have at least as much experience with the law as Gordon Faraday had," Beryl said. "After all, you are a solicitor's daughter. Besides, you have a far better character to boot."

"Beryl is right. And I would be there to advise you on every case, just as I did with Gordon. But I would enjoy advising you much more, I have to admit," Charles said.

Edwina looked over at Beryl.

"Do you really think I should do it?" Edwina asked. "What if it were to interfere with our duties as private enquiry agents?"

"I can only see that it would help. After all, should I be stopped for dangerous driving again, I wouldn't have anything to worry about if you were the magistrate, now would I?" Beryl said with a broad smile.

"I wouldn't be so sure about that, Beryl. I don't plan to be the sort of magistrate who would permit herself to be unduly influenced by personal relationships," Edwina said.

"It sounds as though you've made up your mind to accept the job," Charles said.

"I shall accept it only if Beryl agrees that it won't compromise our business," Edwina said. "I should hate to do anything that would interfere with that."

"I shouldn't think that it would get in the way of your ability to do your job any more than something else would. Like, say, writing a novel?" Beryl said. "Edwina, I think that you could do anything you set your mind to and do it well. I think you could be a private enquiry agent, a magistrate, and a novelist all at the same time. Don't you?" Beryl gave Edwina a long hard look.

So, Beryl had figured out her secret. And Beryl didn't think it was funny. And she didn't think Edwina would fail.

With a little flutter in her heart, Edwina turned towards Charles and said, "I would be delighted to accept. Who knows? Maybe I will write a book about our adventures."